THE COSSACKS

Leo Tolstoy

The Cossacks

A new translation by Peter Constantine

Introduction by Cynthia Ozick

THE MODERN LIBRARY

NEW YORK

Published in the United States by Modern Library, an imprint of The Random
House Publishing Group, a division of Random House, Inc., New York.

MODERN LIBRARY and the TORCHBEARER Design are registered trademarks of
Random House, Inc.

This work was originally published in hardcover by Modern Library,
an imprint of The Random House Publishing Group,
a division of Random House, Inc.

LIBRARY OF CONGRESS CATALOGING-IN-PUBLICATION DATA
Tolstoy, Leo
[Kazaki. English]
The Cossacks / Leo Tolstoy; a new translation by
Peter Constantine; introduction by Cynthia Ozick.
p.   cm.
ISBN 0-8129-7504-9 (alk. paper)
I. Constantine, Peter   II. Title.
PG3366.K4 2004
891.73'3—dc22   2004046875

Printed in the United States of America

www.modernlibrary.com

2 4 6 8 9 7 5 3 1

LEO TOLSTOY

Count Lev (Leo) Nikolayevich Tolstoy was born on August 28, 1828, at Yasnaya Polyana (Bright Glade), his family's estate located 130 miles southwest of Moscow. He was the fourth of five children born to Count Nikolay Ilyich Tolstoy and Marya Nikolayevna Tolstoya (née Princess Volkonskaya, who died when Tolstoy was barely two). He enjoyed a privileged childhood typical of his elevated social class (his patrician family was older and prouder than the Czar's). Early on, the boy showed a gift for languages as well as a fondness for literature—including fairy tales, the poems of Pushkin, and the Bible, especially the Old Testament story of Joseph. Orphaned at the age of nine by the death of his father, Tolstoy and his brothers and sister were first cared for by a devoutly religious aunt. When she died in 1841 the family went to live with their father's only surviving sister in the provincial city of Kazan. Tolstoy was educated by French and German tutors until he enrolled at Kazan University in 1844. There he studied law and Oriental languages and developed a keen interest in moral philosophy and the writings of Rousseau. A notably unsuccessful student who led a dissolute life, Tolstoy abandoned his studies in 1847 without earning a degree and returned to Yasnaya Polyana to claim the property (along with 350 serfs and their families) that was his birthright.

After several aimless years of debauchery and gambling in Moscow and St. Petersburg, Tolstoy journeyed to the Caucasus in 1851 to join his older brother Nikolay, an army lieutenant participating in the Caucasian campaign. The following year Tolstoy officially enlisted in the military, and in 1854 he became a commissioned officer in the artillery, serving first on the Danube and later in the Crimean War. Although his sexual escapades and profligate gambling during this period shocked even his fellow soldiers, it was while in the army that Tolstoy began his literary apprenticeship. Greatly influenced by the works of Charles Dickens, Tolstoy wrote *Childhood,* his first novel. Published pseudonymously in September 1852 in the *Contemporary,* a St. Petersburg journal, the book received highly favorable reviews— earning the praise of Turgenev—and overnight established Tolstoy as a major writer. Over the next years he contributed several novels and short stories (about military life) to the *Contemporary*—including *Boyhood* (1854), three *Sevastopol* stories (1855–1856), *Two Hussars* (1856), and *Youth* (1857).

In 1856 Tolstoy left the army and went to live in St. Petersburg, where he was much in demand in fashionable salons. He quickly discovered, however, that he disliked the life of a literary celebrity (he often quarreled with fellow writers, especially Turgenev) and soon departed on his first trip to western Europe. Upon returning to Russia, he produced the story "Three Deaths" and a short novel, *Family Happiness,* both published in 1859. Afterward, Tolstoy decided to abandon literature in favor of more "useful" pursuits. He retired to Yasnaya Polyana to manage his estate and established a school there for the education of children of his serfs. In 1860 he again traveled abroad in order to observe European (especially German) educational systems; he later published *Yasnaya Polyana,* a journal expounding his theories on pedagogy. The following year he was appointed an arbiter of the peace to settle disputes between newly emancipated serfs and their former masters. But in July 1862 the police raided the school at Yasnaya Polyana for evidence of subversive activity. The search elicited an indignant protest from Tolstoy directly to Alexander II, who officially exonerated him.

That same summer, at the age of thirty-four, Tolstoy fell in love with eighteen-year-old Sofya Andreyevna Bers, who was living with her parents on a nearby estate. (As a girl she had reverently memorized whole passages of *Childhood*.) The two were married on September 23, 1862, in a church inside the Kremlin walls. The early years of the marriage were largely joyful (thirteen children were born of the union) and coincided with the period of Tolstoy's great novels. In 1863 he not only published *The Cossacks* but began work on *War and Peace*, his great epic novel, which came out in 1869.

Then, on March 18, 1873, inspired by the opening of a fragmentary tale by Pushkin, Tolstoy started writing *Anna Karenina*. Originally titled *Two Marriages*, the book underwent multiple revisions and was serialized to great popular and critical acclaim between 1875 and 1877.

It was during the torment of writing *Anna Karenina* that Tolstoy experienced the spiritual crisis which recast the rest of his life. Haunted by the inevitability of death, he underwent a "conversion" to the ideals of human life and conduct that he found in the teachings of Christ. *A Confession* (1882), which was banned in Russia, marked this change in his life and works. Afterward, he became an extreme rationalist and moralist, and in a series of pamphlets published during his remaining years Tolstoy rejected both church and state, denounced private ownership of property, and advocated celibacy, even in marriage. In 1897 he even went so far as to renounce his own novels, as well as many other classics, including Shakespeare's *Hamlet* and Beethoven's Ninth Symphony, for being morally irresponsible, elitist, and corrupting. His teachings earned him numerous followers in Russia ("We have two Czars, Nicholas II and Leo Tolstoy," a journalist wrote) and abroad (most notably, Mahatma Gandhi) but also many opponents, and in 1901 he was excommunicated by the Russian Holy Synod. Prompted by Turgenev's deathbed entreaty ("My friend, return to literature!"), Tolstoy did produce several more short stories and novels—including the ongoing series *Stories for the People*, *The Death of Ivan Ilyich* (1886), *The Kreutzer Sonata* (1889), *Master and Man* (1895), *Resurrection* (1899), and *Hadji Murád* (published posthumously)—as well as a play, *The Power of Darkness* (1886).

Tolstoy's controversial views produced a great strain on his marriage, and his relationship with his wife deteriorated. "Until the day I die she will be a stone around my neck," he wrote. "I must learn not to drown with this stone around my neck." Finally, on the morning of October 28, 1910, Tolstoy fled by railroad from Yasnaya Polyana, headed for a monastery in search of peace and solitude. However, illness forced him off the train at Astapovo; he was given refuge in the stationmaster's house and died there on November 7. His body was buried two days later in the forest at Yasnaya Polyana.

CONTENTS

INTRODUCTION

Cynthia Ozick

Contemplating the unpredictable trajectory of Tolstoy's life puts one in mind of those quizzical Max Beerbohm caricatures, wherein an old writer confronts—with perplexity, if not with contempt—his young self. So here is Tolstoy at seventy-two, dressed like a *muzhik* in belted peasant tunic and rough peasant boots, with the long hoary priestly beard of a vagabond pilgrim, traveling third class on a wooden bench in a fetid train carriage crowded with the ragged poor. In the name of the equality of souls he has turned himself into a cobbler; in the name of the pristine Jesus he is estranged from the rites and beliefs of Russian Orthodoxy; in the name of Christian purity he has abandoned wife and family. He is ascetic, celibate, pacifist. To the multitude of his followers and disciples (Gandhi among them), he is a living saint.

And over here—in the opposite panel—is Tolstoy at twenty-three: a dandy, a horseman, a soldier, a hunter, a tippler, a gambler, a wastrel, a frequenter of fashionable balls, a carouser among gypsies, a seducer of servant girls; an aristocrat immeasurably wealthy, inheritor of a far-flung estate, master of hundreds of serfs. Merely to settle a debt at cards, he thinks nothing of selling (together with livestock and a parcel of land) several scores of serfs.

In caricature, the two—the old Tolstoy, the young Tolstoy—cannot be reconciled. In conscience, in contriteness, they very nearly can. The young Tolstoy's diaries are self-interrogations that lead to merciless self-indictments, pledges of spiritual regeneration, and utopian programs for both personal renewal and the amelioration of society at large. But the youthful reformer is also a consistent backslider. At twenty-six he writes scathingly, "I am ugly, awkward, untidy and socially uncouth. I am irritable and tiresome to others; immodest, intolerant and shy as a child. In other words, a boor. . . . I am excessive, vacillating, unstable, stupidly vain and aggressive, like all weaklings. I am not courageous. I am so lazy that idleness has become an ineradicable habit with me." After admitting nevertheless to a love of virtue, he confesses: "Yet there is one thing I love more than virtue: fame. I am so ambitious, and this craving in me has had so little satisfaction, that if I had to choose between fame and virtue, I am afraid I would very often opt for the former."[1]

A year later, as an officer stationed at Sevastopol during the Crimean War, he is all at once struck by a "grandiose, stupendous" thought. "I feel capable of devoting my life to it. It is the founding of a new religion, suited to the present state of mankind: the religion of Christ, but divested of faith and mysteries, a practical religion, not promising eternal bliss but providing bliss here on earth. I realize," he acknowledges, "that this idea can only become a reality after several generations have worked consciously toward it," but in the meantime he is still gambling, losing heavily, and complaining of "fits of lust" and "criminal sloth."[2] The idealist is struggling in the body of the libertine; and the libertine is always, at least in the diaries, in pursuit of self-cleansing.

It was in one of these recurrent moods of purification in the wake of relapse that Tolstoy determined, in 1851, to go to the Caucasus, an untamed region of mountains, rivers, and steppes. He had deserted his university studies; he was obsessed by cards, sex, illusory infatuation; he was footloose and parentless. His mother had died when he was two, his father seven years later. He had been indulged by adoring elderly aunts, patient tutors, obsequious servants (whom he sometimes had flogged). When the family lands fell to him, he attempted to lighten the bruised and toilsome lives of his serfs; the new threshing machine he ordered failed, and behind his back they called him a madman. Futility and dissatisfaction dogged him. Once more a catharsis was called for, the hope of a fresh start innocent of salons and balls, in surroundings unspoiled by fashion and indolence, far from the silks and artifice of Moscow and St. Petersburg. Not fragile vows in a diary, but an act of radical displacement. If Rousseau was Tolstoy's inspiration—the philosopher's dream of untutored nature—his brother Nicholas, five years his senior, was his opportunity. Nicholas was an officer at a *stanitsa*, a Cossack outpost, in the Caucasus. Tolstoy joined him there as a zealous cadet. The zeal was for the expectation of military honors, but even more for the exhilaration of seeing Cossack life up close. The Cossacks, like their untrammeled landscape, were known to be wild and free; they stood for the purity of natural man, untainted by the affectations of an overrefined society.

So thinks Olenin, the young aristocrat whose sensibility is the motivating fulcrum of *The Cossacks*, the novel Tolstoy began in 1852, shortly after his arrival in the Caucasus. Like Tolstoy himself, Olenin at eighteen

> had been free as only the rich, parentless young of Russia's eighteen forties could be. He had neither moral nor physical fetters. He could do anything he wanted.... He gave himself up to all his passions, but only to the extent that they did not bind him.... Now that he was leaving Moscow he was in that happy, youthful state of mind in which a young man, thinking of the mistakes he has committed, suddenly sees things in a different light—sees that these past mistakes were incidental and unimportant, that back then he had not wanted to live a good life but that now, as he was leaving Moscow, a new life was beginning in which there would be no such mistakes and no need for remorse. A life in which there would be nothing but happiness.

But the fictional Olenin is Tolstoy's alter ego only in part. After months of dissipation, each comes to the Caucasus as a volunteer soldier attached to a Russian brigade; each is in search of clarity of heart. Olenin, though, is a wistful outsider who is gradually drawn into the local mores and longs to adopt its ways, while his creator is a sophisticated and psychologically omniscient sympathizer with the eye of an evolving anthropologist.

After starting work on *The Cossacks,* Tolstoy soon set it aside and did not return to finish it until an entire decade had elapsed. In the interval, he continued to serve in the military for another three years; he published stories and novels; he traveled in Europe; he married. Still, there is little evidence of a hiatus; the narrative of *The Cossacks* is nearly seamless. It pauses only once, of necessity, in Chapter Four—which, strikingly distanced from character and story, and aiming to explain Cossack culture to the uninitiated, reads much like an entry in a popular encyclopedia. Terrain and villages are minutely noted; also dress, weapons, songs, shops, vineyards, hunting and fishing customs, the status and behavior of girls and women. "At the core of [Cossack] character," Tolstoy writes, "lies love of freedom, idleness, plunder, and war. . . . A Cossack bears less hatred for a Chechen warrior who has killed his brother than for a Russian soldier billeted with him. . . . A dashing young Cossack will flaunt his knowledge of Tatar, and will even speak it with his brother Cossacks when he drinks and carouses with them. And yet this small group of Christians, cast off on a distant corner of the earth, surrounded by Russian soldiers and half-savage Mohammedan tribes, regard themselves as superior, and acknowledge only other Cossacks as their equals." On and on, passage after descriptive passage, these living sketches of Cossack society accumulate—so much so that a contemporary critic observed, "A score of ethnological articles could not give a more complete, exact, and colorful picture of this part of our land."[3]

The name "Cossack" appears to derive from a Turkic root meaning freebooter, or, in a milder interpretation, adventurer. As a distinct population group, the Cossacks grew out of a movement of peasants escaping serfdom, who in the fifteenth century fled to the rivers and barren plains of Ukraine and southeastern Russia, seeking political autonomy. Having established self-governing units in areas close to Muslim-dominated communities, whose dress and outlook they often assimilated, the Cossacks were eventually integrated into the Russian military; their villages became army outposts defending Russia against the furies of neighboring Chechen fighters. It is into this history—that of an admirable, courageous, independent people, in gaudy Circassian costume, the women as splendidly self-reliant as the men—that Tolstoy sets Olenin, his citified patrician. And it is vital for Tolstoy to halt his story before it has barely begun—momentarily to obliterate it from view—in order to supply his readers in Moscow and St. Petersburg with a geographical and sociological portrait of the land Olenin is about to encounter. For such readers, as for Olenin, the Cossacks are meant to carry the romantic magnetism of the noble primitive.

But there is a different, and far more sinister, strain of Cossack history, which Tolstoy omits, and which later readers—we who have passed through the bloody portals of the twentieth century—cannot evade. Tolstoy saw, and survived, war. We too have seen war; but we have also seen, and multitudes have not survived, genocide. The most savage of wars boasts a cause, or at least a pretext; genocide pretends nothing other than the lust for causeless slaughter. And it is genocide, it must be admitted, that is the ineluctable resonance of the term "Cossacks." Writing one hundred and fifty years ago, Tolstoy registers no consciousness of this genocidal association—the long trail of Cossack pogroms and butcheries; hence the Cossacks of his tale are merely conventional warriors. Lukashka, a young fighter, coldly fells a Chechen enemy; his companions vie for possession of the dead man's coat and weapons. Afterward they celebrate with pails of vodka. A flicker of humane recognition touches the killer, but is quickly snuffed: "'He too was a man!' Lukashka said, evidently admiring the dead Chechen." To which a fellow Cossack replies, "Yes, but if it had been up to him, he wouldn't have shown *you* any mercy." It is the language of war, of warriors, heinous enough, and regrettable—still, nothing beyond the commonplace.

Then is it conceivable that we know more, or wish to know more, than the majestic Tolstoy? Along with Shakespeare and Dante, he stands at the crest of world literature: who can own a deeper sensibility than that of Tolstoy, who can know more than he? But we do know more: through the grimness of time and the merciless retina of film, we have been witness to indelible scenes of genocide. And it is because of this ineradicable contemporary knowledge of systematic carnage that Cossack history must now, willy-nilly, trigger tremor and alarm. Fast-forward from Tolstoy's eighteen fifties to the year 1920: Isaac Babel, a Soviet reporter, is riding with the Red Cossacks (a brigade that has made common cause with the Bolsheviks); they are hoping forcibly to bring Poland to Communism. Babel, like Olenin, is a newcomer to the ways of the Cossacks, and he too is entranced by nature's stalwarts. In his private diary he marvels at these skilled and fearless horsemen astride their thundering mounts: "inexplicable beauty," he writes, "an awesome force advancing ... red flags, a powerful, well-knit body of men, confident commanders, calm and experienced eyes."[4] And again, describing a nocturnal tableau: "They eat together, sleep together, a splendid silent companionship.... They sing songs that sound like church music in lusty voices, their devotion to horses, beside each man a little heap—saddle, bridle, ornamental saber, greatcoat."[5]

But there is a lethal underside to this muscular idyll. Daily the Cossacks storm into the little Jewish towns of Polish Galicia, looting, burning, torturing, raping, branding, desecrating, murdering: they are out to slaughter every living Jew. Babel, a Jew who will become one of Russia's most renowned writers (and whom the Soviet secret police will finally execute), conceals his identity: no Jew can survive when Cossacks are near. (My own mother, who emigrated from Czarist Russia in 1906 at the age of nine, once confided, in a horrified whisper, how a great-uncle, seized in a Cossack raid, was tied by his feet to the tail of a horse; the Cossack galloped off, and the man's head went pounding on cobblestones until the skull was shattered.)

Tolstoy did not live to see the atrocities of 1920; he died in 1910, and by then he had long been a Christian pacifist; but surely he was aware of other such crimes. The Cossack depredations of the nineteenth century are infamous; yet these, and the mass killings Babel recorded, hardly weigh at all in comparison with the Chmielnicki massacres that are the bloodiest blot on Cossack history. In a single year, between 1648 and 1649, under the leadership of Bogdan Chmielnicki, Cossacks murdered three hundred thousand Jews, a number not exceeded until the rise of the genocidal Nazi regime.

None of this, it goes without saying, forms the background of Tolstoy's novel; *The Cossacks,* after all, is a kind of love story: its theme is longing. The seventeenth century is buried beyond our reach, and already the events of the middle of the twentieth have begun to recede into forgetfulness. All the same, the syllables of "Cossacks" even now retain their fearful death toll, and a reader of our generation who is not historically naïve, or willfully amnesiac, will not be deaf to their sound.

Tolstoy's stories are above all always humane, and his depiction of his Cossacks is exuberantly individuated and in many ways unexpectedly familiar. They are neither glorified nor demeaned, and they are scarcely the monsters of their collective annals; if they are idiosyncratic, it is only in the sense of the ordinary human article. *The Cossacks* was immediately acclaimed. Turgenev, older than Tolstoy by ten years, wrote rapturously, "I was carried away."[6] Turgenev's colleague, the poet Afanasy Fet, exclaimed, "The ineffable superiority of genius!"[7] and declared *The Cossacks* to be a masterpiece; and so it remains, validated by permanence. Then what are we to do with what we know? How are we to regard Tolstoy, who, though steeped in principles of compassion, turned away from what *he* knew?

The answer, I believe, lies in another principle, sometimes hard to come by. Not the solipsist credo that isolates literature from the world outside of itself, but the idea of the sovereign integrity of *story.* Authenticity in fiction depends largely on point of view—so it is not Tolstoy's understanding of the shock of history that must be looked for; it is Olenin's. And it is certain that Olenin's mind is altogether bare of anything that will not stir the attention of a dissolute, rich, and copiously indulged young man who lives, like most young men of his kind, wholly in the present, prone to the prejudices of his class and time. Tolstoy means to wake him up—not to history, not to pity or oppression, but to the sublimeness of the natural world.

So come, reader, and never mind!—set aside the somber claims of history, at least for the duration of this airy novel. *A Midsummer Night's Dream* pays no heed to the Spanish Armada; *Pride and Prejudice* happily ignores the Napoleonic Wars; *The Cossacks* is unstained by old terrors.

A bucolic fable is under way, and Olenin will soon succumb to the mountains, the forest, the village, the spirited young men, the bold young women. His first view of the horizon—"massive mountains, clean and white in their gentle contours, the intricate, distinct line of the peaks and the sky"—captivates him beyond his stale expectations, and far more genuinely than the recent enthusiasms of Moscow: "Bach's music or love, neither of which he believed in."

> All his Moscow memories, the shame and repentance, all his foolish and trivial dreams about the Caucasus, disappeared forever. It was as if a solemn voice told him: "Now it has begun!" ... Two Cossacks ride by, their rifles in slings bouncing lightly on their backs, and the brown and gray legs of their horses blur—again the mountains. ... Across the Terek [River] smoke rises from a village—again the mountains. ... The sun rises and sparkles on the Terek shimmering through the weeds—the mountains. ... A bullock cart rolls out of a Cossack village, the women are walking, beautiful young women—the mountains. ...

And almost in an instant Olenin is transformed, at least outwardly. He sheds his formal city clothes for a Circassian coat to which a dagger is strapped, grows a Cossack mustache and beard, and carries a Cossack rifle. Even his complexion alters, from an urban pallor to the ruddiness of clear mountain air. After three months of hard bivouac living, the Russian soldiers come flooding into the village, stinking of tobacco, their presence and possessions forced on unwilling Cossack hosts. Olenin is no ordinary soldier—his servant has accompanied him from Moscow, and he is plainly a gentleman who can pay well for his lodging, so he is quartered in one of the better accommodations, a gabled house with a porch, which belongs to the cornet, a man of self-conscious status: he is a teacher attached to the regiment. To make room for him, the cornet and his family must move into an adjacent thatch-roofed house: Olenin, like every Russian billeted in the village, is an unwelcome encroachment. "You think I need such a plague? A bullet into your bowels!" cries Old Ulitka, the cornet's wife. Maryanka, the daughter, gives him silent teasing hostile glances, and Olenin yearns to speak to her: "Her strong, youthful step, the untamed look in the flashing eyes peering over the edge of the white kerchief, and her strong, shapely body struck Olenin. . . . 'She is the one!' he thought." And again:

> He watched with delight how freely and gracefully she leaned forward, her pink smock clinging to her breasts and shapely legs, and how she straightened up, her rising breasts outlined clearly beneath the tight cloth. He watched her slender feet lightly touching the ground in their worn red slippers, and her strong arms with rolled-up sleeves thrusting the spade into the dung as if in anger, her deep, black eyes glancing at him. Though her delicate eyebrows frowned at times, her eyes expressed pleasure and awareness of their beauty.

But he cannot approach her. He is solitary, watchful, bemused by everything around him. He sits on his porch, reading, dreaming; alone and lost in the woods, he is overpowered by a spurt of mystical idealism. More and more the abandoned enticements and impressions of Moscow ebb, and more and more he immerses himself in Cossack habits. He befriends a garrulous, grizzled old hunter, Eroshka, a drunkard and a sponger, who teaches him the secrets of the forest and introduces him to Chikhir, the local spirits. In and out of his cups, Eroshka is a rough-cut philosopher, ready to be blood brother to all— Tatars, Armenians, Russians. He mocks the priests, and believes that "when you croak . . . grass will grow over your grave, and that will be that." "There's no sin in anything," he tells Olenin. "It's all a lie!"

And meanwhile Maryanka continues elusive. She is being courted by Lukashka, whom Olenin both admires and envies. Lukashka is all that Olenin is not—brash, reckless, wild, a fornicator and carouser, fit for action, at one with the life of a fighter. He is a Cossack, and it is a Cossack—not Olenin—that is Maryanka's desire. Even when Olenin is finally and familiarly accepted by Old Ulitka, Maryanka resists. At bottom, *The Cossacks* is an old-fashioned love triangle, as venerable as literature itself; yet it cannot be consummated, on either man's behalf. Maryanka may not have Lukashka—violence destroys him. And she must repudiate Olenin: he is a stranger, and will always remain so. Despite the Circassian coat, despite Eroshka's embraces, despite the merrymaking Chikhir, he is, unalterably, a Russian gentleman. He will never be a Cossack. In the end Moscow will reclaim him.

But Tolstoy's art has another purpose, apart from the regretful realism of the tale's denouement and its understated psychological wisdom. It is, in this novel, a young man's art, instinct with ardor—an ardor lacking any tendril of the judgmental. By contrast, the old Tolstoy, at seventy, pledged to religio-political issues of conscience, nevertheless declined to lend his moral weight to a manifesto seeking a reprieve for Alfred Dreyfus, the French Jewish officer falsely accused of treason. Though this was the cause célèbre of the age, Tolstoy was scornful: Dreyfus was hardly a man of the people; he was not a *muzhik;* he was not a pacifist believer. "It would be a strange thing," he insisted, "that we Russians should take up the defense of Dreyfus, an utterly undistinguished man, when so many exceptional ones have been hanged, deported, or imprisoned at home."[8] His polemical engines charged instead into a campaign on behalf of the Dukhobors, an ascetic communal sect that refused to bear arms and, like Tolstoy himself, preached nonresistance to evil. A brutal initiative urged by the Czar had exiled the group to the Caucasus, where at the government's behest bands of Cossack horsemen surrounded the sectarians, whipped and maimed them, and pillaged their houses. Tolstoy was outraged, and in a letter to the Czar protested that such religious persecutions were "the shame of Russia." That among the agents of persecution were the selfsame Cossack daredevils about whom he had written so enchantingly forty years before will perhaps not escape notice.

And again: never mind! The young Tolstoy is here possessed less by social commitment than by the sensory. His visionary lyricism exults in Maryanka's strong legs, and in the mountains, woods, and sparkling rivers of the Caucasus. The Caucasus is his motive and his message. Natural beauty is his lure. Tolstoy's supremacy in capturing heat, weather, dust, the thick odors of the vineyard, culminates in a voluptuous passage:

> The villagers were swarming over the melon fields and over the vineyards that lay in the stifling shade, clusters of ripe black grapes shimmering among broad, translucent leaves. Creaking carts heaped high with grapes

made their way along the road leading from the vineyards, and grapes crushed by the wheels lay everywhere in the dust. Little boys and girls, their arms and mouths filled with grapes and their shirts stained with grape juice, ran after their mothers. Tattered laborers carried filled baskets on powerful shoulders. Village girls, kerchiefs wound tightly across their faces, drove bullocks harnessed to loaded carts. Soldiers by the roadside asked for grapes, and the women climbed onto the rolling carts and threw bunches down, the men holding out their shirt flaps to catch them. In some courtyards the grapes were already being pressed, and the aroma of grape-skin leavings filled the air.... Laughter, song, and the happy voices of women came from within a sea of shadowy green vines, through which their smocks and kerchiefs peeked.

The scene is Edenic, bursting with fecundity, almost biblical in its overflowingness. Scents and juices spill out of every phrase: it is Tolstoy's sensuous genius at its ripest. Olenin will return to Moscow, yes; but his eyes have been dyed by the grape harvest, and he will never again see as he once saw, before the Caucasus, before Maryanka, before the mountains. The novel's hero is the primordial earth itself, civilization's dream of the pastoral. The old Tolstoy—that crabbed puritanical sermonizing septuagenarian who wrote *What Is Art?*, a tract condemning the pleasures of the senses—might wish to excoriate the twenty-something author of *The Cossacks.* The old Tolstoy is the apostle of renunciation. But the young Tolstoy, who opens Olenin to the intoxications of the natural world, and to the longings of love, means to become, at least for a time, an apostle of desire.

———

CYNTHIA OZICK's acclaimed works of fiction include *The Shawl, The Puttermesser Papers,* and *Heir to the Glimmering World.* Her most recent essay collection, *Quarrel & Quandary,* won the National Book Critics Circle Award.

NOTES

1. *Tolstoy,* by Henri Troyat. A biography translated from the French by Nancy Amphoux. Doubleday, 1967, p. 116.
2. Ibid., p. 123.

3. Ibid., p. 284 (the critic was one Annenkov, writing in the *St. Petersburg Review*).

4. *Isaac Babel; 1920 Diary.* Edited by Carol J. Avins, translated from the Russian by H. T. Willetts. Yale University Press, 1995, p. 14.

5. Ibid., p. 61.

6. Troyat, p. 284.

7. Ibid., p. 285.

8. Ibid., p. 564.

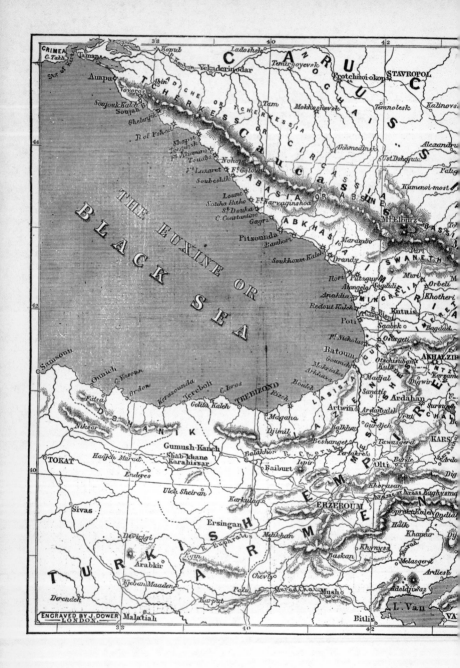

MAP OF THE
CAUCASUS,
AND THE
SEAT OF WAR IN ASIA.

BY J. DOWER, F.R.G.S.
Scale of English Miles.
Russian Versts.
☆ ☆ ☆ Principal Roads
☆ ☆ ☆ Fortified Places

THE COSSACKS

1

Moscow lies silent. From time to time screeching wheels echo in the wintry streets. Lights no longer burn in the windows, and the street-lamps have gone out. The ringing of church bells rolls over the sleeping city, warning of the approach of dawn. The streets are empty. The narrow runners of a nighttime sleigh mix sand and snow as the driver pulls over to a corner and dozes off, waiting for a fare. An old woman walks past on her way to church, where candles, sparse and red, are already burning asymmetrically, throwing their light onto the golden icon stands. The workers of the city are waking after the long winter night and preparing to go to work.

But fashionable young gentlemen are still out on the town.

Light flickers illegally from behind the closed shutters in one of Chevalier's windows. A carriage, sleighs, and cabs are huddling in a line by the entrance. A troika is waiting to leave. A porter, bundled in a heavy coat, stands crouching behind the corner of the house as if hiding from someone.

"Why do they keep blathering, on and on?" a footman sitting in the hall at Chevalier's wonders, his face drawn. "And always when it's my shift!"

From the brightly lit room next to the hall come the voices of three young men. One is small, neat, thin, and ugly, and gazes with kind, weary eyes at his friend, who is about to leave on a journey. The second, a tall man, is twiddling his watch fob as he lies on a sofa next to a table covered with the remains of a banquet and empty wine bottles. The man about to leave on a journey is wearing a new fur jacket and is pacing up and down the room. From time to time he stops to crack an almond with his thick, strong fingers, whose nails are meticulously clean. For some reason he is continually smiling. A fire burns in his eyes. He speaks passionately, waving his arms. But it is clear that he is searching for words, and that the words which come to him seem inadequate to express what has moved him. He is constantly smiling. "Now I can tell you everything!" he says. "It's not that I am trying to justify myself, but I want you, of all people, to understand me as well as I understand myself—I don't want you to see things the way a vulgar person would. You say that I have done her wrong!" He turns to the small man, who is gazing at him with kindly eyes.

"Yes, you have done her wrong," the small, ugly man answers, and it seems that even more kindness and weariness are reflected in his eyes.

"I know your point of view," the man about to leave continues. "You feel that there is as much happiness in being the object of love as there is in loving—and that if you attain it once, it's enough for a lifetime!"

"Oh yes, quite enough, my dear fellow! More than enough!" the small, ugly man says with conviction, opening his eyes wide and then closing them.

"But why not experience love oneself?" the man setting out on a journey says. He becomes pensive for a moment and then looks at his friend as if pitying him. "Why not love? I don't mean 'Why not be loved?' No, being loved is a misfortune! It's a misfortune because you feel guilty that you cannot return the same feelings, that you cannot reciprocate. Lord!" He waves his hand disparagingly. "If only this could all happen reasonably. But it seems to have a will of its own. It's as if I had made her fall in love with me. I know that's what you think—I know you do. Don't deny it! But will you believe me if I tell you that of all the bad and foolish things I have done in my life, this is the only one I do not and cannot repent of! I did not lie to her, not at the beginning and not later! I really thought I had finally fallen in love, but then I realized that the whole thing was an unintentional lie, that one cannot love that way. So I simply could not continue. And yet she did. Is it my fault I couldn't? What was I to do?"

"Well, it's all over now!" his friend said, lighting a cigar to chase away his drowsiness. "But one thing is clear: you have not yet loved, and you don't know what love is!"

The young man about to set out on a journey clasped his head in his hands, again wanting to express something, but unable to find words. "You are right! I have never loved! But I have a desire within me to love, a burning desire! Yet the question remains: Does such a love exist? Somehow everything is so incomplete. But what's the point of even talking about it! I have made a mess of my life, a complete mess! But you're right, it's all over now. I feel that I am about to embark on a new life!"

"A new life that you'll also make a mess of," the man on the sofa cut in.

But his friend did not hear him. "I am sad to be leaving but also happy," he continued. "Though I have no idea why I am sad." He began to speak about himself, not noticing that the others did not find the topic as interesting as he did. A person is never so much an egoist as in moments of rapture. He feels that at such times there is nothing more splendid or interesting than himself.

A young house serf wrapped in a scarf and wearing a heavy coat came into the room. "Dmitri Andreyevich, the driver says he cannot wait any longer—the horses have been harnessed since midnight, and it's already four in the morning!"

Dmitri Andreyevich looked at his serf Vanyusha. In the serf's coarse scarf, his felt boots, and his drowsy face, he heard the voice of another life calling to him—a life full of hardship, deprivation, and work.

"Yes, we must leave! Farewell!" he said, patting the front of his jacket to see if any of the hooks were unclasped. The others urged him to tip the driver to wait a little longer, but he put on his hat and stood for a moment in the middle of the room. The friends kissed good-bye—once, twice, then stopped and kissed a third time. He walked up to the table, emptied a glass, took the small, ugly man by the hand, and blushing said, "I must speak my mind before I go. . . . I must be straightforward with you, because I love you dearly, my friend. . . . You are the one who loves her, aren't you? I sensed it from the beginning . . . no?"

"Yes, I love her," his friend replied, smiling even more gently. "And perhaps . . ."

"Excuse me, but I have been ordered to put out the candles," one of the sleepy waiters said, hearing the last words of the conversation and wondering why gentlemen always kept saying the same things. "Who should I make the bill out to? To you, sir?" he asked, turning to the tall man, knowing very well that he was the one who was to pay.

"Yes, to me," the tall man said. "How much do I owe?"

"Twenty-six rubles."

The tall man thought for an instant but said nothing and slipped the bill into his pocket.

The other two friends were continuing their farewell. "Good-bye, you are a splendid fellow," the small, ugly man said.

Their eyes filled with tears. They went out onto the front steps.

"Oh, by the way," Dmitri Andreyevich said, blushing as he turned to the tall man. "Take care of the check, will you? And then send me a note."

"Don't worry about it!" the tall man said, putting on his gloves. "Ah, how I envy you!" he added quite unexpectedly.

Dmitri Andreyevich climbed into the sleigh and wrapped himself in a heavy fur coat. "Well, why don't you come along?" he said, his voice shaking. He even moved over and made room. But his friend quickly said, "Good-bye, Mitya! God grant that you . . ." He could not end his sentence, as his only wish was for Dmitri Andreyevich to leave as soon as possible.

They fell silent for a few moments. One of them said another farewell. Someone called out, "Off you go!" And Dmitri Andreyevich's driver set off.

One of the friends shouted, "Elizar, I'm ready!" And the cabbies and the coachman stirred, clicked their tongues, and whipped their horses. The wheels of the frozen coach creaked loudly over the snow.

"Olenin is a good fellow," one of the two friends said. "But what an idea to set out for the Caucasus, and as a cadet of all things! Not my notion of fun! Are you lunching at the club tomorrow?"

"Yes."

The two friends drove off in different directions.

Olenin felt warm in his heavy fur, even hot, and he leaned back in the sleigh and unfastened his coat. The three shaggy post-horses trudged from one dark street to the next, past houses he had never seen before. He felt that only travelers leaving the city drove through these streets. All around was darkness, silence, and dreariness, but his soul was filled with memories, love, regrets, and pleasant, smothering tears.

2

"I love them! I love them dearly! They are such wonderful fellows!" he kept repeating, on the verge of tears. But why? Who were these wonderful fellows? Whom did he love? He wasn't quite sure. From time to time he looked at one of the houses and was astonished at how odd it was. There were moments when he was surprised that the sleigh driver and Vanyusha, who were so alien to him, were sitting so close, rattling and rocking with him as the outrunners tugged at the frozen traces. Again he said, "What fine fellows, I love them dearly!" He even burst out, "I'm overcome! How wonderful!" And he was taken aback at saying this, thinking, "I'm not drunk, am I?" Olenin had drunk a good two bottles of wine, but it was not only the wine that had affected him: He remembered the words of friendship that had seemed so sincere, words that had been uttered shyly, impulsively, before his departure. He remembered his hands being clasped, looks, moments of silence, the special tone in a voice saying, "Farewell, Mitya!" as he was sitting in the sleigh. He remembered how sincere he had been. All this had a touching significance for him. He felt that it was not only good friends and acquaintances who had rallied around him before his departure. Even men indifferent to him, who actually disliked him, or indeed were hostile to him, had somehow resolved to like him and to forgive him, as one is forgiven in the confessional or at the hour of one's death.

"Perhaps I will never return from the Caucasus," he thought and decided that he loved his friends, and the others too. He felt sorry for himself. But it was not his love for his friends that raised his soul to such heights that he could not restrain the foolish words that spontaneously burst from him; nor was it love for a woman which had reduced him to this state. (He had never been in love.) What made him cry and mutter disconnected words was love for himself— a young, burning love filled with hope, a love for all that was good within his soul (and he felt at this moment that everything within his soul was good). Olenin had not studied anywhere, was not employed anywhere (except for some nominal appearances he put in at an office), had already squandered half his fortune, and though he was twenty-four had not yet chosen a career or done anything in life. He was what Moscow society calls "a young man."

At eighteen, Olenin had been free as only the rich, parentless young of Russia's eighteen forties could be. He had neither moral nor physical fetters. He could do anything he wanted. He had no family, no fatherland, no faith, and wanted for nothing. He believed in nothing and followed nothing. And yet he was far from being a dry, bored, or somber young man. Quite the contrary. He was fascinated by everything. He decided that love did not exist, but whenever he happened to be in the presence of an attractive young woman, he found himself rooted to the spot. He had always been of the opinion that honors and titles were nonsense, and yet had felt an involuntary pleasure when Prince Sergei walked up to him at a ball and spoke a few pleasant words. He gave himself up to all his passions, but only to the extent that they did not bind him. The instant he immersed himself in a certain activity and felt the imminence of a struggle, the tiresome struggle of everyday life, he instinctively hurried to tear himself away and reassert his freedom. This was how he had approached work, society, dabbling in agriculture, music (which for a while he had thought of devoting himself to), and even the love of women, in which he did not believe. He thought a great deal about where he should direct the power of youth that is granted a man only once in a lifetime. Not the power of mind, spirit, or education but the power to make of himself and of the whole world whatever he wants. Should he direct this power toward art, science, love, or toward some practical venture? There are people who lack this drive, who the moment they enter life slip their heads beneath the first yoke that comes their way and diligently toil beneath it to the end of their days. But Olenin was too aware of the presence of the all-powerful god of youth, the capacity to stake everything on a single aspiration, a single thought, the capacity to do what one sets out to do, the ability to dive headfirst into a bottomless abyss without knowing why or what for. He bore this awareness within him, was proud of it and unconsciously pleased with it. Until now he had loved only himself and could not do otherwise, because he expected nothing but good. He had not yet had time to be disappointed in himself. Now that he was leaving Moscow he was in that happy, youthful state of mind in which a young man, thinking of the mistakes he has committed, suddenly sees things in a different light—sees that those past mistakes were incidental and unimportant, that back then he had not wanted to live a good life but that now, as he was leaving Moscow, a new life was beginning in which there would be no such mistakes and no need for remorse. A life in which there would be nothing but happiness.

As always happens between the first two or three post stages during a long journey, one's imagination lingers at the place one has left, but then suddenly, as one wakes up on the first morning on the road, one's imagination shifts to the journey's end, where it builds castles in the air. This is how it was with Olenin, too.

Outside Moscow, he gazed at the snow-covered fields and was happy that he was alone in the vast expanse. He wrapped himself in his fur, lay down in the bottom of the sleigh, calmed down and, no longer agitated, began to doze. The farewells had shaken him, and he thought of the past winter he had spent in Moscow. Images interrupted by vague thoughts and reproaches began springing up in his mind despite himself. He remembered the friend who had seen him off, and his affection for the young woman they had spoken of. She was rich. "How could he love her, in spite of the fact that she loved me?" he wondered, and a nasty suspicion came into his mind. "There seems to be a lot of dishonesty in people. But why have I never loved?" he asked himself suddenly. "They keep telling me that I have never loved. Can it be that I am some sort of moral cripple?" And he began thinking about his past infatuations. He remembered the sister of one of his friends in the days when he first entered society. He had spent many evenings sitting with her at a table, a lamp lighting the lower part of her delicate face and her slim fingers at their embroidery. He remembered the long, faltering conversations, their awkwardness in each other's presence, and the unease and persistent annoyance he felt in the face of this awkwardness. An inner voice kept saying: "This isn't quite right, this isn't quite right." And it wasn't. Then he remembered a ball, and a mazurka he had danced with the beautiful D. "I was so much in love that night! How happy I was! And how ill and vexed I was the next morning when I woke up and realized I felt completely free! Where is love? Will it not come and bind me hand and foot?" he thought. "No! Love does not exist! The young lady next door, who told me that she loves the stars in the sky, which she also told Dubrovin and my bailiff, was also 'not quite right.' " Olenin remembered his farming venture in the village, but in this memory too there was nothing he could dwell on with pleasure.

"I wonder how long they'll be talking about my leaving?" he suddenly thought but was not clear about who "they" might be. The following thought, which made him knit his brow, was of his tailor, Monsieur Cappelle, and the 678 rubles that Olenin still owed him. He recalled the words with which he had asked the tailor to wait another year to be paid, and the expression of bewilderment and resignation on the tailor's face. "O God, o God!" Olenin said, screwing up his eyes and trying to chase away the unbearable thought. "And yet, in spite of everything, she did love me!" he mumbled, thinking of the young woman he and his friend had mentioned during their farewell. "If I had married her I would have been able to pay off all my debts, and now I also owe so much money to Vasilyev." He thought of how he had played cards with Vasilyev the night before at the club, to which he had gone directly after seeing her, and how he had then humiliated himself by begging to play on after his money had run out, and Vasilyev's cold refusal. "A year of thrift and I will pay everything off, and then they can all go to Hell!" But despite this reassurance he again began to count up the debts he still owed, their terms, and when they were due.

"And I owe Morel quite a bit of money, too," he remembered, thinking of the long night in which he had piled up that substantial debt. It had been a night of wild carousing (there had even been a gypsy orchestra), organized by a group of aristocrats from St. Petersburg: Sashka B., an aide-de-camp to the Czar, and Prince D.—another elderly gentleman of some importance. "Though one wonders why those gentlemen are so pleased with themselves," Olenin thought. "And the arrogance with which they have set up their little circle, which one is supposed to feel so flattered to join! Just because they're high-ranking officers? It's terrible how foolish and vulgar they think everyone else is. I showed them in no uncertain terms that I had little if any interest in being part of all that—though I am sure that my steward Andrei would be quite stunned to hear me address a gentleman like Sashka B., a real colonel and an aide-de-camp to the Czar, as 'my dear fellow.' That evening nobody drank more than I did. I taught the gypsies a new song, and everyone sat listening to it. Even if I've done a lot of foolish things in my life I am, after all, a very, very impressive young man," Olenin thought.

Morning found Olenin at the third post stage. He drank tea, surprised Vanyusha by helping him reload the bundles and trunks, and then sat stiff-backed in the sleigh among his belongings, organized, punctilious, and extremely pleased at knowing where everything was. He knew where his money was and how much he had, where his passport and traveling papers were, and everything seemed to him set up so practically and so nicely organized that he became quite cheerful and saw the long journey ahead as nothing more than an extended jaunt.

Throughout the morning and well into the day he was immersed in calculations: how many versts* he had traveled, how many remained to the next post stage, how many to the first town, how many till lunch, till evening tea, till Stavropol, and what fraction of the whole journey he had already put behind him. He also calculated how much money he had: how much was left, how much was needed to pay off all his debts, and what part of his income he could live on every month. By evening, as he drank his tea, he had calculated that the road to Stavropol was seven-elevenths of the whole journey, that these debts amounted to one-eighth of his assets, and that with some economizing he could pay them off within seven months. He complacently wrapped himself in his coat, made himself comfortable in the sleigh, and dozed off.

* A verst is about two-thirds of a mile.

His imagination now dwelt on the future in the Caucasus. All his dreams involved Ammalat-beks,* Circassian† maidens, mountains, raging torrents, and looming dangers. His visions were hazy and obscure, but beckoning glory and menacing death gave this future a veneer of excitement. With remarkable bravery and breathtaking strength, he saw himself slaughtering and subjugating hordes of wild Chechens, and then again he imagined himself a Chechen fighting the Russians for independence, shoulder to shoulder with his comrades. As his dreams grew more detailed, familiar faces from Moscow appeared: Sashka B. fighting against him alongside the Russians, or then again fighting him alongside the Chechens. Even the tailor, Monsieur Cappelle, somehow ended up celebrating with the victors. But now, when old humiliations and mistakes came to mind, the memory was pleasant. It was clear that in the Caucasus, surrounded by mountains, torrents, Circassian maidens, and danger, such mistakes would not be repeated. He had now confessed these errors to himself, and that was that.

But there was another dream, the sweetest of them all, that merged with the young man's dreams of the future. It was about a woman. She stood there in the mountains, a Circassian slave girl, slender, with a long braid and deep, docile eyes. He imagined a solitary hut high in the mountains, with her waiting by the door as he came home tired and covered with dirt, blood, and glory. He imagined her kisses, her shoulders, her sweet voice, her docility. She was beautiful but uneducated, wild, and rough. During the long winter nights he would begin to educate her. She was clever and quick-witted and would soon learn all the essentials. And why not? She would also have a knack for languages, read French novels, and even understand them—she would surely love *Notre-Dame de Paris*. And she would be able to speak French. In a drawing room she would have more poise than a lady of the highest society. And she could sing—simply, with strength and passion.

---

* The romantic hero of Aleksandr Bestuzhev-Marlinsky's popular novella *Ammalat-bek* (1831).

† Circassia is a region in the northern Caucasus.

"Ah, sheer nonsense!" Olenin said to himself. They had arrived at a post stage, and he had to climb into a new sleigh and pay a tip. But he quickly fell back into his nonsensical dreams, and again imagined Circassian maidens, glory, a return to Russia, the rank of colonel, a beautiful wife.

"But there's no such thing as love, and honors are sheer nonsense!" he said to himself. "And what about the 678 rubles? But the conquered lands of the Caucasus will give me all the wealth I need! Though now I think of it, it wouldn't really be proper to keep it all for myself. No, I will have to distribute it. But to whom? I'll start off by giving Cappelle 678 rubles, and then we'll see." The images that clouded his thoughts became hazier, and only Vanyusha's voice and the sleigh stopping interrupted his healthy, sound sleep. In a drowsy stupor he changed sleighs at a new post stage, and they drove on.

The following morning brought the same stages, the same tea, the same bouncing horse cruppers, the same short conversations with Vanyusha, the same vague dreams and evening slumber, followed by a night of tired, healthy sleep.

3

The further Olenin traveled from the heart of Russia, the more distant all his memories seemed, and the nearer he drew to the Caucasus, the lighter his heart became. "I don't ever want to go back or show my face in society again!" he thought. "Here the people are not really *people*— I mean, none of them know me or will ever move in my circles in Moscow or hear anything about my past. Nor is it likely that anyone in Moscow will ever find out anything I do here." A new sense of being free of his past overcame Olenin among the rough and simple men he met along the road, whom he did not acknowledge as "people" on the level of his Moscow acquaintances. The rougher the people and the fewer the signs of civilization, the freer he felt. He hated Stavropol, through which he had to travel: There were signboards everywhere, some even in French, ladies in carriages, cabbies waiting in squares, a boulevard, and a gentleman in a hat and coat eyeing all who drove by. "It wouldn't surprise me if these people knew some of my acquaintances," he muttered to himself, and again thought of the club, the tailor, the cards, and Moscow society. But beyond Stavropol everything was most satisfactory—wild and, above all, beautiful and dangerous. Olenin became more and more cheerful. He regarded the Cossacks, coachmen, and innkeepers as simple men with whom he could chat and joke without having to think about what class they belonged. They were all part of mankind, toward which Olenin felt an unconscious natural warmth, and they were all friendly to him.

While still in the land of the Cossacks of the river Don, he changed from sleigh to cart, and beyond Stavropol the weather was so warm that he rode without his coat. It was suddenly spring—an unexpected, joyful spring for Olenin. At night he was warned not to venture out of the fortified Cossack villages, for they said it was dangerous after dark. Vanyusha was becoming anxious, and a loaded gun lay beside him in the cart. Olenin became increasingly cheerful. At one of the post stages, he was told that there had been a terrible murder on the road not too long ago. He now saw armed men by the wayside. "It's beginning!" Olenin said to himself, eager to see the snow-covered mountains about which he had been told so much. One afternoon a Nogai* driver pointed his whip at some mountains shrouded in clouds. Olenin peered at them avidly, but the light was fading and they were hidden by the clouds. He saw something white, something gray, but try as he would, he could not find anything attractive in these mountains about which he had heard and read so much. He thought the mountains and clouds looked alike, and the extraordinary beauty of snow-covered peaks that everyone went on about was as much an invention as Bach's music or love, neither of which he believed in.

His enthusiasm for the mountains faded. The following day, as he rode in the troika early in the morning, he was awakened by a chilly breeze and looked around indifferently. The morning air was completely clear. Suddenly, not more than twenty paces away, as he first thought, he saw massive mountains, clean and white in their gentle contours, the intricate, distinct line of the peaks and the sky. He suddenly grasped the great distance between himself, the mountains, and

---

* The Nogai are seminomadic Turkic people living in northern Caucasia.

the sky, the immensity of the mountains, and the boundlessness of this beauty, and was afraid that this might be only an illusion, a dream. He shook himself to wake up—but the mountains were still there.

"What are they? Can you tell me what they are?" he asked the driver.

"Mountains," the Nogai answered indifferently.

"I've been looking at them too," Vanyusha said. "What a sight! No one back home would believe it!"

As the troika sped over the smooth road, the mountains looked as if they were running along the horizon, the rose-colored peaks sparkling in the rising sun. At first the mountains merely took Olenin aback, then they filled him with joy; but then, the more he looked at the chain of mountains that rose not from behind other mountains but straight out of the steppe, the more he *felt* them. At that moment everything he saw, everything he thought, everything he sensed, took on the stern and majestic character of the mountains. All his Moscow memories, the shame and repentance, all his foolish and trivial dreams about the Caucasus, disappeared forever. It was as if a solemn voice told him: "Now it has begun!" The road, the outline of the river Terek visible in the distance, the Cossack villages, and the people—all this now seemed to him no longer trivial. He looks at the sky and sees the mountains. He looks at himself, at Vanyusha—again the mountains. Two Cossacks ride by, their rifles in slings bouncing lightly on their backs, and the brown and gray legs of their horses blur—again the mountains. . . . Across the Terek smoke rises from a village—again the mountains. . . . The sun rises and sparkles on the Terek shimmering through the reeds—the mountains. . . . A bullock cart rolls out of a Cossack village, the women are walking, beautiful young women—the mountains. . . . Chechen marauders roam the steppes, I am riding along the road, but I am not frightened of them, I have a gun, strength, youth—the mountains. . . .

4

The stretch of the Terek along which the Greben Cossack villages lie, about eighty versts in length, unifies the terrain and the people. The river flows swift, turbid, and broad, eternally washing gray sand onto the flat right bank, overgrown with reeds, while eroding the steep, low-lying left bank with its tangled roots of century-old oak trees, rotting plane trees, and young brushwood. The Terek separates the lands of the Cossacks from those of the hill tribes: peaceful but restless Chechen villages lie on the right bank, while on the left bank, half a verst or so from the water, are the Cossack villages, seven or eight versts from one another. In the old days, most of these villages had been built on the riverbank, but every year the Terek shifted northward and washed over them, and now nothing remains of them but overgrown ruins, kitchen gardens, and pear, plum, and poplar trees entwined with wild brambles and grapevines. No one lives there anymore, and the sandbanks are dotted only by the tracks of deer, wolves, hares, and pheasants. A road runs through the forest linking the Cossack villages that are just over a cannon shot distant from one another, and along the road are watchtowers, with sentinels and military checkpoints manned by Cossacks. Only a thin strip of fertile, wooded land about half a mile wide is under Cossack control. Beyond it lie the rolling dunes of the Nogai and Mozdok steppes that stretch far into the north, emptying God knows where into the Turkmen, Astrakhan, and Kyrgyz-Kaisak steppes. South of the Terek lie Chechnya, the Kochkalykov Range, the Black Mountains, another range, and then the snow-covered massifs whose peaks have been seen but never climbed.

From time out of mind a handsome, warriorlike Russian population of Old Believers,* called the Greben Cossacks, have lived on this wooded strip of land by the river. A long time ago their forefathers had fled Russia and settled among the Chechens by the banks of the Terek on the Greben, the first ridge of the forest-covered mountains of Chechnya. The Cossacks intermarried with the Chechens and adopted their customs and way of life, but they retained both the Russian language and the Old Beliefs in all their purity. A legend prevails among the Cossacks that Czar Ivan the Terrible came to the Terek, called the Greben elders into his presence, and granted them

---

* Old Believers were religious dissenters who refused to accept the liturgical reforms imposed upon the Russian Orthodox Church by Nikon, who was patriarch of Moscow from 1652 to 1658.

the land on the Russian side of the river. He urged them to live in friendship with Russia and promised not to force his rule upon them or to compel them to change their faith. To this day, the Greben Cossacks claim kinship with the Chechens. At the core of their character lies love of freedom, idleness, plunder, and war. Russia's influence expresses itself only in negative ways: the disallowing of elections, the removal of bells, the army stationed there or constantly marching through. A Cossack bears less hatred for a Chechen warrior who has killed his brother than for a Russian soldier billeted with him to defend his village, and who has blackened the walls of his hut with tobacco smoke. A Cossack will respect an enemy tribesman but despise the Russian soldier, whom he sees as an oppressor with strange and alien ways. In fact, to the Cossack the Russian peasants are foreign, wild, and contemptible. The only ones he has met are itinerant peddlers or settlers from the Ukraine, whom the Cossacks scornfully call *shapovali*, "hat pounders." To the Cossack, the epitome of style is dressing in Circassian fashion. The best weapons are bought or stolen from the hill tribes, as are the best horses. A dashing young Cossack will flaunt his knowledge of Tatar, and will even speak it with his brother Cossacks when he drinks and carouses with them. And yet this small group of Christians, cast off on a distant corner of the earth, surrounded by Russian soldiers and half-savage Mohammedan tribes, regard themselves as superior and acknowledge only other Cossacks as their equals.

A Cossack spends most of his time at the checkpoints, on campaigns, or hunting and fishing. He almost never works at home. Even his presence in the village is an exception; he will return there only for the feasts of the holy days, and then he carouses. All Cossacks make their own wine, and drunkenness is not so much a general tendency as a ritual, neglecting which would be considered apostasy. A Cossack regards a woman as an instrument of his well-being: A girl might be allowed to enjoy herself, but a married woman, from her youngest years to advanced old age, has to work hard and fulfill the requirements of obedience and labor prevalent in the East. As a result, women, notwithstanding their apparent subjugation, are well-developed both physically and morally, and have far more authority in the home than do women in the West. A Cossack woman's seclusion and habituation to heavy work give her all the more power within the home. A Cossack considers it unseemly to speak to his wife needlessly or with tenderness in front of others, but when he is alone with her he is aware that she is superior to him. His house, all he owns, his entire property, are amassed and maintained through her work. A Cossack lives in the firm conviction that manual labor is demeaning and appropriate only for a woman or a Nogai workman. But he does have a vague sense that everything he calls his own is a product of women's work, and that it is in the power of women—mothers and wives—whom he considers his slaves, to deprive him of everything. Furthermore, the constant heavy work the Greben women do has given them a uniquely independent and masculine character, and has developed in them physical strength, healthy understanding, decisiveness, and firmness of character. Most of the women are stronger, cleverer, and better looking than the men. The beauty of the Greben women is particularly striking, as it combines the purest features of a Circassian face with a strong and robust Russian body. The Cossack women dress in Circassian fashion—in a Tatar tunic, a quilted jacket, and slippers—but tie their head scarves as Russian women do. They insist on style, cleanliness, and elegance, both in dress and in the decoration of their homes. The women, particularly unmarried girls, enjoy freedom in their dealings with men.

The village of Novomlinskaya has preserved more than any other place the customs of the old Greben, and the women of this village have always been renowned throughout the Caucasus for their beauty. The Cossacks live off their vineyards, orchards, and watermelon and pumpkin fields, from the planting of corn and millet, from fishing and hunting, and from the spoils of war. Novomlinskaya lies three versts from the Terek and is separated from it by a stretch of dense woodland. On one side of the road through the village lies the river, while on the other lie the vineyards and orchards, beyond which stretch the dunes of the Nogai steppe. The village is surrounded by an earthen rampart and prickly blackthorn bushes, and one can enter or leave only through a tall gate covered by a small, reed-thatched roof. Next to it stands a monstrous cannon on a wooden cart, captured in the distant past by the Cossacks and not fired in over a hundred years. A Cossack in uniform, armed with saber and rifle, sometimes stands guard at the gate, and sometimes not. Sometimes he presents arms to a passing officer, and sometimes not. A white board with black painted letters hangs below the gate's thatched roof: 266 houses, 897 male souls, 1,012 female souls.

The Cossacks' houses stand on posts about two or three feet off the ground, have tall gables, and roofs neatly thatched with reeds. All the houses, even the older ones, are solid, clean, and have high porches in front of them varying in shape. They are not huddled against each other but scattered along broad streets and lanes. Boldly shining sunflowers and climbing vines and creepers grow outside the houses next to dark green poplars and tender, pale-leafed acacias with fragrant white blossoms towering above the roofs. On the broad village square, three little stores sell bales of cloth, sunflower seeds, pea pods, and gingerbread. And beyond a tall fence and a row of old poplars lies the house of the commander of the regiment, a house with casement windows that is bigger and taller than any of the other houses. On weekdays there are few people in the streets, particularly in summer. The young men are on duty at the checkpoints or away on campaigns, while the old men are out hunting, fishing, or working with the women in the vineyards and orchards. Only the very old, the very young, and the sick remain at home.

5

It was one of those rare evenings found only in the Caucasus. The sun had set behind the mountains, but darkness had not yet fallen. The evening glow stretched over a third of the sky, and the dull, white vastness of the mountains stood out sharply. The air was delicate, still, and filled with sound. A long shadow stretched several versts from the mountains over the steppe. The steppe, the riverbank, the paths were empty. Only rarely did mounted men appear, and then the Cossacks at their checkpoints and the Chechens in their villages watched them with surprise and suspicion, wondering who they might be.

As darkness falls people huddle in their houses in fear of one another, and only birds and beasts, unafraid of man, roam freely in the vast emptiness. As the sun sets, chattering Cossack women come hurrying out of the vineyards where they were tying up the vines, and the vineyards and orchards stand empty, like the steppe all around. At this time in the evening the village comes alive as people arrive from all directions on foot, on horseback, and on creaking carts. Girls with hitched-up smocks carry brushwood and talk cheerfully as they hurry to the village gate, where the cattle are being herded in a cloud of dust and mosquitoes brought from the steppe. The well-grazed cattle scatter through the streets, and women in bright quilted jackets push their way among them, their shrill voices and cheerful shrieks and laughter mingling with the lowing of the beasts. An armed, mounted Cossack, on leave from his checkpoint, rides up to a house and leans from his saddle to knock on a window. The face of a beautiful young Cossack woman appears, and tender, smiling words follow. A Nogai laborer with high cheekbones, dressed in rags, is bringing a load of reeds from the steppe. He drives his creaking cart into the yard of the Esaul,* raises the yoke from the oxen's tossing heads, and he and his master call out to one another in Tatar. A puddle stretches across almost the whole width of the street, and a barefoot Cossack woman with a bundle of firewood on her back, her hitched-up smock revealing her white legs, is edging by the fence on the roadside as she tries to get past. A huntsman back from the woods jokingly shouts, "Lift it higher, you shameless girl!" He points his rifle at her, and the woman lowers her smock and drops the firewood. An old Cossack with rolled-up trousers, his gray chest bare, comes home from a day of fishing. Slung over his shoulder is a net full of thrashing silvery fish. He crawls through his neighbor's broken fence rather than going all the way around. His coat gets caught on the fence, and he tugs it free. A woman is dragging a dry branch along the street, and from around the corner comes the sound of an ax. Children are shrieking as they chase hoops along the level parts of the street. Women are climbing over fences to get to their yards more quickly. The fragrant smoke of dried dung rises from every chimney. The heightened bustle that precedes the silence of night echoes from every courtyard.

* An Esaul was a Cossack captain.

Old Ulitka, the wife of the Cossack cornet* and schoolmaster, has come to the gate of her courtyard like many of the other women, and waits for the cattle that her daughter, Maryanka, is chasing along the road. Before Ulitka can even open the gate, a large, bellowing cow barges into the yard in a cloud of mosquitoes, followed by well-fed cattle trudging slowly, evenly swatting their sides with their tails, their large eyes recognizing Ulitka. Maryanka, beautiful and lithe, follows the cattle into the yard, throws down her switch, closes the gate, and then hurries on nimble feet to drive the animals into their stalls.

"Take off those damn slippers, you devil's wench!" her mother shouts. "Soon they'll be hanging off your heels in tatters, the way you wear them out!"

Maryanka is not in the least offended that her mother calls her a devil's wench: to her the words are an endearment, and she cheerfully continues what she is doing. Maryanka's face is covered by a kerchief tied around her head. She is wearing a pink smock and a green jacket. She disappears into the cattle shed behind a large, fat cow, and her gentle, urging words ring out. "Won't you hold still? There you go, good girl, good girl!"

A little later, mother and daughter come out of the cattle shed carrying large pails of milk, the yield of the day, and cross over into the milk shed. The smoke of burning dung begins to rise from the shed's clay chimney as the milk is turned into curd. Maryanka stokes the fire, while the old woman goes out to the gate. Twilight has already settled over the village, and the air is filled with the smell of vegetables, cattle, and the fragrant smoke of burning dung. Women are hurrying into their yards carrying burning rags. All that can be heard now is the snorting and calm chomping of the milked cows in the sheds, and the voices of women and children. It is unusual to hear a drunken man's voice on a weekday.

An old, mannish woman comes over to Ulitka from the yard across the street to get some fire. She brings a rag with her.

"Are you done with your chores?" the old woman asks Ulitka.

* A cornet was a cavalry officer.

"My girl's in there stoking the fire," Ulitka replies. "You need some?" she adds, pleased to be able to oblige her neighbor.

The two Cossack women go inside the house. Ulitka's rough hands, unused to delicate objects, tremble as she carefully opens the lid of a precious matchbox, a rarity in the Caucasus. The mannish woman sits down on the porch, obviously meaning to chat. "Your old man's still away at the school?" she asks Ulitka.

"He's forever teaching those children. He sends word that he'll be back for the festival," Ulitka replies.

"He's a clever man. That's always good."

"Very true. It's always good."

"My son Lukashka is serving at the checkpoint, but they won't let him come home," the old woman says, though Ulitka knows that well enough. The old woman needs to talk about her son, whom she has just fitted out for the Cossack regiment, and whom she wants to marry off to Ulitka's daughter, Maryanka.

"So he's at the checkpoint, is he?"

"That's where he is. He hasn't been back since the last festival. The other day I sent him some shirts with Fomushkin, who tells me not to worry, his captain's pleased enough with him. He tells me they're out looking for Chechen marauders again. He tells me not to worry— Lukashka's happy there."

"Well, God be praised," Ulitka says. "They don't call him Snatcher for nothing." Lukashka had been nicknamed Snatcher for his bravery because he had snatched a drowning boy from the water, and Ulitka brought up his nickname in order to flatter Lukashka's mother.

"I thank God that he is a good son, a good boy! Everyone's pleased with him," the old woman says. "If only he would get married, then I could die a happy woman!"

"It's not like there's a lack of girls in our village," Ulitka answers nimbly, carefully replacing the lid on the matchbox with her large, callused hand.

"Oh, there are many girls, many," Lukashka's mother agrees, nodding her head. "But your Maryanka, now she's a girl one doesn't find every day."

Ulitka knows what Lukashka's mother has in mind, and though considers Lukashka a good Cossack, she shrinks from this conversation: She is a cornet's wife and well-to-do, while Lukashka is the son of a simple Cossack, and is now fatherless; furthermore, she is not in a hurry to part with her daughter. But the main reason for her reticence is that custom requires a mother to be restrained. "Well, when Maryanka comes of age, she'll be marriageable enough," Ulitka says coolly.

"I'll send the matchmaker over. After we finish with the grape picking, we will come bow to you and Ilya Vasilyevich."

"Ilya?" Ulitka replies haughtily. "It's me you have to speak to. But all in good time."

Lukashka's mother sees in the severe look of the cornet's wife that this is not the moment to say more. She lights the rag with the match and rises to go. "Remember our chat," she says, "and don't turn us down when the time comes. I'm off, I have to light the fire," she adds, and as she crosses the street waving the burning rag in her outstretched hand, she sees Maryanka, who bows to her.

"What a fine girl, and a hard worker too," the old woman thinks, eyeing Maryanka. "Ulitka says when she comes of age! It's high time the girl got married, and married into a good house like ours! She must marry my Lukashka!"

But Old Ulitka has her own worries, and she remains sitting on the porch, deep in thought, until her daughter calls her.

6

The men of the Cossack villages spend their lives on campaigns and at military checkpoints, or "posts" as the Cossacks call them. It was late afternoon, and Lukashka the Snatcher, whom the two old women in the village had been talking about, was standing on a watchtower of the Nizhnye Prototsky checkpoint on the bank of the Terek. Leaning on the tower's parapet, he narrowed his eyes, looking far over the river and then down at his comrades, exchanging a few words with them. The sun was already nearing the snowy range that sparkled white above the clouds which were rolling over its foothills, taking on darker and darker shadows. Translucency poured through the evening air. A coolness emanated from the wild, overgrown forests, but the area around the checkpoint was still hot. The Cossacks' voices rang out more sonorously, hanging in the air. The moving mass of the swift, brown Terek stood out more distinctly from its immovable banks. Its waters were receding, and here and there wet sand lay brown on the riverbanks and shoals. The side of the river across from the checkpoint was deserted, and an endless waste of reeds stretched all the way to the mountains. A short distance down the low riverbank were a few mud huts, with the flat roofs and funnel-shaped chimneys of a Chechen village. From the watchtower, Lukashka's sharp eyes peered through the evening smoke of the peaceful village at the bustling figures of the Chechen women in their blue and red dresses.

The Cossacks at the checkpoint were not particularly vigilant, even though Chechen marauders were expected to attack from the Tatar side of the river, for it was May, and the woods along the Terek were now so thick that they were almost impassible, and the river was so shallow that one could easily wade across at any point. Nor were the Cossacks particularly concerned that a messenger had been sent by the commander of the regiment ordering them to heighten their vigil: scouts had reported that a party of eight Chechen marauders was preparing to cross the river. The Cossacks, unarmed and unperturbed, their horses unsaddled, spent their time fishing, hunting, and drinking. Only the horse of the man on duty was saddled, wandering with hobbled legs past the brambles by the woods, and only the watchman was wearing his Circassian coat and holding his rifle and saber at the ready. The sergeant, a tall, lean Cossack with an extraordinarily long back and small hands and feet, sat with his jacket unbuttoned on a small earthen mound that ran along the wall of a hut. His eyes were closed, and his head, propped in his hands, lolled from one palm to the other. He wore the expression of boredom and laziness of a man in charge. An older Cossack with a large, black beard that was beginning to gray and a shirt belted with a black strap, lay by the edge of the river, lazily gazing at the monotonously swirling waters. Other men, also half-dressed and drained by the heat, were washing their clothes in the river, plaiting bridles, or lying on the hot sand of the riverbank, humming songs. One Cossack, his thin face burnt black by the sun, lay flat on his back in a drunken stupor outside one of the huts, which two hours earlier had been in the shade but on which the hot, slanting rays of the sun now fell.

Lukashka, standing on the watchtower, was a tall, handsome young man of about twenty, who bore a striking resemblance to his mother. His face and his whole constitution, despite the awkwardness of youth, exuded great physical and moral strength. Though he had only recently joined the Cossack regiment, it was clear from the assured expression on his face and his unruffled poise that he already had the proud, warriorlike carriage typical of Cossacks and men who carry arms. His wide Circassian coat was torn in places, he wore his hat cocked to the back in Chechen fashion, and his leggings were rolled down below the knees. His clothing was simple, but he wore it with the Cossack flair that imitates Chechen warriors, whose clothes are always loose, torn, and careless; only their weapons are expensive. But Lukashka's weapons and ragged clothes were sported in a certain manner that not everyone can manage, and that immediately strikes the eye of a Cossack or Chechen. He had the look of a Chechen warrior. His hands resting on his saber, he narrowed his eyes and peered at the distant Chechen village. If one looked at his features separately, they were not handsome, but anyone looking at his stately form and his intelligent, black-browed face would have to say, "A fine young man indeed!"

"Look at all those women pouring out of that village!" he called from the tower, idly flashing his bright white teeth, not addressing anyone in particular.

Nazarka, lying below, quickly raised his head and called back, "They must be going for water."

"I should frighten them with a shot," Lukashka said, laughing. "That would scatter them soon enough!"

"It won't reach them."

"What do you mean? I can shoot farther than that! Wait till their next feast comes up, and watch me visit Girei Khan and drink a mug of Tatar beer with him!" Lukashka replied, angrily swatting at the mosquitoes that clung to him.

A rustling in the thicket drew the Cossacks' attention. A spotted mongrel hunting dog, sniffing a trail and wagging its hairless tail, ran excitedly up to the checkpoint. Lukashka recognized the dog as belonging to Uncle Eroshka, a hunter who lived next door to him in the village, and he saw the hunter's figure moving through the underbrush.

Uncle Eroshka was a giant of a Cossack, with a wide chest and broad shoulders and a big beard gray as the moon. His strong limbs were so well proportioned that in the forest, where there was nobody to compare him to, he seemed rather small. He was wearing a white, tattered hat, a frayed, tucked-up coat, and uncured buckskin shoes that were tied to his feet with cords. Slung over one shoulder was a blind, behind which he hid to shoot pheasants, and a bag with a chicken and a small falcon for baiting hawks. Over his other shoulder he carried a slaughtered wildcat strung on a leather strap. Another bag filled with bullets, gunpowder, and bread hung from his belt in back, along with a horse's tail to swat away mosquitoes, a large dagger in a torn sheath spattered with dried blood, and two dead pheasants. He peered at the checkpoint and stopped.

"Heel, Lyam!" he shouted to his dog, in such a sonorous bass that the echo resounded deep into the woods. He slung the large percussion musket that the Cossacks call a *flinta* onto his shoulder and raised his hat.

"A good day to you!" he called to the Cossacks in the same strong, cheerful bass, completely effortless but loud, as if he were calling to the opposite bank of the river.

"And a good day to you, Uncle! A good day to you!" the voices of the young Cossacks called back from all directions.

"Tell me if you've seen any game!" Uncle Eroshka shouted, wiping the sweat off his broad, handsome face with the sleeve of his jacket.

"There's a fine hawk nesting in that plane tree over there! The moment the sun sets he starts hovering right overhead," Nazarka said with a wink, clownishly jerking his shoulders.

"Tall tales!" the old man said incredulously.

"No, it's true, Uncle! If you lie in wait here for the next few hours, you'll see!" Nazarka replied with a chuckle.

The Cossacks began to laugh. Nazarka had never seen a hawk hovering above the checkpoint, but the young men stationed there liked to tease Uncle Eroshka whenever they saw him.

"You fool, you're always lying!" Lukashka called down from the tower to Nazarka, who immediately fell silent.

"If you think I should lie in wait, then I'll lie in wait!" the old man said, to the great amusement of the Cossacks. "Have you seen any boars?"

"Boars? Do you think we're keeping a lookout for boars here?" the sergeant said, leaning forward and scratching his back with both hands, pleased at the opportunity for some distraction. "It's Chechen marauders we're hunting, not wild boars! *You've* not heard anything, have you?" he added, narrowing his eyes and showing his white, close-set teeth.

"Chechen marauders?" the old man repeated. "No, I haven't heard anything. Do you have any good Chikhir wine? Give me a drink, I'm all worn out! When I get a chance, I'll bring you some nice fresh meat. Give me a drink!"

"So what are you going to do, lie in wait for game?" the sergeant asked, as if he had not heard what the old man had said.

"I was going to lie in wait all night," Uncle Eroshka replied. "I was thinking that I might, God willing, bag some game for the festival—then I'll give you some too, I swear!"

"Hey, Uncle Eroshka!" Lukashka called from the tower, and all the Cossacks looked up. "Head over to the runlet upstream—I see a big litter of boars there! I'm not joking, I swear! The other day one of our men shot a beast there. I swear I'm not joking!" he added in a serious tone, slinging his rifle behind his back.

"Ah, Lukashka the Snatcher is here!" the old man said, looking up at the tower. "Where was it that your friend shot the beast?"

"Didn't you see me? I suppose I'm too high up," Lukashka said. "He shot it right by the runlet," he added. "We were walking along there when we heard a crackling sound, but my rifle was in its sling. So Ilyaska shot it. I'll show you where it was—it's not that far. Just wait a moment, I know all the paths here!"

Lukashka looked over to the sergeant and with a decisive, almost commanding tone, called down from the watchtower, "Uncle Mosyev!

It's time to change shifts!" He grabbed his rifle and began climbing down without waiting for the sergeant's response.

"You can come down!" the sergeant called and looked around at the other men. "It's your turn, Gurka, isn't it? Get up there!" He turned back to the old man and said, "That Lukashka of yours has turned into quite a good hunter. He's just like you, roaming the woods, never staying in his quarters! You should have seen the beast he bagged the other day!"

7

The sun had set, and the shadows of night were spreading from the woods. The Cossacks finished what they were doing around the checkpoint and gathered in the hut to eat supper. Only the old man remained beneath the plane tree, holding his falcon by a string tied to its leg as he waited for the hawk to appear. There was a hawk in one of the trees, but it did not swoop down upon the chicken that the old man was using as bait. Lukashka was humming tunes as he set out nooses to catch pheasants in the thickest brambles. Though he was tall and had big hands, it was clear that anything he put his mind to, whether fine or rough, responded to his touch.

"Hey, Luka!" Nazarka's shrill voice came from nearby in the underbrush. "The men have all headed back for supper!"

Nazarka pushed his way through the brambles out onto the path, holding a live pheasant under his arm.

"Where did you get that bird?" Lukashka asked him. "From one of my traps?"

Nazarka was the same age as Lukashka, was his friend and neighbor in the village, and like him had only joined the company that spring. He was an ugly young man, thin and sickly, with a piercing voice that rang in one's ears. Lukashka was sitting cross-legged like a Tatar among the weeds, setting out the traps.

"I don't know whose bird this is, it must be yours."

"If it was behind the pit by the plane tree, then it's mine. I set the trap yesterday."

Lukashka got up and looked at the pheasant. He stroked the bird's dark blue head, which it stretched out in terror, its eyes rolling.

"Let's make a pilaf with it. Go kill and pluck it," he said.

"Should we eat it ourselves or give it to the sergeant?"

"Why give it to him?"

"I don't know how to butcher these things," Nazarka said apprehensively.

"Then give it to me!"

Lukashka drew a knife. The bird fluttered up, but before it could spread its wings, its blood-drenched head slumped and quivered.

"That's how it's done!" Lukashka said, dropping the bird on the ground. "It'll make a good pilaf!"

Nazarka looked at the bird and shuddered.

"Just watch that devil send us out again tonight to lie in ambush!" he said, picking up the pheasant. (The devil he was referring to was the sergeant.) "He sent Fomushkin to get some Chikhir wine the night it was his turn, and so we always end up being sent out there! It's us every night!"

Lukashka walked toward the checkpoint whistling a tune. "Here, take that noose trap with you!" he shouted. Nazarka took it.

"I'll give him a piece of my mind, I swear!" Nazarka continued. "We should tell him we won't go, that we're tired out, and that's that! Though I guess maybe you should tell him, he listens to you."

"That's enough," Lukashka said absently. "Who cares, anyway? If we were being sent out of the village, I'd be the first to speak up. In the village you can drink and have fun! But out here? If you ask me, being inside the hut all night or lying out in ambush is all the same! You're just—"

"Will you be coming back to the village with us?" Nazarka asked.

"I'll be going back for the festival."

"Gurka says that your Dunaika has started seeing Fomushkin," Nazarka said suddenly.

"She can go to the Devil!" Lukashka replied, his white teeth flashing, but not in a smile. "You think I can't find another girl?"

"Gurka said he went to her house and her husband was out, but that he found Fomushkin there, eating a pie. He stayed for a bit, but as he left he passed by the window and heard her say, 'Thank God that idiot is gone! Won't you finish the pie, darling? You can stay the night, if you like.' And Gurka, outside the window, said to himself, 'Well, how about that!' "

"You're lying!"

"I swear it's true!"

Lukashka said nothing for a few moments. "Well, if she's with someone else, then she can go to Hell! The village is full of girls! I was getting tired of her anyway."

"You're a fool. You should go for the cornet's daughter, Maryanka. Surely she's the kind who'll look twice at a man."

Lukashka frowned. "Maryanka? Well, I don't care."

"So try her."

"Why, do you think there aren't enough girls in the village?"

Lukashka began whistling again and walked to the checkpoint, plucking leaves off twigs. He came to some bushes and, seeing a smooth sapling, stopped, drew his knife, and cut it off.

"That'll make a nice cleaning rod for my rifle," he said, whipping the sapling through the air so it whistled.

The Cossacks were sitting on the dirt floor in the clay-walled front room of the hut, eating their supper around a low Tatar table, when the question of whose turn it was to lie in ambush that night came up.

"Well, who's got to go tonight?" one of the Cossacks called through the open door to the sergeant in the other room.

"Yes, whose turn is it?" the sergeant called back. "Uncle Burlak has been, Fomushkin has been," he added, hesitating. "Will the two of you go—you and Nazarka?" the sergeant said to Lukashka. "And Ergushov too—that is, if he's slept off his liquor."

"You never sleep off your liquor, why should he?" Nazarka muttered, and everyone laughed. Ergushov was the man who had been lying drunk outside the hut. He had just come staggering into the room, rubbing his eyes. Lukashka was already up, cleaning his rifle.

"Well then, get a move on! Eat your supper and go!" the sergeant said, coming into the room and closing the door without waiting for an answer, as he evidently did not expect Lukashka and the two others to agree. "I wouldn't be sending you out if I hadn't been ordered to," he continued. "But the captain could turn up here any moment, and we all know word has it that eight Chechens have crossed the river!"

"Of course we have to go!" Ergushov said. "An order's an order! We have to be out there at times like this! I say we go!"

Lukashka had picked up a large chunk of pheasant meat in both hands and was holding it in front of his mouth. His eyes darted from the sergeant to Nazarka. He laughed, apparently indifferent to the mounting tension between the two men. Suddenly Uncle Eroshka, who had been waiting in vain for the hawk under the plane tree, came into the darkening room. "Well, boys!" his bass voice thundered, drowning out all the others. "I'm coming along! You lie in wait for Chechens, and I'll lie in wait for boars!"

8

Darkness had fallen by the time the three Cossacks, wrapped in their cloaks, their rifles slung over their shoulders, left the checkpoint with Uncle Eroshka and walked along the Terek to where they were to lie in wait. Nazarka had not wanted to go, but Lukashka spoke some sharp words to him, and they all set out. They walked along a runlet in silence, then headed toward the riverbank on a path that was barely visible among the reeds. A thick, black log had washed onto the bank, flattening the reeds around it.

"Why don't we hide here?" Nazarka asked.

"Good!" Lukashka replied. "Stay here, and I'll be right back. I want to show Uncle Eroshka where I saw the boar."

"Yes, this is a very good place!" Ergushov agreed. "The Chechens won't be able to see us, but we'll see them. Let's stay here—it's the best place!"

Nazarka and Ergushov spread their cloaks on the ground and settled down behind the log, while Lukashka continued along the path with Uncle Eroshka.

"It's near here," Lukashka whispered, walking noiselessly a few steps ahead of the old man. "I'll show you where that boar is hiding. I'm the only one who knows."

"Yes, show me!" the old man whispered back. "You're a good lad, Snatcher!"

Lukashka stopped, crouched down by a pool of water, and whistled softly. "You see this? It stopped here to drink," he said barely audibly, pointing at a fresh print.

"God bless you!" the old man said. "The boar will be holed up beyond that ditch! I'll stay here, you go back now!"

Lukashka wrapped himself in his cloak and headed back toward the river, eyeing the wall of reeds to his left and the Terek, seething in its banks, to his right. "Those Chechens must be creeping around here somewhere!" he thought. Suddenly a loud rustling noise and a splash made him shudder and reach for his rifle. A boar leapt panting over the embankment, and its black shape, outlined for an instant against the gleaming surface of the water, disappeared into the reeds. Lukashka quickly took aim, but the boar was gone before he could shoot. He spat in fury and walked on. When he came to the log where Nazarka and Ergushov were lying in wait, he stopped and whistled softly. His whistle was returned, and he joined his comrades.

Nazarka lay asleep, curled up in his cloak. Ergushov was sitting cross-legged and moved a little to the side to make room for Lukashka.

"This is fun! And it's a great hideout!" Ergushov whispered. "Did you show Uncle Eroshka the place?"

"Yes," Lukashka replied, spreading his cloak on the ground. "You should have seen the boar I just shied up from the riverbank! It must have been the one we were looking for. You heard all the crackling, no?"

"Yes, I thought right away you must have flushed out something," Ergushov said, pulling his cloak tighter around his shoulders. "I'll get some sleep now. Wake me when the first cock crows," he added. "We have to do this right: I'll catch a few winks now while you're on watch, and then you can get some sleep while I watch."

"As it is, I don't feel like sleeping," Lukashka replied.

The night was dark and warm. Stars shone in one part of the sky, the larger part by the mountain was overcast. A single, large black cloud that blended with the peaks in the windless night slowly spread further and further, standing out starkly from the deep, starry sky. All Lukashka could see was the Terek and the distance beyond. Behind him and to his sides was a wall of reeds. At times they began to sway and rustle against one another for no apparent reason. Seen from below, their swaying tops looked like tender, leafy branches against the light part of the sky. At his feet lay the riverbank, beyond which the torrent was seething. Further out, the glossy mass of brown water rippled monotonously past banks and shoals, and further still the water, the opposite bank, and the clouds faded into the impenetrable darkness. Black shadows, which Lukashka's sharp eye recognized as driftwood that the current was carrying downstream, were drifting along the surface of the river. Rare flashes of summer lightning sparked in the water as in a black mirror, revealing the outline of the sloping bank on the other side. The even sounds of the night, the rustling of the reeds, the snoring of the Cossacks, the humming of the mosquitoes, and the flowing water were interrupted from time to time by a distant gunshot, the gurgling of a chunk of the riverbank falling into the water, the splash of a big fish, and the crackling of an animal in the wild undergrowth. An owl flew along the river, its wings flapping together with every second beat, and right above the Cossacks' heads it turned and flew toward the forest, its wings now touching at every beat. It hovered over a gnarled plane tree and then settled in its branches. At every unexpected sound Lukashka listened intently, narrowing his eyes, and slowly reached for his rifle.

The greater part of the night had passed. The black cloud had stretched westward, revealing the clear, starry sky from within its torn edges, and the tilted, golden crescent of the moon shone reddish above the mountains. There was now a chill in the air. Nazarka woke, muttered a few words, and fell asleep again. Lukashka was bored, got up, and began stripping the sapling he had found earlier in the evening into a rod for cleaning his rifle. His head was filled with thoughts of the Chechens living in the mountains, and how their young fighters crossed the Terek, unafraid of the Cossacks; but they might be crossing at some other point. He leaned out from his hiding place and looked up and down the river, but saw nothing. He gazed at the opposite bank, which stood out weakly against the water in the timid light of the moon, and stopped thinking about the Chechens. He was now only waiting for it to be time to wake his comrades so they could all return to the village for the festival. He imagined Dunaika there, his "sweet soul," as the Cossacks call their mistresses, and he was filled with anger. He saw the first signs of morning—a silvery mist whitening over the water, and young eagles nearby whistling shrilly and flapping their wings. Finally the first cockcrow came from the distant village, followed by a second, which was answered by others.

"It's time to wake them up," Lukashka thought. He had finished stripping the rod, and his eyes were growing heavy. He turned to his comrades and tried to figure out which legs belonged to whom; but suddenly he thought he heard a splash from the opposite bank of the river. He again glanced at the brightening mountains on the horizon beneath the moon's tilted sickle, at the outline of the opposite bank, at the river, and at the driftwood now clearly visible floating downstream. He felt as if it was he who was moving while the river with its driftwood was stationary—but this feeling was only momentary. He fixed his eyes again on the driftwood. A large, black log with a branch sticking out of it caught his attention. There was something strange about it. It was floating along in the middle of the river without swaying or rolling. It did not look as if it were being carried downstream by the current but more as if it were cutting across the river toward the shallows. Lukashka carefully leaned forward and watched its progress. The tree trunk floated toward a sandbank, stopped, and then began to shift strangely. Lukashka thought he saw a hand appear from behind the log.

"I'm going to get that Chechen myself!" he muttered, reaching for his rifle. He set up his rifle rest with calm, quick movements, leaned the rifle on it, held it there silently, cocked the trigger, and holding his breath, his eyes darting up and down the river, took aim. "No, I'm not going to wake the others first," he thought. His heart began beating so fast that he had to stop. He listened. The log suddenly jolted forward and once more began floating toward him. "I mustn't miss!" he thought, and suddenly, in the weak light of the moon, he saw the head of a Chechen bob up in front of the log. He aimed directly at the head, it seemed quite near, right at the end of the rifle barrel. He peered over it.

"Yes, it's a Chechen all right!" he thought with a surge of joy and, rising to his knees, once more took aim and peered at his target, just visible at the end of his long rifle. "In the name of the Father and the Son," he said, in the Cossack way he had learnt in his earliest years, and pulled the trigger. For an instant a flash of lightning lit the reeds and the water. The sharp, piercing sound of the shot carried across the river and turned into a rumble somewhere far away. The log was no longer floating across the river but bobbing and rolling downstream.

"Grab him!" Ergushov yelled, snatching for his rifle and scrambling up from behind their hideout.

"Shut up!" Lukashka hissed through clenched teeth. "Chechens!"

"Who did you shoot?" Nazarka asked.

Lukashka did not answer but immediately reloaded his gun and watched the floating log. A little way down the river it stopped in the shallows, and something large floated out from behind it.

"What did you shoot? Why won't you tell us?" the Cossacks repeated.

"I told you, a Chechen!" Lukashka said.

"You're pulling our leg! I bet your gun just went off!"

"I killed a Chechen—that's what the shot was!" Lukashka said, jumping to his feet, his voice shaking. "There was a man swimming across, and I killed him! Look over there!" He pointed to the shallows.

"You're lying!" Ergushov said, rubbing his eyes.

"No, I'm not! Look over there! Look!" Lukashka said, grabbing him by the shoulder and pulling him with such force that Ergushov gasped.

Ergushov looked to where Lukashka was pointing. He saw the body in the water and immediately changed his tone. "Well, look at that! But, as God is my witness, I'm sure there'll be others coming, too!" he said quietly and began loading his rifle. "That man you shot was a scout! The others must be close by—somewhere up that riverbank, as God is my witness!"

Lukashka began unfastening his belt and slipped off his Circassian coat.

"Where do you think you're going?" Ergushov hissed. "If you so much as show yourself, you'll be done for, as God is my witness! You've already shot that Chechen, it's not like he's going to get away now! Give me some powder—you have some? Nazarka, get back to the checkpoint as fast as you can, but don't go along the riverbank, otherwise they'll pick you off!"

"Go back on my own?" Nazarka snapped angrily. "You go!"

Lukashka, having removed his jacket, crawled toward the riverbank.

"Don't go in the water!" Ergushov said, priming the pan of his rifle with powder. "Can't you see he's not moving? It's almost morning—let's wait till our mounted patrol gets here! Go back to the checkpoint, Nazarka! Look at him, he's frightened! There's no need to be frightened, as God is my witness!"

"Lukashka, hey, Lukashka!" Nazarka called out. "You didn't say how you shot him!"

Lukashka suddenly stopped, having changed his mind about going into the river.

"Why don't the two of you head back to the checkpoint! I'll keep watch here! Tell the others to send the patrol; those Chechens might well be on this side of the river by now, we have to catch them!"

"My point exactly! They'll get away!" Ergushov said, getting up. "They have to be caught, that's for sure! Stay here and don't move! You'll be done for if they see you! Keep your eyes peeled, do you hear?"

"I know, I know," Lukashka said. Examining his rifle again, he crouched back down behind the log. Ergushov and Nazarka crossed themselves and headed back to the checkpoint over the forest path, cutting their way through the brambles to avoid the riverbank.

Lukashka sat alone, watching the shallows and listening for the Cossack patrol. It was a long way to the checkpoint, but he was plagued by impatience—he was worrying that the Chechens following the man he had killed might manage to escape. He was just as furious as he had been when the boar had gotten away the evening before. He kept glancing around, looking up and down the bank, expecting to see a man any moment. He had set up his rifle rest and was ready to shoot. That he might be the one who could be shot never crossed his mind.

9

It was growing light. The Chechen's body, bobbing gently in the shallows, was now clearly visible. There was a rustling in the reeds next to

Lukashka; he heard steps and saw the tops of the reeds moving. He cocked his rifle and whispered, "In the name of the Father and the Son," but as the rifle catch clicked the footsteps fell silent.

"Hey there, Cossacks! Don't shoot old Uncle Eroshka!" a calm bass voice called, and the old man stepped out from the reeds.

"By God, I almost killed you!" Lukashka said.

"What did you shoot?" The old man's sonorous voice echoed through the forest and down the river, breaking the silence and mystery of the night that had enveloped Lukashka. It was as if everything around suddenly became clearer and brighter.

"You might not have shot anything last night, but I certainly did," Lukashka said, uncocking his rifle and getting up with remarkable calmness.

The old man stared at the Chechen's back, now clearly glistening in the water rippling around it.

"He was swimming behind the log, but I saw him, and . . . Hey, look at that! Can you see it? He has a rifle! Do you see it?" Lukashka asked.

"Of course!" the old man said angrily, his face serious and stern. "You killed a Chechen warrior!" he added with a touch of sadness.

"I was sitting here, and looked over there and wondered what that black thing was. I spotted him while he was on the other side—it looked as if a man had been walking along the bank and suddenly fallen into the river. 'How strange!' I thought. And the log, a nice big log, comes floating along, not downstream, but across the river! I'm watching the log, and suddenly I see a head poking out. 'Really strange!' I think. I look out from the reeds where I'm crouching and see nothing. I get up, and I'm sure the bastard hears me, he swims over to the shallows, where he looks around. 'Ha!'—I think to myself— 'You're not going to get away!' I felt like something was stuck in my throat! I get my rifle ready and wait, not moving a hair! The Chechen waited a bit, waited some more, and then swam on, and the moment he swam into the moonlight I could see his back! 'In the name of the Father and the Son, and the Holy Ghost!' Then I look through the smoke of my rifle and see him floundering. He was moaning—at least I thought he was. Ah, God be praised, I've killed him! And when he floated over to the shallows, I could see him clearly. He tried to get up but didn't have the strength. He kept thrashing about and then just lay there. I saw it all clearly! He wasn't moving, so he had to be dead, is what I thought. Nazarka and Ergushov ran back to the checkpoint to get the others, in case there are more Chechens around."

"And so you got him!" the old man said. "He is far away now, my boy!" And again he shook his head sadly.

Cossack horsemen and foot soldiers came crashing through the underbrush along the riverbank, talking loudly among themselves.

"Did you bring the boat?" Lukashka shouted to them.

"Good man, Luka! Let's haul the Chechen out of the water!" one of the Cossacks called.

Lukashka, not waiting for the boat, began undressing, his eyes fixed on his prey.

"Wait! Nazarka is bringing the boat!" the sergeant called.

"You fool!" another Cossack shouted. "The Chechen might just be pretending to be dead! Take your dagger with you!"

"Nonsense!" Lukashka shouted back, taking off his trousers. He undressed, crossed himself, jumped into the water with a splash, and swam toward the shallows against the current, his white arms arcing high, his back rising out of the water. The Cossacks were talking loudly among themselves on the riverbank, and three mounted men rode off to patrol the area. The boat appeared at the bend in the river. Lukashka stood up in the shallows, bent over the body, and shook it twice. "He's dead all right!" he called back sharply.

The bullet had hit the Chechen in the head. He was wearing blue trousers, a shirt, and a Circassian coat, and had a gun and a dagger slung over his shoulder. There was also a large branch tied to his back, which at first had misled Lukashka.

"That's a big fish you've landed!" one of the Cossacks said as the Chechen's body was pulled out of the boat and rolled onto the riverbank, pressing down the weeds.

"How yellow he looks!" another Cossack said.

"Where did our men go to hunt down the other Chechens?" a third asked. "I'm sure they're still all on the other bank. This one had to be a scout if he was swimming like that, otherwise why would he have been alone?"

"He must have been a good fighter, with a sharper mind than the others! A brave warrior!" Lukashka said mockingly, shivering in the cold. "His beard is dyed and clipped."

"And he had a coat in that sack tied to his back, so he could swim better," one of the Cossacks added.

"Lukashka, you take the dagger and coat, and I'll give you three rubles for the gun," the sergeant said tentatively, holding out the dead man's rifle. "You can see it's all dented here," he added quickly, blowing into the barrel. "I just want it for a keepsake."

Lukashka did not answer. He was angry at the sergeant's deviousness but knew he could not avoid giving him the rifle.

"That Chechen bastard! He could have had a good coat instead of this rag," Lukashka said, glowering and hurling the Chechen's coat on the ground.

"At least you can use it as a sack for kindling wood," one of the Cossacks said.

"I'm heading back to the village," Lukashka told the sergeant, forgetting his anger and ready to put the sergeant's three rubles to good use.

"Yes, go ahead," the sergeant said. Still eyeing the rifle, he turned to the Cossacks. "Boys, drag the body back to the checkpoint! And cover him with branches so he doesn't lie in the sun—the Chechens might come down from the mountains to ransom him."

"But it's not yet all that hot," one of the men said.

"What if the jackals get at the body? That wouldn't be good, would it?" another Cossack cut in.

"We'll set up a watch. It would be bad if they come to ransom him and he's been torn to pieces."

"Well, Lukashka, like it or not, you have to stand all the men here a hefty bucket of vodka!" the sergeant called out cheerfully.

"That's the custom!" the Cossacks chimed in. "See how God has favored you? Still green behind the ears, and you've already felled a Chechen warrior!"

"Buy the dagger and the coat, and throw in a few more rubles and you can have the trousers too!" Lukashka said. "They don't fit me—he was a bony devil!"

One of the Cossacks bought the coat for a ruble. Another bought the dagger for two buckets of vodka.

"You'll drink your fill, boys! I'm standing you all a bucket of vodka!" Lukashka called out. "I'll bring it myself from the village."

"And cut the trousers up into kerchiefs for the girls!" Nazarka said. The Cossacks guffawed.

"Enough horsing around!" the sergeant said. "Drag the body back to the checkpoint! And remember not to leave the carcass to rot outside the hut!"

"What are you waiting for? Take the Chechen away!" Lukashka shouted with authority at the Cossacks, who grudgingly picked up the body, as if Lukashka were their commander. They dragged the body a few steps, then let its legs drop lifelessly to the ground. They stepped aside and stood for a few moments in silence. Nazarka walked up to the corpse and straightened its head, which had slumped to the side, so that the dead man's face and the bloody bullet wound above his temple could be seen.

"Look at the mark it made! Right in the brain!" he said. "But at least his people will still recognize him when they come for him."

The Cossacks said nothing, the angel of silence flying over them. The sun had already risen and lit the dew-covered grass with its splintered rays. The river was seething nearby. From throughout the awakened forest, pheasants were greeting the morning. The Cossacks stood silent and motionless around the dead man. The brown body, bare except for the wet, blue trousers girdled by a sash over the taut stomach, was handsome and strong. His muscular arms lay straight by his sides, and his bluish and freshly shaven head with its clotted wound was thrown back, his smooth, sunburnt forehead standing out sharply against the shaven part of the head. His glassy, wide-open eyes stared blankly upward with sunken pupils. His delicate lips, drawn out at the edges and prominent beneath his red, well-trimmed mustache, seemed set in an easy, good-natured smile. His slender hands were covered in reddish hairs, and the nails on his clenched fingers were painted red. Lukashka had not yet dressed and was still wet, his neck more flushed and his eyes brighter than usual. His broad cheekbones quivered. Faint steam was rising from his white, healthy body in the fresh morning air.

"He too was a man!" Lukashka said, evidently admiring the dead Chechen.

"Yes, but if it had been up to him, he wouldn't have shown *you* any mercy," one of the Cossacks replied.

The angel of silence flew away. The Cossacks began bustling and talking. Two men set out to cut some brushwood to cover the body. Others strolled off toward the checkpoint. Lukashka and Nazarka hurried to get ready to go to the village, and within half an hour were making their way through the thick forest, almost running, and talking continually.

"But don't tell Dunaika I sent you!" Lukashka was saying in a sharp voice. "Just go find out if her husband is home."

"I'll also drop in to see Yamka, maybe we can all carouse and have some fun!" Nazarka said.

"When should we carouse, if not today!" Lukashka replied.

Lukashka and Nazarka arrived at the village, drank a little, and then lay down to sleep till nightfall.

10

On the third day after the events just described, two companies of the Caucasus Infantry were stationed in the village of Novomlinskaya. Army carts were standing around the square unharnessed. The company cooks dug a pit, stole some loose firewood from nearby yards, and began boiling kasha. The sergeant majors were busy calling the roll. The men from the cart units were hammering tethering posts into the ground. The quartermasters walked the streets as if they were from the village and showed officers and soldiers where their lodgings were. Green boxes stood in rows. There were carts and horses everywhere, and caldrons of boiling kasha. The captain, the lieutenant, and Onisim Mikhailovich, the sergeant major, were standing around. The companies had been ordered to quarter in this village, so they made themselves at home. No one told the Cossack villagers why these soldiers were being stationed here, where they were from, or whether they were Old Believers, nor were the villagers asked if they minded the soldiers being billeted on them.

Off duty, exhausted, and covered in dirt, the soldiers fill the streets and squares like a noisy and disordered swarm of bees. Completely ignoring the villagers' hostility, they enter the houses in twos and threes, chatting merrily, their rifles jangling, hang up their bullet belts, unpack their sacks, and make coarse remarks to the women. A large group of them is standing around the soldier's favorite spot, the caldron filled with boiling food. They smoke pipes and watch the steam rising faintly into the hot sky, where it thickens into a white cloud, and the flames of the fires quiver in the air like melting glass. They make fun of the Cossack villagers for their un-Russian ways. Soldiers appear in every yard. One can hear their laughter, one can hear the angry, piercing cries of the Cossack women defending their homes, refusing to give the soldiers water or kitchenware. Boys and girls, clinging to their mothers' aprons and each other, watch the soldiers' every move with terror and excitement—these are the first soldiers they have ever seen—and run after them, keeping a careful distance. Old Cossacks come out of their huts, sit on the earthen mounds that encircle every Cossack abode, and in somber silence, as if they neither knew nor cared what would come of all of this, watch the soldiers go about their business.

Olenin, who had signed up three months earlier as a cadet in the Caucasus Regiment, was billeted on one of the best houses in the village, the house of Cornet Ilya Vasilyevich—in other words, Old Ulitka's house.

"I wonder where all this will end, Dmitri Andreyevich!" Vanyusha called, catching his breath. Olenin, sporting a Circassian coat, had just ridden into the courtyard on a horse he had bought in Grozny and was in the best of spirits after the regiment's five-hour march.

"Why, what's the matter, Ivan Vasilich?" Olenin asked, patting his horse and looking cheerfully at Vanyusha, who had ridden in on a baggage cart and who, sweating and disheveled, was now anxiously unloading Olenin's bags and trunks. By all appearances, Olenin was very much a changed man. A youthful mustache and beard covered his formerly clean-shaven face, and a healthy, reddish tan on his cheeks, forehead, and neck had replaced the yellowish pallor of late nights and revelry. He now carried a rifle, and his new black tailcoat had been replaced by a dirty white Circassian coat with wide folds. Instead of a fresh, stiff collar, the thin red band of a quilted silk shirt girded his sunburnt neck. He wore Circassian clothes, but he did not wear them well. It was plain to see that he was Russian, not a Circassian warrior. Everything was right—but not quite. And yet, his whole appearance exuded health, cheerfulness, and self-satisfaction.

"You seem to think this is all a joke," Vanyusha said, "but just try speaking to these people! They don't give you a chance, not a chance! You can't squeeze a word out of them!" Vanyusha angrily hurled an iron bucket down on the doorstep. "Somehow these people aren't Russian!"

"You should have a word with the village chief."

"How can I if I don't know where his ... his locationality is!" Vanyusha spluttered in an offended tone.

"Who has upset you?" Olenin asked, looking around.

"The Devil only knows! Damn! There's no real master in this house—they say he's gone off to a *kriga** or something. And the old woman inside is such a devil that only God can save us!" Vanyusha said, clutching his head. "I don't know how we'll live here. These people call themselves Christians, but they're worse than Tatars! Even a Tatar is more noble. 'He's gone off to the *kriga*'! Not that I have the slightest idea what a damn *kriga* is!" Vanyusha turned away.

"You mean, things here aren't quite what they are back home?" Olenin asked mockingly, still in his saddle.

"Can I please take your horse now?" Vanyusha asked, visibly distraught at the new order of things but resigning himself to his fate.

"So, even a Tatar is more noble, is he?" Olenin said, dismounting and tapping the saddle with his hand.

"You're laughing, you think this is funny!" Vanyusha said angrily.

---

* A *kriga* is a place on the riverbank with a wattle fence for catching fish. [Tolstoy's note]

"Come now, don't be angry, Ivan Vasilich!" Olenin said, still smiling. "I'll go speak to the people in the house right away and arrange everything. Don't worry, we are going to have a wonderful time here!"

Vanyusha did not answer. He narrowed his eyes, shook his head, and contemptuously watched his master walk toward the house. Vanyusha thought of Olenin only as his master, and Olenin saw Vanyusha only as his servant, and both men would have been taken aback had anyone suggested that they were friends. And yet they were friends, even though they did not know it. Vanyusha had been taken into Olenin's house when he was eleven and Olenin too was eleven. When Olenin was fifteen, he had spent some time teaching Vanyusha to read French, of which Vanyusha was extremely proud. And now, whenever Vanyusha was in a good mood he dropped French words, always laughing foolishly when he did so.

Olenin hurried onto the porch of the house and pushed open the door to the front room. Maryanka, wearing the kind of pink Tatar smock that Cossack women usually wear in the house, jumped back startled from the door and shrank against the wall, covering her nose and mouth with her wide sleeve. Olenin opened the door further and in the dim light saw the young Cossack woman's tall, shapely figure. With the quick and hungry curiosity of youth, he noticed despite himself the strong, virginal lines that stood out beneath the thin calico smock, and her beautiful black eyes that were fixed on him with childish terror and wild curiosity. "She is the one!" Olenin thought. "And yet I'm sure there are many more around here like her" was the thought that immediately followed, and he completely opened the door. Old Ulitka, also in a smock, was bent over with her back toward him, sweeping the floor.

"Greetings, I've come about my lodgings," he began.

Without straightening up, the Cossack woman turned her severe but still beautiful face toward him. "What have you come for, to scoff at us? I'll teach you scoffing, may the Black Plague strike you down!" she shouted, glaring at him venomously from the corner of her eyes.

Olenin had imagined that the gallant, battle-worn Caucasus Infantry, to which he belonged, would be welcomed enthusiastically everywhere, particularly by the Cossacks, who were, after all, brothers-in-arms. He was therefore quite taken aback at this reception. Not to be put off, he began explaining that he was perfectly willing to pay for the lodgings, but the old woman would not let him speak. "What have you come for? Who needs a plague like you, may the pox rot your ugly mug!" she shrieked. "Wait till my husband comes home, he'll show you your place! I don't need your dirty money—as if I don't have my own! He wants to foul up my house with his tobacco, and then give me money! You think I need such a plague? A bullet into your bowels!"

"I see Vanyusha is right," Olenin thought. "Even a Tatar is more noble." And followed by Old Ulitka's curses, he went outside. As he walked out the door, Maryanka, still in her pink smock but now wearing a kerchief that covered her whole face except for her eyes, unexpectedly slipped past him out of the front room, her bare feet pattering nimbly over the porch. She stopped for an instant and looked back with laughing eyes before disappearing around the corner of the house. Her strong, youthful step, the untamed look in the flashing eyes peering over the edge of the white kerchief, and her strong, shapely body struck Olenin with even more force than before. "She is the one!" he thought, and went out into the yard to Vanyusha, looking back at Maryanka and thinking even less than before about his lodgings.

"You see, here even the young girls are wild!" Vanyusha said, still bustling about the cart, but now a little more cheerfully. "She's just like a wild little mare! *La femme!*" he added in a loud, portentous voice, and then burst out laughing.

11

Toward evening the cornet came home from fishing, and hearing that he was going to be paid for billeting Olenin, calmed his wife down and quickly provided Vanyusha with everything he needed. Ulitka and the cornet moved to the older, heated house, while Olenin was given the new, still unheated one for three rubles a month.

Olenin ate and took a nap. He woke up toward evening, washed and tidied himself, and ate dinner. Lighting a cigarette, he sat by the window that looked out onto the street. The heat had subsided. The slanted shadow of the house with its ornately carved gables lay across the dusty street and fell onto the lower part of the house across the way, whose thatched roof was glowing in the rays of the setting sun. The air grew fresher. The village had fallen silent. All the soldiers had settled quietly into their lodgings. The herds had not yet been driven back to the cowsheds, and the villagers had not returned from the fields and orchards.

Olenin's lodgings were almost at the edge of the village. From time to time dull gunshots echoed from far across the Terek, from the Chechen and Kumik lands through which the army had marched. After three months of hard bivouacking, Olenin felt comfortable. His face felt clean and fresh, and his rested body and limbs, not used to cleanliness during the long months of the campaign, felt calm and strong. His soul too was fresh and clear. He thought of the campaign and the dangers that were now past. He thought how well he had carried himself, that he had not behaved worse than the next man, and how the valiant Cossacks had accepted him as a comrade. By now his thoughts of Moscow had all but disappeared. His old life had been wiped away, and a life that was new, completely new, had begun, and there had not yet been time for mistakes. A new man among new men, he could acquire a new reputation. He experienced a youthful feeling of irrational joy in life, and as he looked out the window at little boys chasing hoops in the shadows by the house, and looked around his tidy new lodgings, he thought how well he was going to settle into this new way of life in the Cossack village. He also looked at the mountains and the sky, and a stern feeling of the majesty of nature mingled with all his memories and dreams. His new life had not begun the way he had imagined it would on his journey from Moscow, but it had begun unexpectedly well. Mountains, mountains, and more mountains were at the heart of everything he thought and felt.

"He kissed his dog good-bye, he licked the barrel dry!" the children who had been chasing hoops suddenly began chanting, peering around the corner into the side street. "He kissed his dog good-bye!" they shouted and began edging backward.

The taunts were directed at Uncle Eroshka, who was returning from the hunt with his rifle slung over his shoulder and three pheasants hanging from his belt.

"I have sinned, I have sinned, children!" he called out, waving his hands briskly and looking into the windows of the houses on both sides of the street. "I sold my poor dog for drink, sinner that I am!" he said, vexed at himself but trying to act as if he did not care.

Olenin was surprised at the children's behavior toward the old man but was even more taken aback by the man's strong frame and expressive, intelligent face.

"Uncle!" he called out to him. "Can you come here a moment?"

The old man looked into the window and stopped. "Greetings, my friend," he said, raising his hat over his close-cropped head.

"Greetings, my friend," Olenin answered. "What are those brats shouting at you?"

Uncle Eroshka walked over to the window. "They are making fun of me, old man that I am. But I don't mind. I like it. Why shouldn't they have a little fun at their old uncle's expense?" he said in his strong, resonant voice. "Are you the commander of the soldiers?"

"No, I'm a cadet. Where did you catch those pheasants?"

"I caught these three hens in the forest," the old man answered, turning his broad back to the window, showing Olenin the pheasants that hung with their heads wedged in his belt, staining his coat with blood. "Never seen pheasants before?" he asked. "Here, take a pair. There you go." And he handed Olenin two birds through the window. "Are you a hunter yourself?"

"Yes I am," Olenin answered. "During the campaign I shot four."

"Four? That's a lot!" the old man said with a mocking twinkle in his eye. "You a drinker? You drink Chikhir wine?"

"Do I drink Chikhir wine! I love drinking!"

"Ha! I see you're a fine fellow! We will be true blood brothers, you and I!" Uncle Eroshka called out.

"Come on in!" Olenin said. "Let's drink some Chikhir!"

"I'll come in," the old man answered. "But here, first take the pheasants."

Eroshka's face clearly showed that he liked the cadet—he realized he could drink here for free and that his gift of the two pheasants would not go to waste. A few moments later Eroshka appeared at the door. It was only now that Olenin realized how big and strong his frame was, youthful in spite of the old man's thick white beard and the deep lines of age and toil. The muscles of his arms, legs, and shoulders were full and strong, like those of a young man. Deep scars were visible on his head beneath his cropped hair. His thick, sinewy neck was covered in crisscrossing folds like that of a bull, his rough hands scratched and battered. He entered the room with a light step, slung his rifle from his shoulder, and put it in the corner, sizing up Olenin's belongings with a quick glance. Stepping softly in his rawhide shoes, he walked through the room, bringing with him a penetrating but not unpleasant odor of Chikhir, vodka, gunpowder, and congealed blood. He bowed before the icons, smoothed his beard, walked over to Olenin, and reached out his strong, swarthy hand.

"Hoshgildi!" he said. "In Tatar that means 'Good day, peace be with you'—that's what it means in their language."

"Hoshgildi! I know," Olenin replied, giving him his hand.

"No, no! That's not how it's done, you fool!" Uncle Eroshka said, shaking his head reproachfully. "If someone says *'Hoshgildi'* to you, you're supposed to say, *'Allah pazi bo sun!'* which means, 'May God save you!' That's what you're supposed to say, not *'Hoshgildi.'* I'll teach you all of that. We had a fellow here called Ilya Moseyich, one of you Russians, and he and I were blood brothers. A drinker, horse rustler, and hunter—and what a hunter! I taught him everything he knew!"

"What are you going to teach me?" Olenin asked with growing interest.

"I'll take you hunting, I'll teach you how to fish, I'll show you Chechens, and if you want a pretty little sweet soul, I'll get you one. That's the kind of man I am, someone who knows how to have fun!" Uncle Eroshka burst out laughing. "Let me sit down, my friend—I'm worn out! *Karga?"*

"What does *karga* mean?"

"It means 'all right' in Georgian. That's what I always say, it's my favorite word. When I say *karga,* it means I'm ready for some fun. So, my friend, won't you call for some Chikhir? You have an orderly, don't you? Ivan!" the old man shouted. "All of your soldiers are called Ivan. Your man's an Ivan too, isn't he?"

"Yes, he is. Vanyusha! Go get some Chikhir from our landlord, and bring it here."

"Ivan or Vanyusha, it's all the same. Why are all your soldiers Ivans? Ivan!" the old man called out. "Tell them to give you Chikhir from the barrel they just started. They have the best Chikhir in the village— and don't pay more than thirty kopecks, because you'll only give that old witch something to gloat about. It's a curse how stupid our people are," Uncle Eroshka confided after Vanyusha had left. "They don't see you Russians as men. To them you are worse than a Tatar. They say all Russians are worldly sinners. But if you ask me, even though you're a Russian soldier, you're still a man—you have a soul in you. Why do I say that? My friend Ilya Moseyich was a Russian soldier, and he was a man of gold! And you know what, my friend, that's why my people don't like me, but I don't care! I'm a fun-loving man, I love everyone, I, Eroshka! That's how it is, my friend!"

And the old man patted the young man tenderly on the shoulder.

12

Vanyusha was in the best of spirits. He had prepared Olenin's lodgings, managed to get himself shaved by the company barber, and pulled his trouser legs out of his boots as a sign that the company was now at rest and comfortably billeted. He eyed Eroshka with wary misgiving, as if he were some unknown wild beast. He shook his head at the floor Eroshka had soiled with his shoes, took two empty bottles from under the bench, and headed over to Old Ulitka.

"Good evening to you, dear mistress," he said, intent on being particularly amiable. "The gentleman sent me to buy some Chikhir from you—will you be so kind as to pour me some?"

The old woman did not answer. Her daughter was standing in front of a small Tatar mirror, tying a kerchief around her head. She turned and looked at Vanyusha.

"I will give you good money," Vanyusha said, jingling the coins in his pocket, and then added, "Be nice to us, and we'll be nice to you— it will be better that way."

"You want a lot of Chikhir?"

"Just an eighth."

"Go and tap some for him," Old Ulitka told her daughter. "And mind, sweetie, that it's from the barrel we just started."

The girl brought a ring of keys and a jug, and Vanyusha followed her out of the house.

Olenin saw her walk past the window. "Who is that woman?" he asked Uncle Eroshka.

The old man winked and nudged him with his elbow.

"Watch this," he said, leaning out the window. He cleared his throat and bellowed, "Maryanka! Darling Maryanka! Won't you fall in love with me, my sweetheart?" He turned to Olenin and whispered, "I'm always good for a joke!"

Without looking back, Maryanka walked on with the strutting gait of the Cossack woman, smoothly swinging her arms. Then she slowly turned her black, long-lashed eyes toward the old man.

"Love me and I promise you happiness!" Eroshka shouted, and with a wink looked at Olenin as if expecting him to say something. "What you need is a quick tongue—just a bit of fun," he added. "She's a fine girl, isn't she?"

"A beauty," Olenin said. "Call her over."

"No, no!" the old man replied. "She's been promised to Lukashka. Luka is a good Cossack, a fighter, he killed a Chechen warrior the other day. I'll find you a better girl—I'll find you one dressed in silk and silver. I said I'll find you one, and find you one I will! A real beauty, you'll see!"

"An old man like you saying such things!" Olenin exclaimed. "What you're suggesting is a sin!"

"A sin? What do you mean, a sin?" the old man snapped. "Is it a sin to look at a pretty girl? Is it a sin to have some fun with her? Or is it a sin to love her? Is that how things are back where you're from? No, my dear friend, it is not sin, it is salvation! God made you and God also made women. He made everything. So how can it be a sin to look at a pretty woman? That's what she was made for—to be loved and taken delight in. That's how *I* see things!"

Maryanka crossed the courtyard and entered the dark, cool storeroom filled with barrels. She walked over to one, spoke the customary words of prayer, and put in the siphon. Vanyusha stood in the doorway, smiling. He found it very funny that she was only wearing a smock, and that the smock was tight behind and tucked up in front, and even funnier that she was wearing a coin necklace. He thought all this was very un-Russian, and imagined how everyone back home in the servant quarters would laugh if they saw such a girl. "But *la fille il c'est très bien!*" he thought. "I will tell my master."

"You're blocking the light, you devil!" the girl suddenly said. "You'd do better to give me that jug!"

Maryanka filled the jug with cold red wine and handed it to Vanyusha.

"No, give Mother the money," she said, pushing away his hand with the coins.

Vanyusha laughed.

"Why are you so unkind, you sweet girl?" he asked good-naturedly, shifting from one foot to the other while Maryanka stopped up the barrel.

She burst out laughing. "Are *you* perhaps kind?"

"The gentleman and I are both very kind," Vanyusha said emphatically. "We are so kind that wherever we have been quartered, the people putting us up were grateful to us. My master is a nobleman."

Maryanka stood and listened. "So, is your master married?" she asked.

"No! My master is young and unmarried—because noblemen can never marry young," Vanyusha said in a superior tone.

"Too young? An ox of a man like that too young to marry? Is he the commander of all you men here?"

"My master is a cadet. That means he's not an officer yet. But actually he is higher up than a general, because he's so important. The Czar himself knows him," Vanyusha said with pride. "We aren't poor riffraff like the other soldiers. My master's father was a senator, he had more than a thousand serfs, and my master is sent a thousand rubles a month. That's why wherever we've been quartered the people loved us. Another man might be an army captain, but if he has no money, then what's the good of that, as—"

"I'll go lock up," the girl interrupted.

Vanyusha carried the wine to Olenin, proclaiming, *"La fille il c'est très jullie!"* And with a foolish laugh he quickly left the room.

13

Meanwhile, a bugle sounded tattoo in the village square. The villagers were returning from work. The cattle were lowing by the gates in a dusty golden cloud. Women and girls hurried through streets and yards, driving the cattle toward the sheds. The sun sank below the distant snow-covered mountain range, and a bluish shadow spread over earth and sky. The first stars appeared dimly over the darkening orchards, and the bustle in the village gradually fell silent. After tending the cattle, the women gathered on the street corners to sit in groups on the earthen mounds surrounding the houses, cracking sunflower seeds with their teeth. Maryanka, having milked the cows, joined a group of women and girls who were talking to an old man about the Chechen warrior whom Lukashka had killed. The old Cossack was telling the tale, and the women were asking questions.

"I bet he'll get a good reward, won't he?" one of the women asked.

"Of course he will. Word has it they'll give him a medal."

"But Mosyev tried to get the better of him—he took his rifle, but the commanders in Kizlyar heard about it."

"He's mean-spirited, Mosyev is!"

"I heard Lukashka has come back to the village," one of the girls said.

"He and Nazarka have already drunk half a bucket at Yamka's." Yamka was a dissolute, unmarried Cossack woman who kept a drinking house.

"That Lukashka the Snatcher is a lucky man!" one of the women added. "A real snatcher! That's for sure a fine boy! His father, old Kiryazh, was a fine man too, and Luka's just like him. When old Kiryazh was killed, the whole village wailed. Ah, look, here they come," the woman said, pointing at three men walking toward them along the street. "Ha, that drunkard Ergushov managed to join them!"

Lukashka, Nazarka, and Ergushov had drunk half a bucket of

vodka among them. The faces of all three were redder than usual, particularly that of old Ergushov, who was tottering. Laughing loudly, he kept nudging Nazarka in the ribs.

"Hey there, girls!" he called out. "How about a song!"

"Greetings, greetings!" the girls called out.

"Why should we sing, it's not a feast day!" one of the women said. "It's you who's full of drink—*you* sing!"

Ergushov guffawed and nudged Nazarka. "Why don't you start, and I'll sing along. I'm the best singer you ever heard!"

"Hey, have you fallen asleep, my beauties?" Nazarka shouted. "We've come back from the checkpoint to drink your health! But as you can see, we've already drunk Lukashka's!"

As Lukashka approached the group, he slowly raised his sheepskin hat and stopped in front of the girls. His neck and wide cheekbones were flushed. He stood and spoke quietly and deliberately; but in his quietness and deliberateness there was more vitality than in all of Nazarka's antics. Lukashka was like a playful stallion that had suddenly stopped in midgallop, snorting and flicking its tail. He spoke little, glancing at his drunken comrades and then back at the girls with a twinkle in his eye. When Maryanka joined the group at the corner, he raised his sheepskin hat in an unhurried sweep, stepped aside for her to pass, and then stepped back in front of her, one foot a little forward, his thumbs hooked into his belt and toying with his dagger. Maryanka acknowledged his greeting with a slight bow, sat down on the earthen mound, and took a bag of sunflower seeds from between her breasts. Lukashka watched her with unmoving eyes. Everyone had fallen quiet when Maryanka appeared.

"So, how long are you boys here?" one of the Cossack women asked, breaking the silence.

"We're going back tomorrow morning," Lukashka answered coolly.

"Well, may God grant that everything go well for you!" the old Cossack said. "I was just telling the others the same thing."

"And so say I!" drunken Ergushov chimed in with a guffaw. "Look how many guests we have here!" he added, pointing at a soldier walking by. "The soldiers' vodka is good—I love it!"

"I've been saddled with three of those devils!" one of the women said. "Grandpa's already gone to the village council, but they say nothing can be done!"

"Aha! You've had trouble with them?" Ergushov exclaimed.

"Have they smoked you out of the house too with that damn tobacco of theirs?" one of the women asked. "I told them they can smoke all they want out in the yard, but not inside the house. Even if the village elder comes himself and demands I let them smoke inside, I won't! And how do I know they won't rob me? The village elder isn't quartering any of them, the old devil!"

"I see you don't like them!" Ergushov said.

"I've also heard tell that the girls have to make the soldiers' beds and pour them Chikhir with honey," Nazarka said, putting his foot forward like Lukashka and, like him, jauntily pushing back his sheepskin hat.

Ergushov laughed out loud and embraced the girl sitting closest to him.

"Get away from me!" the girl burst out. "I'll tell your old woman!"

"So tell her!" Ergushov shouted. "What Nazarka says is true: There was a decree, and you know he can read. It's true!" And he threw his arms around the next girl sitting in the row.

"What do you think you're doing, you beast!" rosy, round-faced Ustenka squealed, laughing and raising her hand to hit him.

Ergushov staggered back and almost lost his balance. "And they say girls aren't strong! You almost killed me!" he guffawed.

"I wish you'd stayed at the checkpoint. The Devil himself sent you back here!" Ustenka said as she turned away, still laughing. "You were asleep when the Chechen came—if he'd slit your throat, we'd all have been better off!"

"I'm sure you'd have wailed at his funeral!" Nazarka said, laughing.

"Yes, just as much as I'll be wailing at yours!"

"You see, she has no heart!" Ergushov said, turning to Nazarka. "You'd think she'd wail at my death, no? What do you say?"

Lukashka was gazing silently at Maryanka, who was obviously embarrassed. "I hear they have billeted the army commander on you," he said, moving closer.

Maryanka, as always, did not answer immediately but slowly raised her eyes and looked at the three Cossacks. There was a spark in Lukashka's eyes as if something special, not related to the conversation, was taking place between him and Maryanka.

"At least they are lucky enough to have two houses," an old woman answered for Maryanka. "Look at Fomushkin—they saddled him with one of the commanders. The whole place is filled with his things, and the family has nowhere to go. Has anyone ever heard of a wild horde like this let loose on a village? But what can you do? It's as if the Black Plague had come down on us!"

"I've heard tell they're going to build a bridge over the Terek," one of the girls said.

"And I've heard tell that they're going to dig a pit for all the girls who're not nice to young men," Nazarka crooned, sidling up to Ustenka.

Ergushov passed Maryanka, who was sitting beside the girl he had just hugged, and threw his arms around the old Cossack woman next to her.

"What, you're not going to hug Maryanka?" Nazarka shouted. "You're supposed to hug all the girls, one after the other!"

"No, this one here is sweeter," Ergushov shouted, kissing the old woman, who was struggling to push him away.

"He's choking me!" she cried out, laughing.

The even sound of stamping feet at the end of the street interrupted the banter. Three soldiers in army coats, their rifles on their shoulders, marched in step to relieve the men standing guard by the ammunition wagon. The corporal, a distinguished old soldier, glaring angrily at the Cossacks, marched his men directly at the group, so that Lukashka and Nazarka, who were in the middle of the street, would have had to move in order to let them pass. Nazarka stepped aside, but Lukashka stayed where he was, narrowing his eyes and turning his broad back toward the soldiers. "We're standing here, so walk around us," he said, contemptuously nodding his head back over his shoulder at the marching men.

They marched silently around him, stamping their boots on the dusty street. Maryanka laughed out loud, and the other girls joined in.

"What handsome uniforms!" Nazarka said. "Such fine military men!" And he marched along the street, mimicking them.

Again the villagers laughed.

Lukashka slowly went over to Maryanka. "Where have you put up the commander who's been billeted on you?" he asked.

Maryanka thought for a moment. "In our new house."

"Is he old or young?" Lukashka asked, sitting down beside her.

"You think I've asked?" she said. "I was sent to get him some Chikhir, and through the window I saw a redheaded fellow sitting with Uncle Eroshka. They brought in a whole cartload of his things." She lowered her gaze.

"I'm glad I managed to get leave from the checkpoint!" Lukashka said, moving closer and looking into her eyes.

"Have you come for a long time?" Maryanka asked with a faint smile.

"Till morning," he said. "Give me some seeds," he added, stretching out his hand.

Maryanka smiled and unbuttoned the collar of her smock.

"Don't take them all, though," she said.

"I was so lonely without you at the checkpoint!" Lukashka said in a restrained whisper, as she took the bag from between her breasts. Moving even closer, he whispered something to her with a twinkle in his eye.

"No, I won't come! I won't!" Maryanka said abruptly, leaning away from him.

"But I want to tell you something," Lukashka whispered. "By God, you must come, Mashenka!"

Maryanka smiled and shook her head.

"Maryanka, Maryanka!" her little brother shouted, running along the street toward them. "Mummy says dinner's ready!"

"I'm coming! Go back on your own, darling, and I'll be there in a minute."

Lukashka stood up and raised his hat. "I think I'll go home too," he said coolly, but struggling to repress a smile, and disappeared behind the corner of the house.

Night had completely descended on the village. Bright stars were strewn across the sky. The streets were dark and empty. Nazarka stayed behind with the Cossack women on the earthen mound, their laughter ringing out. Lukashka, having left nonchalantly, crouched like a cat and then suddenly ran silently toward Maryanka's house, holding down his swinging dagger. He passed two streets, went around the corner, and lifting the tails of his Circassian coat, sat down and waited by the fence. "She's a typical cornet's daughter!" he thought. "Won't even go in for some fun! We'll see!"

The sound of a woman's quick footsteps caught his attention. He listened and chuckled. Maryanka, her head lowered, was walking straight toward him, tapping her cattle switch against the palings of the fence. Lukashka stood up.

"You devil! You startled me!" she said, laughing. "I see you didn't go home after all."

Lukashka put one arm around her and with the other touched her face. "I wanted to tell you something!" he said, his voice trembling.

"What can you have to tell me in the middle of the night?" Maryanka asked. "My mother is waiting for me, and I'm sure your sweet little soul is waiting for you."

She freed herself from his embrace and hurried to the gate of her yard, Lukashka running beside her, still trying to talk her into staying awhile. She stopped and turned to him, smiling. "What did you want to tell me, you night owl?"

"Don't make fun of me, Maryanka! What does it matter that I have a sweet little soul—she can go to Hell for all I care! Just say a word, and I will love you, I will do whatever you want!" He jingled the coins in his pocket. "Hear that? Now we can really live! Other men find happiness, but what about me? Can't I find some with you, Maryanka?"

She remained silent. She stood in front of him, breaking her switch into small pieces with nimble fingers. Lukashka suddenly clenched his fists. "Why do I have to wait and wait?" he exclaimed, seizing both her hands with a dark frown. "Don't I love you, my sweetheart? Do whatever you want with me!"

Maryanka did not turn her face away from him as she spoke. "Don't try to bully me, Lukashka, but there is something I want to tell you," she said, her calm expression and voice not changing. She stepped back but did not pull her hands away from his. "I know I am just a girl, but I want you to listen to me. It's not for me to say, but if you love me, then this is what we should do." She tried to pull away from him. "If you let go of me, I'll tell you. I will marry you, but don't expect any nonsense beforehand."

"You will marry me? But it isn't for us to decide if we can marry! What I'm asking you is to love me, Maryanka!" Lukashka said, suddenly humble and gentle. He smiled and gazed into her eyes. Maryanka embraced him tightly and kissed him vehemently on the lips. "My darling!" she whispered, pressing him against her. Then she suddenly tore herself away and ran through the gate and into her yard, in spite of his entreaties.

"Go! They will see us!" she called back. "Go! I think that devil of a Russian quartered with us is loitering about in the yard!"

"That cornet's daughter!" Lukashka thought. "Ha, she'll marry me! Marriage is nice and fine, but what I want is love."

He found Nazarka at Yamka's, and the two men walked to Dunaika's, where Lukashka spent the night, despite Dunaika's unfaithfulness.

14

Olenin had in fact been in the yard when Maryanka came through the gate, and he heard her say, "That devil of a Russian quartered with us is loitering about in the yard!" He had spent the whole evening with Uncle Eroshka on the porch of his new lodgings. He had called for a table, a samovar, wine, and a lighted candle, and over a glass of tea and a cigar had listened to the tales of the old man, who sat at his feet on the porch. Though the breeze was mild, the candle dripped and the flame danced in all directions, now lighting up the porch's columns, now the table and the plates, now the old man's white, close-cropped head. Moths circled in the air, dust sprinkling from their wings. They thrashed about on the table and in the glasses, flew into the flame of the candle, or disappeared into the black air beyond the circle of light.

Olenin and Eroshka drank five bottles of Chikhir. Eroshka kept filling the glasses, always handing one to Olenin, drinking his health and talking tirelessly. He spoke of the Cossacks' old way of life, of his father, who had been called Broad-back. He had been known to carry a dead boar weighing upward of ten pood* on his shoulders, and could drink two whole buckets of Chikhir in a single sitting. He talked of his youth and of his friend Girchik, with whom he had carried felt cloaks across the Terek during the plague. He talked of hunting, and how one morning he had killed two deer, and of his sweet little soul who used to come out to the checkpoint at night. He told all this with such passion that Olenin did not notice how much time had passed.

"Ah yes, my friend," Eroshka told him, "you did not know me in my best years—back then I could have shown you a thing or two! And now the children sing, 'He kissed his dog good-bye, he licked the barrel dry!' but in those days the name Eroshka thundered through the whole regiment. Who had the best horse? Who had a genuine Gurda sword? Who was the man to go drinking and carousing with? Who was sent to the mountains to kill Ahmet Khan? Eroshka, that's who! Who did the girls love? Eroshka! And that's because I was a true warrior. A drinker, a horse rustler—I seized whole herds up in the mountains. A singer! There was nothing I couldn't do. Today there aren't any more Cossacks like that. It turns my stomach even to look at them! From the time they are this high," he added, holding his hand a few feet from the ground, "they put on foolish little boots and spend the day staring at them—their only pleasure! Or they drink themselves into a stupor, but even that they can't do like real men! But who was I? I was Eroshka the horse rustler. I barely came down to the village—I was always up in the mountains! Princes who were my blood brothers came to see me. In those days I was blood brother to all: Tatars, Armenians, Russian soldiers and officers. I didn't care who a man was as long as he could hold his drink. They tell me I must stop mixing with others, not drink with Russian soldiers, not eat with Tatars."

"Who tells you that?" Olenin asked.

"Our priests. But you should hear a mullah or a Tatar qadi! He'll say: 'You are unbelieving infidels! Why do you eat pork?' You see, everyone has his own rules. But if you ask me, it's all the same. God made everything for man's pleasure. There's no sin in anything. Take a beast: a beast will live in the Tatar's reeds as well as in ours—wherever it goes,

* A pood is approximately thirty-six pounds.

the beast's at home. Whatever God gives it, it will eat. But our priests say we'll have to lick frying pans in Hell. I think it's all a lie!"

"What's all a lie?"

"What the priests say. I'll tell you something—in Chervlenaya, the Cossack colonel himself was my blood brother. He was as fine a fellow as I was. He was killed in Chechnya. He used to say that the priests had made the whole thing up. When you croak, he used to say, grass will grow over your grave, and that will be that." Eroshka laughed. "What a wild fellow he was!"

"How old are you?" Olenin asked.

"God only knows! I'd say I'm about seventy. I was no longer a stripling when you Russians still had a czarina on the throne—so you count up how old I might be. About seventy, no?"

"That sounds right. But you're still a fine fellow!"

"Well, I thank God that I'm healthy, very healthy. But that witch of a woman ruined my life!"

"What do you mean?"

"She ruined it!"

"So when you die, grass will grow?" Olenin asked.

Eroshka clearly did not want to explain himself. He was silent for a few moments.

"What do *you* think? Come on, drink!" he shouted, handing Olenin another cup of wine with a broad smile.

15

"What was I saying?" Eroshka continued, trying to remember. "Yes, that's the kind of man I am! I'm a hunter! There was none like me in the whole regiment. I can find and show you every single beast, every bird. I know what's where. And I have dogs, two rifles, nets, a blind, and a hawk—I have everything, thank God. If you're a real hunter and not just full of talk, I'll show you everything! What kind of man am I? The moment I see a track, I know what animal it was, where it will lie, where it will drink, where it will wallow in the mud. I make myself a perch and wait there all night. What's the point of sitting around at home? You only fall into sin, get roaring drunk, and then the women's tongues start wagging, the boys start catcalling, and you only get crazier. It's much better to go out at dusk, look for a nice little place, press down the reeds, and sit and sit, waiting, like a good hunter. You know everything that's going on in the forest. You look up at the sky, the stars come out, you watch them and they tell you how much time has passed. You look around—the forest is rustling, you wait and wait, suddenly there's a sound, a boar has come to wallow in the mud. You hear the young eagles call, cocks crowing in the distant village, geese cackling. If it's geese, it isn't midnight yet. All this I know. You hear a rifle shot somewhere far away, and you think to yourself: Who fired that? A Cossack hunter lying in wait like me? Did he kill the beast or just injure the poor thing, its blood dripping onto the reeds, all for nothing. Oh, I don't like that! I don't like that at all! Why did he just injure the beast? The fool! The fool! Or you think: Maybe a Chechen warrior killed some silly Cossack boy! All this goes through your head.

"Once I was sitting by the edge of the river, I look, and I see a cradle floating downstream! A nice cradle, only the top edge crushed. The thoughts that came to my head! Whose cradle is that? Those damn Russian soldiers must have raided a Chechen village, grabbed the women, and some devil must have killed the child, seized it by its little feet, and flung it against the wall. You think they don't do such things? Some men have no soul! Those thoughts came to my head, and I was filled with pity. I thought: They threw away the cradle, hunted down the mother, burnt the house, and then the Chechen warrior comes over to our side of the river and pillages us. You sit there all night and think. And when you hear a litter of boars come breaking through the reeds, your heart pounds in your chest. Come here, my sweethearts! They'll smell my scent, you suddenly think. You sit still, not moving a hair, and your heart goes thump, thump, thump, hard enough to throw you into the air. This spring I came across a really good litter, there was a shimmer of black in the reeds. I was ready to shoot and whispered 'In the name of the Father and the Son,' when the sow grunts to her litter: 'Disaster, my children! A man is lying in wait!' and the whole litter flees into the bushes. I was so furious I could have eaten her alive!"

"How could the sow tell her litter that a man is lying in wait?" Olenin asked.

"Why, you think these beasts are fools? No, my friend, a beast is cleverer than a man, even though you might call the beast a sow. A beast knows everything. A man might walk along a sow's track without noticing, but the moment a sow comes across your track she takes one sniff and runs away. She knows you cannot smell her scent, but she can smell yours. And there's this to be said: You want to kill her, but she wants to roam through the forest. You have your law, she has hers. She's a sow, but that does not make her baser than you—she too is a creature of God. Ha! Man is a fool, a fool, such a fool!" Eroshka said and hung his head, deep in thought.

Olenin was also deep in thought. He climbed down from the porch and paced the yard in silence, with one arm behind his back.

Rousing himself from his thoughts, Eroshka looked up and peered intently at the moths circling and tumbling into the candle's flickering flame.

"You silly things!" he said. "Look where you're flying! So silly! So silly!"

He got up and began waving the moths away with his fat fingers.

"You'll burn, you silly things! Here, fly this way, there's so much space there!" he said tenderly, his fingers carefully trying to catch a moth by its wings and then release it away from the flame. "You're flying to your own ruin, and I pity you."

Eroshka sat talking and drinking from the bottle, while Olenin paced up and down the yard. Suddenly a whisper by the gate caught Olenin's attention. Holding his breath despite himself, he heard a woman's laughter, a man's voice, and the sound of a kiss. He walked to the other side of the yard, rustling the grass under his feet on purpose. The wicker gate creaked. A Cossack in a dark Circassian coat and white sheepskin hat (it was Lukashka) was going along the fence, and a tall woman in a white kerchief walked past Olenin. Maryanka's assured step seemed to say, "I have nothing to do with you, and you have nothing to do with me." Olenin followed her with his eyes until she reached the porch of her house, and through the window he even saw her take off her kerchief and sit down on the bench. Suddenly Olenin was gripped by the anguish of loneliness, a dim yearning and hope, and a vague feeling of jealousy.

The last lights went out in the houses. The last sounds in the village fell silent. The wicker fences, the cattle shimmering in the yards, the roofs of the houses, and the stately poplar trees all seemed immersed in the healthy, quiet sleep of toil. Only the endless croaking of frogs came from far away in the wet marshes. In the east, the stars faded and seemed to diffuse in the growing light, but above Olenin's head they became more dense. The old man was sleeping, his head resting on his arm. A cock crowed in the courtyard across the street. But Olenin kept pacing the yard, deep in thought. A song sung by a few voices wafted into the courtyard. He walked over to the fence and listened. Young Cossack voices were singing cheerfully, one voice standing out sharply in its strength.

"Do you know who that is, singing there?" the old man asked, waking up. "It's Lukashka, a true warrior! He killed a Chechen—how he's rejoicing! But why is he rejoicing? The fool, the fool!"

"Have you ever killed anyone?" Olenin asked.

The old man suddenly raised himself on both elbows and turned to look at him.

"Damn it!" he shouted. "What kind of question is that? One doesn't talk about such things! Killing a man is a difficult matter, ah, how difficult it is! Good-bye, my friend, I'm filled with food and drink. Shall I take you hunting tomorrow?"

"Yes."

"Get up early—if you oversleep, there'll be a fine to pay."

"I might well get up earlier than you," Olenin replied.

The old man left. The song fell silent. Olenin heard steps and lively talk. A few moments later the singing started up again, but further away, and Eroshka's loud bass had joined the other voices.

"What people, what a life!" Olenin thought. He sighed and returned alone to his lodgings.

16

Uncle Eroshka lived alone, retired from active service in the Cossack Regiment. Some twenty years earlier his wife had converted from the Old Beliefs to the Russian Orthodox faith, run away, and married a

Russian sergeant major. Eroshka had no children. He was not bragging when he said that in the old days he had been the most dashing young man of the village. Everyone in the Cossack Regiment still knew him from his old feats. He had more than one dead Chechen or Russian on his conscience. He had gone horse rustling in the mountains, stolen from the Russians, and twice been thrown in prison. The greatest part of his life had been spent hunting in the forest, where for days he lived off a single piece of bread and drank only water. But when he got back to the village, he did nothing but carouse from morning to night.

After returning from Olenin's lodgings, Eroshka slept for two hours and woke up before dawn. He lay in bed and weighed the man he had met the evening before. He liked Olenin's straightforwardness— straightforwardness in the sense that Olenin did not begrudge him his wine. And he liked Olenin himself. He was surprised that all Russians were so straightforward and so rich, and could not understand why they knew absolutely nothing, even though they were all so educated. He thought about these questions and what he might be able to get out of Olenin.

Uncle Eroshka's house was quite large and new, but the absence of a woman was evident. In contrast to the Cossacks' usual meticulous cleanliness, Eroshka's room was filthy and untidy. He had thrown his bloodstained coat on the table, and next to it lay a half-eaten piece of flatcake and a plucked, mangled jackdaw, which he had been feeding his hawk. Strewn on the benches were his rawhide shoes, rifles, his dagger, his sack, and a tangle of rags and wet clothes. Another pair of rawhide shoes was soaking in a tub of stinking, dirty water in the corner, next to which stood his hunting blind and his rifle. On the floor lay a net and a few dead pheasants. A hen with a foot tied was pecking in the dirt near the table. A dented pot filled with some sort of milky liquid stood on the unlit stove, and next to it a screeching falcon was trying to break free of its tether. A molting hawk sat calmly on the edge of the stove, watching the hen out of the corner of its eye, bending its head from time to time right and left.

Uncle Eroshka lay on his back in his short bed, which he had set up between the wall and the stove, and was picking at the scabs on his hands from the beak of the hawk, which he always carried without gloves. He was wearing a shirt, and his strong legs were propped up against the stove. The air in all the rooms, and particularly around Eroshka, was filled with that strong yet not unpleasant blend of smells that always accompanied him.

"Are you home, Uncle?" came a strong voice in Tatar through the window. Eroshka immediately recognized it as that of Lukashka.

"I'm home, I'm home, come in," Eroshka called back in Tatar. "So, Luka Marka, you've come to visit your uncle? Are you off to the checkpoint?"

The hawk started up at its master's booming voice, fluttered its wings, and tugged at its cord.

The old man liked Lukashka, the only one among the young generation of Cossacks he excluded from his contempt. Furthermore, Lukashka and his mother were neighbors and gave the old man wine and produce, like clotted cream. But Uncle Eroshka always looked at things from a practical standpoint. "Why not? These people are well enough off," he would say to himself. "I give them fresh meat or a bird, and they don't forget me either, and bring me a pie or a nice piece of flatcake."

"Hello, Marka! I'm glad to see you," the old man called out cheerfully, nimbly swinging his bare feet off the bed and jumping up. He took a few steps over the creaking floor, looked down at his turned-out feet, and suddenly found them funny. He smiled and stamped his heel on the floor, stamped it again, and then did a little jig.

"That was pretty good, wasn't it?" he said, his small eyes twinkling.

Lukashka smiled faintly.

"So you're off to the checkpoint?" the old man repeated.

"I brought the Chikhir I promised you the other day."

"May Christ smile upon you!" the old man said. He picked up the trousers and the quilted coat that were lying on the floor, put them on, and tied a strap around his waist. He poured some water on his hands from a pot, wiped them on his trousers, and then smoothed out his beard with a broken piece of comb.

"I'm ready," he said, going up to Lukashka, who took a mug, wiped it clean, poured the wine into it, and sitting down on a stool, handed it to him.

"To your health! In the name of the Father and the Son!" the old man said, solemnly taking the wine. "May you always get what you desire, may you always be valiant and earn yourself that medal!"

Lukashka also uttered a benediction, drank some wine, and put the mug down on the table. The old man got up, placed some dried fish on the doorstep, and began pounding it with a stick to soften it. He picked up the fish with his coarse hands, placed it on his only plate, and put it on the table.

"I lack for nothing, God be praised, I even have tasty things to eat," he said proudly. "So what's all this about Mosyev?"

Lukashka, eager for the old man's opinion, told him how Sergeant Mosyev had taken the rifle that was rightfully his.

"Forget the rifle," the old man said. "If you don't let him keep it there won't be any rewards."

"But, Uncle, they say if you're not yet a mounted Cossack, you can't expect much of a reward—and the rifle's a good one. It's Crimean, worth a good eighty rubles!"

"Forget it! That's how I once got into a fight with a lieutenant—he wanted my horse. 'Give me your horse,' he tells me, 'and I'll have you made a cornet.' I wouldn't give it to him, and so I didn't get to be a cornet."

"But, Uncle, I have to buy myself a horse, and they say you can't get one across the river for less than fifty rubles, and Mother hasn't sold the wine yet!"

"Ha! In my day we never bothered paying for horses," the old man said. "When Uncle Eroshka was your age, he had rustled whole herds of horses from the Nogai and driven them over the Terek. I'd sometimes give a man a good horse for no more than a jug of vodka or a nice cloak."

"You would hand over a horse for so little?"

"Marka, Marka, what a fool you are!" the old man said dismissively. "A man steals so that he doesn't have to be a miser. I doubt you boys have ever seen how horses are rustled. Have you?"

"What can I say, Uncle," Lukashka replied. "We are not the kind of Cossacks you were."

"Marka, Marka, what a fool you are! 'Not the kind of Cossacks you were'!" the old man said, mimicking Lukashka. "You're definitely not the kind of Cossack I was at your age!"

"What do you mean?"

The old man shook his head contemptuously. "Your uncle Eroshka was straightforward, and never asked the price of anything. That is why I was a blood brother to every Chechen. A blood brother would come visit me, I'd get him drunk on vodka, go carousing with him, give him a bed for the night—and when I'd go visit him, I'd always bring him a present, a *peshkesh*. That's how things should be done, not the way they're done nowadays! The only fun you boys know is cracking sunflower seeds and spitting out the shells," the old man said scornfully, miming young Cossacks cracking seeds and spitting out shells.

"I know," Lukashka said. "You're right."

"If you want to be a real Cossack, you must be a brave warrior and not a muzhik.* Even a muzhik can get his hands on a horse—he pays the money and the horse is his."

The two men sat in silence.

"There's no fun to be had anywhere, Uncle. Not in the village and not at the checkpoint, either. There's nowhere a man can carouse. You should see what a coward everyone is, even Nazarka. The other day we were in a Chechen village—Girei Khan sent word that we should rustle some horses from the Nogai, but none of our men would go! What could I do? Go on my own?"

"Why didn't you ask me? You think I'm all dried up? Well I'm not! Get me a horse, and I'll ride to the Nogai with you!"

"Why talk of it now, Uncle?" Lukashka said. "The real question is how one is to handle Girei Khan. He says that if we get the horses to the Terek, even if it's a whole herd, he'll see to it that they're all sold. But he's a Chechen himself, how can you trust him?"

"You can trust Girei Khan and all his clan, they are good people. His father was a true blood brother of mine. Just listen to your uncle Eroshka, I only teach you what's right: Make Girei Khan take an oath, and then you can be sure he'll stick to it. But when you ride with him, be sure to keep your rifle at the ready, especially when the horses are

---

* A muzhik is a Russian peasant.

being divided up. I once almost got killed by a Chechen that way—I asked him to pay ten rubles for a horse. It's nice to be trusting, but don't lie down to sleep without a rifle at your side."

Lukashka listened intently to the old man's words. After a few moments of silence he said, "By the way, Uncle, word has it you have some break-in weed."

"I don't have any, but I can tell you how to get some. You're a good boy, and I'm sure you won't forget your old uncle. You want to know how?"

"Yes, tell me."

"The tortoise, as you know, is a devilish animal."

"That it is."

"Look for a tortoise nest, and build a wall around it so the tortoise can't get back in. The tortoise will come to its nest, go around the wall, first this way, then that. When it realizes it can't get in, it'll go off to find some break-in weed and then use it to break through the wall. The next morning you go to the nest, and where the wall is broken you'll find the break-in weed. Take it with you wherever you go, and no lock or bolt can ever withstand you again."

"You've tried it, Uncle?"

"No, I haven't, but some good men told me about it. The only spell I've ever used is reciting the 'All Hail' whenever I mount a horse. And as you can see, no one has killed me yet."

"Which 'All Hail' is that, Uncle?"

"You don't know it? Oh, these young Cossacks! Well, I'm glad you asked! Recite this spell after me:

> Hail you who live in Zion
> Behold your king!
> We mount our horse
> Sophonia weepeth
> Zakharias speaketh
> Father Mandreth
> Kind mankind loveth.

"Kind mankind loveth," the old man repeated. "You know it now? Recite it!"

Lukashka laughed. "You are telling me this is why you've never been killed?"

"You young ones have gotten too clever! Learn it and recite it. It won't harm you. Recite it, and you'll be fine." The old man laughed too. "But you'd better not go to the Nogai."

"Why?"

"These are other times now, and you young men are not up to it— you've become shit Cossacks. And now all these Russians have descended on us! They'll throw you in jail. Just forget the whole thing. You youngsters could never pull it off. Now Girchik and me, back when we . . ." And the old man was about to launch into one of his endless stories, but Lukashka looked out the window and said, "It's light already, I have to be off. Come by the checkpoint when you have a chance."

"May Christ smile upon you! I'm going over to see the Russian soldier. I promised to take him hunting. He seems a good enough fellow."

17

Lukashka left Eroshka's house and headed home. A damp fog was rising from the earth and enveloping the village. The sound of unseen cattle stamping and rustling came from all directions. Cocks crowed more often and more strongly. The air gradually began to fill with light, and the villagers were starting to wake up. It was not until Lukashka stood in front of his house that he could see the fence, still wet from the fog, and the porch and the open gate. Through the fog he could hear the sound of an ax chopping wood. He went into the house. His mother was already up, throwing wood into the stove. His little sister was still asleep.

"Ah, Lukashka, had enough carousing?" his mother asked quietly. "Where were you all night?"

"In the village," he replied reluctantly, taking his rifle out of its sling and examining it.

His mother shook her head.

Lukashka poured some gunpowder onto the rifle pan, took some empty cartridges out of a pouch, and began filling them, stopping them up carefully with a bullet wrapped in a strip of cloth. He checked the cartridges, tugging at them with his teeth, and then put the pouch away.

"Mother, don't forget that my bags need mending," he said.

"Yes, yes. Your sister, the deaf-mute one, was mending something yesterday evening. Do you have to go back to the checkpoint already? I haven't seen you at all!"

"As soon as I get my things ready, I have to be off," Lukashka replied, tying up his gunpowder bag. "Where's my sister? Is she out in the yard?"

"I think she's chopping wood. She's been very worried about you. She says she never gets to see you anymore. She points to her face, clicks her tongue, and then presses her hands to her heart, as if she's telling me she's sad. Shall I call her? She understood everything about the Chechen."

"Yes, call her," Lukashka said. "And I had some lard somewhere—can you find it for me? I need to grease my sword."

The old woman went outside, and a few minutes later Lukashka heard his deaf-mute sister's shuffling footsteps as she entered the house. She was six years older than her brother and would have looked remarkably like him if she had not had that dull yet abruptly changing expression common to deaf-mutes. She wore a rough, patched smock, an old, light blue kerchief, and her feet were bare and mud-spattered. Her neck, hands, and face were sinewy, like those of a man. It was clear from her clothes and appearance that she was used to doing a man's rough work. She had brought in a bundle of wood, which she threw into the stove. Then she came up to her brother with a happy smile that creased her whole face, touched his shoulder, and began making quick signs with her hands, her face, and her whole body.

"That's nice, Stepka, very nice!" Lukashka replied, nodding his head. "It's very nice that you prepared and fixed everything! Good girl! Here, take this!" And he took two pieces of spice cake out of his pocket and gave them to her.

The mute girl's face flushed, and she hummed wildly with pleasure. She took the spice cake and began making signs even faster, often pointing in one direction, running a thick finger over her eyebrow and face. Lukashka understood her and kept nodding with a slight smile. She was saying that her brother should give the spice cake to the girls, that the girls liked him, and that one of the girls, Maryanka, was better than the rest, and that she was in love with him. She indicated Maryanka by quickly pointing in the direction of Maryanka's yard and then at her eyebrows and face, while clicking her tongue and wagging her head. "She loves you," she signed by pressing her hand against her breast, then kissing her hand and stretching it out as if she were about to embrace someone. Their mother came back into the house, and seeing what her daughter was saying, smiled and shook her head. The girl showed her the pieces of spice cake and again hummed with joy.

"I told Maryanka's mother the other day that I was going to send the matchmaker over," their mother said. "She took my words well enough."

Lukashka looked at his mother silently for a moment and then said, "You have to get the wine carted off and sold—I need a horse."

"I'll have it carted when the time comes. I'll get the barrels ready," she said, clearly not wanting her son to interfere in household matters. "When you leave," she added, "don't forget to take along the sack that's in the front room. It's all the things the neighbors brought along for you to take to the checkpoint. Or do you want me to stuff the things into one of your saddlebags?"

"Yes, that would be better," Lukashka said, preparing to go. "And if Girei Khan rides in from across the river, send him to the checkpoint, because it'll be quite a while before I get another leave. I have business to see to with him."

"I'll send him over, Lukashka, don't worry," the old woman said. "You and the other boys were drinking at Yamka's? I got up in the night to see to the cattle, and I was sure I heard you singing."

Lukashka did not answer but went into the front room, hung the bag over his shoulder, straightened his coat, took his rifle, and stopped for a moment by the door.

"Farewell, Mother."

His mother walked with him to the gate.

"Send me a keg of Chikhir with Nazarka," he said to her, closing the gate behind him. "I promised the boys at the checkpoint. Nazarka will come for it."

"God be with you, Lukashka, and may Christ smile upon you! I'll send it with Nazarka. I'll get it from the new barrel!" the old woman called out, walking up to the fence. Leaning over it she added, "But there's something I want to say to you."

Lukashka stopped.

"You've been carousing and having fun here in the village, though why shouldn't a young man enjoy himself? It is after all God who gave man happiness. It is as it should be, God be praised. But be careful that you don't cross your sergeant. I will sell the wine and get the money for you to buy the horse, and I'll arrange the marriage with the girl."

"Fine, fine!" Lukashka replied with a frown.

His sister called out to catch his attention. She pointed at her head and her hand, which meant "shaved head," in other words, "Chechen." Frowning and mimicking the aiming of a rifle, she shrieked and began humming, shaking her head. She was telling Lukashka to kill another Chechen.

Lukashka smiled, and with light, quick steps, his rifle slung over his shoulder beneath his cloak, he disappeared into the thick fog.

The old woman stood silently awhile at the gate, went back into the milk shed, and immediately returned to her work.

18

While Lukashka was on his way to the checkpoint, Uncle Eroshka whistled to his dogs, climbed over the fence, and took the back lane to Olenin's lodgings. When he was going out to hunt, he did not like women to cross his path. Olenin was still asleep, and Vanyusha, who had awakened but not gotten up, was looking around the room wondering whether it was time to get out of bed. Uncle Eroshka, in full hunting gear, his rifle on his shoulder, swung open the door.

"Get up! Grab a cudgel! Chechens!" he shouted in his deep voice. "Ivan! Light the samovar for your master!" He turned to Olenin. "As for you, get up! Get a move on! That's how we do things here, my friend! Even the girls are up already! Look out the window—look, that girl there's already fetching water, and you're still asleep!"

Olenin woke up and jumped out of bed. The sound of the old man's voice made him feel fresh and cheerful. "Get a move on, Vanyusha! Get a move on!" Olenin called out.

"So that's how you set out for a hunt?" the old man shouted, as if the hut were filled with a large crowd. "Everyone's eating breakfast, and you're still asleep? Lyam, here boy!" he called to his dog. "So, are the rifles ready?"

"I know I should have been up already," Olenin said. "Vanyusha! Gunpowder! Cartridges!"

"You'll have to pay a fine for oversleeping!" the old man shouted.

"Du thé voulez vous?" Vanyusha asked with a grin.

"You're not one of us, you devil!" the old man yelled, baring the stumps of his teeth. "What you're babbling there is foreign!"

"As it's my first offense, you'll have to pardon me," Olenin joked, pulling on a pair of big boots.

"Your first offense will be pardoned, but if you ever oversleep again you'll be fined a bucket of Chikhir. Once the day warms up you won't find any deer out there."

"And even if we do find some, they're bound to be cleverer than we are," Olenin replied cheerfully, repeating what the old man had said the night before. "You can't trick them."

"Yes, laugh all you like! Kill one first, and then talk! Come on now, get a move on! Look, your landlord is coming to see you," Eroshka said, glancing out the window. "Look at that, he's all dressed up and has even put on a new coat so you can see he's an officer! Oh, these people, these people!"

A few moments later Vanyusha announced that the landlord wished to see his master. *"L'argent,"* he added gravely, alerting his master to the reason for the cornet's visit. The smiling cornet appeared close on Vanyusha's heels. He entered the room with a swagger, in a new Circassian coat with officers' shoulder stripes and polished boots—quite unusual for a Cossack—and welcomed Olenin to his new quarters.

Cornet Ilya Vasilyevich was an "educated" Cossack, who had been to Russia, was a schoolmaster, and most important, was a noble—or rather he wished to appear noble. But one could not help feeling that beneath the grotesque affectation of vivacity, self-assuredness, and his outrageous manner of speaking, he was just like Uncle Eroshka. That was also apparent from his sun-browned face, his hands, and his reddish nose. Olenin asked him to sit down.

"Greetings, Ilya Vasilyevich!" Eroshka said, rising and bowing with what Olenin thought was mock humility.

"Hello, Uncle! Here already?" the cornet replied with an offhand nod.

He was a trim, lean man of about forty, quite handsome for his age, with a gray, pointed beard. He was visibly worried that Olenin might take him for an ordinary Cossack and was eager for his importance to be immediately apparent.

"This here is our Egyptian Nimrod,"* the cornet said, pointing at the old man with a self-satisfied smile. "A hunter before the Lord. Our first and foremost man. I see it has already pleased you to make his acquaintance."

Uncle Eroshka looked down at his feet in their wet rawhide shoes and shook his head, as if amazed at the cornet's learning and way with words. "Egg-gyptian Ninnrod!" he muttered. "The things he comes up with!"

"We are about to go hunting, as a matter of fact," Olenin said.

"I see that, sir, I see that indeed!" the cornet said. "But there is a trifling little matter."

"How may I help you?"

"As you are a nobleman," the cornet began, "and as I can also see myself as having the denomination of officer, for which reason we can always by degrees involve one another in discussion, like all men of noble rank—" Here the cornet stopped for a moment and smiled at Olenin and the old man. "But should you entertain the desire, with my consent, as my wife is a foolish woman in our social rank and could not at the present time fully comprehend your words of yesterday's date— Therefore my lodgings could go to the regimental adjutant for six rubles without the stable—as I, having noble connections myself, could always ablate it from myself free of charge. But, since it meets with your approval, I, having the denomination of officer, can come to an agreement with you on all matters personally like an inhabitant of

* In Genesis, Nimrod is a skillful hunter, and a great-grandson of Noah.

these lands and not leave it to the womenfolk, as is custom with us, but I can observe the conditions on all matters—"

"The clarity with which he speaks!" the old man muttered.

The cornet continued talking for quite a while in a similar vein, and Olenin finally gathered, not without some difficulty, that the cornet was hoping to rent the lodgings to him for six silver rubles a month. Olenin readily accepted and offered the cornet a glass of tea. The cornet declined.

"According to our foolish customs," he said, "we consider it a sin to drink from a worldly glass. I, however, as an educated man, look down on this custom, but my wife, due to her human weakness—"

"So, would you like a glass of tea?"

"If you will permit me, I shall bring my own glass, my particular glass, you could say," the cornet replied. He went out on the porch and shouted across the yard: "A glass!"

A few moments later the door of the room opened and a young, sun-browned arm in a pink sleeve appeared. The cornet walked to the door, took the glass, and whispered something to his daughter outside. Olenin poured some tea into the cornet's "particular" glass, and then into Eroshka's "worldly" glass.

"However, I do not wish to detain you," the cornet said, scalding his lips but downing the whole glass of tea. "I myself am a devotee of fishing, I am here only on a short leave, a recreation from my duties, one could say. I, too, have a wish to experience luck and see if Fate will not throw my way the gifts of the river Terek. I hope that you will visit me sometime to drink the wine paternal to these regions, as is the custom in our village."

The cornet shook hands with Olenin, said good-bye, and left. As Olenin was preparing his hunting gear, he heard the cornet's commanding, matter-of-fact voice giving orders to his household. A few minutes later, Olenin saw him walk past the window in a tattered jacket, his trousers rolled up to the knees, a fishing net slung over his shoulder.

"He's a cheat!" Uncle Eroshka said, drinking down the tea in his worldly glass. "Are you really going to pay him six rubles? Has anyone ever heard such a thing? The best house in all the village can be had for two rubles! What a devil! Why, I'd give you mine for three!"

"No, I'm staying here," Olenin said.

"Six rubles! A waste of money!" the old man replied. "Ivan! Some Chikhir!"

At about eight o'clock, after breakfast and a vodka for the road, Olenin and the old man went out into the street. At the village gate they came across an oxcart. Maryanka, wearing a jacket over her smock and in heavy boots, a white kerchief covering her face, was leading with one hand a pair of oxen by a rope tied to their horns, while in her other hand she held a long switch.

"Sweetheart!" the old man called out, moving as if to embrace her.

Maryanka waved her switch at him and looked at the two men cheerfully.

Olenin felt increasingly animated. "Off we go, off we go!" he said, flinging his rifle onto his shoulder, feeling the girl's eyes on him.

"Git! Git!" Maryanka's voice rang out behind them, calling out to the oxen, the wheels of the cart creaking loudly.

As the two men walked along the road that led through the pastures behind the village, Eroshka went on talking. He could not forget the cornet and kept cursing him.

"But why are you so angry with him?" Olenin asked.

"He's a skinflint! I don't like that!" the old man said. "After all, when he drops dead he can't take it with him! What's he hoarding up all his money for? He's already built two houses and snatched away another orchard from his brother! And when it comes to writing things for people, you should see what a dog he is! They come from other villages asking him to write documents for them. And whatever way he decides to write things down, that's what you get! No doubt about it! But what is he hoarding up all that money for? He's got only one brat of a boy and that girl. Once he marries her off, that'll be that!"

"Maybe he's saving up for her dowry," Olenin said.

"What dowry! She's a splendid girl—they'll take her as she is! But he's such a devil that he'll only give her to a rich man. He wants to get his hands on a nice fat sum of bride-money. There's a Cossack called Luka, a nephew of mine and a neighbor. He's the brave young fellow who just killed a Chechen. He's been wooing her for a long time now, but the cornet won't give her to him. There's always an excuse: now he's saying the girl is too young! But I know what the cornet wants, he wants them to keep kowtowing to him. The shame of it all! And yet in the end they will marry her off to Lukashka because he's the best Cossack in the village, a warrior, he killed a Chechen fighter, and he'll get a medal!"

"But let me tell you something," Olenin said. "Yesterday, when I was out walking in the yard, I saw the cornet's daughter kissing some Cossack."

"Nonsense!"

"By God, I did!"

"That girl's a devil," Eroshka said, reconsidering. "What Cossack was she kissing?"

"I couldn't see."

"What color sheepskin was his hat, was it white?"

"Yes."

"And a red coat? More or less your build?"

"No, a little taller than me."

"That's him!" Eroshka said, laughing out loud. "That's him, that's my boy Marka—Lukashka, I mean, I'm only joking when I call him Marka. I love the boy! He's just like me when I was his age! It's no good trying to keep an eye on those girls. My own sweet little soul used to sleep with her mother and her sister-in-law, but I still managed to crawl in. She'd be upstairs, and her mother was a real devil of a witch! She hated me with a passion. I used to go there with my best friend, Girchik. I'd climb up to the window on his shoulders, push it open, and grope around. She'd be sleeping on the bench. Once I woke her, and you should have seen how she jumped up! She didn't recognize me. Who goes there? But I couldn't answer, her mother had begun to stir in her sleep. I took my hat off and stuffed it into her mouth. Then she knew right away it was me, because of the tear in my hat, and so she climbed out the window with me. Back then I lacked for nothing. Clotted cream, grapes—she'd bring out everything," Eroshka added, in his practical way. "And she wasn't the only one. That was life then!"

"And what about now?"

"Now we'll follow the dogs, we'll wait for a pheasant to settle in a tree, and then you can shoot it."

"Why don't you give Maryanka a try yourself?"

"You watch the dogs. Tonight I'll show you," the old man said, pointing at Lyam, his favorite.

They fell silent. They walked another hundred paces, talking, and suddenly the old man stopped and pointed at a branch lying across the path. "What do you think that is?" he asked. "You think it's just a branch? Well it isn't! It's lying wrong."

"What do you mean it's lying wrong?"

The old man smiled.

"You don't know anything! Listen! When a branch is lying like that, then don't step over it. Either walk around it or throw it off the path like this and say, 'To the Father, the Son, and the Holy Ghost.' Then you can walk on and know that God's blessing is with you, and that nothing bad will happen. That's what the old men taught me."

"What nonsense!" Olenin said. "I'd rather you told me more about Maryanka. So is she seeing Lukashka?"

"Shh, quiet now," the old man whispered, again avoiding Olenin's question. "Just listen. We'll go into the forest now."

And the old man, treading silently in his rawhide shoes, walked ahead on the narrow path leading into the wild, overgrown forest. From time to time he looked back at Olenin with a frown. Olenin was rustling and stamping about in his big boots, his rifle getting tangled in the branches of the trees growing along the path.

"Not so loud, soldier!" the old man whispered at him angrily.

There was a feeling in the air that the sun had risen. The fog was beginning to lift but still covered the treetops. The forest seemed incredibly high. With every step the two men took, the surroundings changed. What seemed to be a tree turned out to be a bush, and what seemed to be reeds turned out to be trees.

19

The fog lifted enough to reveal the wet tops of the reeds. Here and there the fog turned to dew that dampened the road and the weeds by the fences. Smoke poured from all the chimneys. The Cossacks were heading out of the village, some to work, some to the river, some to the checkpoints. Olenin and Uncle Eroshka walked beside one another over the damp, overgrown weeds of the path. The dogs, their tails wagging and looking up at their masters, ran alongside. Clouds of mosquitoes buzzed through the air after the hunters, covering their backs, eyes, and hands. There was a smell of grass and forest dampness.

It was quiet. Sounds from the village that had been audible before no longer reached the hunters. Only the dogs rustled through the bushes, and from time to time a bird called. Olenin knew that the forest was dangerous, that Chechen warriors were hiding in the underbrush. But he also knew that a rifle was powerful protection for a man on foot in the forest. It was not that Olenin really felt afraid, but he thought someone else in his position might feel afraid. He looked intently into the misty undergrowth, listening to the faint, sparse sounds, and touching his rifle he experienced a pleasant feeling that was new to him. Uncle Eroshka, walking ahead, stopped at every puddle where there were animal tracks, pointing them out to Olenin after carefully examining them.

The path along which they were walking had been made by carts but had long since been covered by grass. The forest of elms and plane trees on both sides was so thick and overgrown that nothing could be seen. Wild vines entwined almost every tree from bottom to top, and the ground was covered by thick, dark brambles. Every small clearing was dense with blackberry bushes and reeds with swaying gray tops. Large animal tracks and grooved pheasant prints led from the path into the thicket. The vitality of the forest, never penetrated by cattle, amazed Olenin at every step: He had never seen anything like it. The forest, the danger, the old man with his mysterious whispering, Maryanka with her lithe, strong frame, and the mountains, all seemed to him like a dream.

"A pheasant has settled," the old man whispered, looking around and pulling his hat over his face. "Cover your face—a pheasant!" He waved angrily at Olenin and crept forward, practically on all fours. "A pheasant hates a man's face!"

Olenin was still behind him when the old man stopped and began examining a tree. The pheasant squawked from the tree at the dog, which was barking at it, and Olenin saw the bird. But at that instant a shot, as from a cannon, rang out from Eroshka's sturdy rifle, and the bird, fluttering up, shed feathers and fell to the ground. Olenin, as he walked over to the old man, flushed out another pheasant. He drew his rifle from its sling, aimed, and fired. The bird whirled into the air and then fell like a stone, catching in the branches and tumbling into the bushes.

"Good man!" Eroshka called with a guffaw, as he himself would have been hard put to hit the bird in flight.

They gathered up the pheasants and walked on. Olenin, excited by the commotion and the praise, kept talking to the old man.

"Stop! We'll go this way!" Eroshka interrupted him. "Yesterday I saw deer tracks here."

They headed about three hundred paces into the thicket, then made their way into a clearing that was partly flooded and overgrown with reeds. Olenin kept falling behind. Uncle Eroshka, some twenty paces ahead, bent down, nodded his head, and quickly waved him over. Olenin saw that the old man was pointing at a human footprint.

"You see that?"

"Yes. So what?" Olenin said, trying to speak as calmly as possible. "A man's footprint, isn't it?" Cooper's *Pathfinder** and Chechen warriors flashed through his mind. He noticed the furtiveness with which the old man now trod and decided not to ask any questions, uncertain whether it was the hunt or impending danger that led to Eroshka's caution.

"It's my own footprint," the old man said simply and pointed to the grass, beneath which an animal's tracks were barely visible.

The old man walked on. Olenin was now managing to keep up with him. They moved forward some twenty paces to lower ground, until they came to some bushes under a large pear tree, the earth beneath it black and covered with fresh animal dung. The place was overgrown with wild vines and looked like a dark, cool arbor.

"The stag was here this morning," the old man said with a sigh. "You see, its lair is still damp and fresh."

Suddenly there was a loud rustling and crashing in the underbrush not more than ten paces away. Both men were startled and reached for

---

* James Fenimore Cooper's 1840 Leatherstocking novel, *The Pathfinder*.

their rifles but could see nothing. They only heard more branches breaking. The even, quick thud of hooves sounded for an instant; the loud rustle turned into a gallop that became fainter and fainter in the silent forest. It was as if something clutched at Olenin's heart. He peered in vain into the green underbrush, and finally turned and looked at the old man. Uncle Eroshka stood motionless, pressing his rifle to his chest. His hat was cocked backward, his eyes shone with an unusual sparkle, and his open mouth, in which his yellow, decayed teeth flashed maliciously, seemed to have frozen.

"An antlered one," he said and, throwing down his rifle in despair, started tugging at his gray beard. "He was right here! We should have come around by the path! What a fool I am! What a fool!" And he tore angrily at his beard. The hooves of the fleeing stag sounded fainter and fainter. It was as if something were flying over the forest above the fog.

It was dusk when Olenin—tired, hungry, but invigorated—returned to the village with the old man. Dinner was ready. He ate and drank with Eroshka and, feeling warm and cheerful, went out on the porch. Once more the mountains rose before his eyes in the sunset. Once more the old man told his endless tales of hunting, Chechen warriors, sweet little souls, and the bold and carefree way of life the Cossacks used to lead. Once more beautiful Maryanka went in and out of the yard, her young, powerful body outlined beneath her smock.

2 0

The following day Olenin set out alone to find the place where he and the old man had come across the stag. Instead of walking down to the gate, he climbed over the hedges as the villagers did, and before he had time to pull off the thorns that had stuck to his coat, his dog had already flushed out two pheasants. As soon as he entered the underbrush, birds fluttered up at every step. (The old man had not shown him this place the day before, intending to keep it for teaching him how to hunt from a blind.) Olenin hit five pheasants out of the twelve he shot at, but scampering after them through the brambles was so exhausting that he was covered in sweat. He called back his dog, uncocked his rifle, brushed away the mosquitoes with the sleeve of his jacket, and quietly made his way to where he and Eroshka had been the day before. But he could not hold back the dog, which had come across a scent on the path. Along the way Olenin shot two more pheasants, and since he had to search for them in the brambles, it was midday by the time he reached the stag's lair.

The day was bright, still, and hot. The morning freshness had dried out even in the forest, and mosquitoes swarmed over his face, back, and hands. The dog had turned from gray to black, its back completely covered with mosquitoes. Olenin's shirt, through which they plunged their stings, had also turned black. Olenin wanted to flee and suddenly felt it would be impossible to live through the summer in the village. He wanted to head back but, at the sudden thought that the villagers bore these things well enough, decided to brave the swarm and gave himself up to be devoured. And strangely enough, by midday the sensation actually became pleasant. It even seemed to him that if he were not enveloped by mosquitoes and the mosquito paste that his hand mashed over his sweating face, his whole body covered by a consuming itch, the forest would lose its character. This cloud of insects went so well with this wild, insanely lavish vegetation, with the forest's countless animals and birds, the dark verdure, the hot, aromatic air, the rivulets of murky water seeping out of the Terek and gurgling somewhere beneath overhanging leaves, that Olenin found pleasant what he had previously found unbearable. He walked around the place where they had seen the stag the day before and, not finding anything, decided to rest a little. The sun stood high above the forest, and whenever he came upon a path or clearing, it relentlessly cast its harsh rays on his head and back. The seven pheasants hanging from his belt weighed him down painfully. He looked for the track the stag had left the day before, crawled beneath the bush into the thicket where its lair was, and lay down. He looked at the dark foliage around him, at the damp spot where the animal had lain, at yesterday's dung, the stag's knee marks, the torn-up clump of black earth, and at his own footprints from the day before. He felt cool and comfortable. He thought of nothing, desired nothing. Suddenly he was gripped by such a strange feeling of groundless joy and love for everything that, in a habit he had had from childhood, he began crossing himself and expressing his thankfulness. He suddenly saw with the utmost clarity: "Here I am, Dmitri Olenin, so distinct from all other beings, and I am alone, God knows where, in the lair of a magnificent stag, who perhaps has never seen a man before, in a place where no man has ever been or thought such thoughts. I am here, surrounded by trees old and young, one entwined with coils of wild vines. Pheasants dart through the underbrush, chasing one another, and perhaps scenting their dead brothers." He prodded the pheasants hanging from his belt, examined them, and wiped his hand, spattered with warm blood, on his coat. "Perhaps the jackals can scent it too, and slink off with sullen faces. Mosquitoes are hovering all around, buzzing among the leaves—to them gigantic islands—one mosquito, two, three, four, a hundred, a thousand, a million, humming something, humming about something, all around me, each as distinct from the next as I, Dmitri Olenin, am from them.

He vividly imagined what they were thinking and humming. "Over here, boys! Here's someone we can devour!" they hum, and swarm over him. And he felt that he was not simply a Russian nobleman, a member of Moscow society, a relative of such-and-such, a friend of so-and-so, but that he was as much a mosquito, a pheasant, or a stag as the beings around him. "I shall live and I shall die, just like them, just like Uncle Eroshka. And he is right when he says that grass will grow and that will be that!

"But does it matter that grass will grow?" was Olenin's next thought. "I still have to live, have to be happy. Because there is only one thing I want—happiness. It is of no importance what I am, even if I am no more than an animal over which grass will grow. Or I am a frame holding a part of our one-and-only God. But I still need to live the best way I can. And yet how shall I live to be happy, and why was I not happy before?"

He began thinking of his former life and felt disgusted with himself. He had been such an egoist, when he really had not needed anything. He kept looking around at the translucent foliage, the setting sun, and the clear sky, and felt as happy as he had that first moment. "Why am I happy, and what did I live for in the past?" he thought.

"How I used to want everything for myself, how I schemed, all for nothing but shame and sorrow! But I see I don't need anything to be happy!" Suddenly it was as if a new world had opened. "This is what happiness is!" he said to himself. "Happiness is to live for others. How clear it is. The need for happiness is within every man—so happiness must be legitimate. One might try to attain happiness selfishly—in other words, seek riches, glory, luxury, and love—and yet circumstances might not allow one to attain these things. So these are the things that aren't legitimate, not the need for happiness. But what can always be attained, regardless of circumstances? Love and selflessness!"

He was filled with such joy and excitement at discovering this new truth that he jumped up, and in his impatience began wondering who he could sacrifice himself for, who he could do good to, who he could love. "As one needs nothing for oneself, why not live for others?" he thought.

He picked up his rifle and scrambled out of the bushes to hurry back home in order to think everything through and find an opportunity of doing good. He came out into a clearing and looked around. The sun was no longer visible. It was growing cooler over the treetops. The terrain seemed completely unfamiliar and very unlike that surrounding the village. Everything had suddenly changed: the weather, the feel of the forest, the sky that had clouded over, and the wind whistling through the trees. All around him there was nothing but reeds and the ancient, rotting forest. He called his dog, which had run off to chase some animal, and his voice echoed back as if through a wasteland. He was frightened. He was suddenly seized by dread. His mind filled with Chechen warriors and the murders he had heard about, and he waited. Any second a Chechen might leap out from behind a bush and he would have to fight for his life and die, or try to scamper away in fear. He thought of God and of his future life as he had not done in a long time. And all around was the same dark, grim, wild nature. "Is it worth living just for oneself, when one might die any moment," he wondered, "die without having done anything good, die in a way that no one will know?"

He headed in the direction where he imagined the village to be. He no longer thought of hunting and felt a desperate exhaustion. He eyed every bush and tree, almost in terror, expecting at any moment to be called to account for his life. He wandered in circles, until he came upon a rivulet in which cold, sandy water from the Terek flowed, and so as not to stray any further he decided to follow it, not knowing where it would lead. Suddenly the reeds behind him rustled. He shuddered and reached for his rifle. Ashamed, he saw that it was only his dog—it threw itself panting and excited into the cold water and began lapping at it. Olenin also drank and then followed the dog, hoping it might lead him back to the village.

Despite the dog's company, everything around him seemed even murkier. The forest was darkening, the wind was blowing harder through the tops of the old, decaying trees, and strange, large birds hovered screeching above their nests. The vegetation became sparser, and there were now more whispering reeds and barren, sandy clearings covered with animal tracks. Through the droning wind Olenin could hear other cheerless, monotonous sounds. He felt increasingly downcast. He groped for the pheasants hanging from his belt behind him. One of them was missing. Its body had fallen off, only its blood-drenched head and neck were still jutting out from beneath his belt. He felt terror like never before. He began to pray to God, afraid now of only one thing: that he would die without doing good. He wanted so much to live, to live so that he could perform a great feat of selflessness.

2 1

Suddenly it was as if his soul was filled with sunlight: He heard the sound of Russian being spoken, heard the fast, even flow of the Terek, and only two paces away saw the river's brown, moving surface stretching out before him, the drab, wet sand of its banks and shallows, the distant steppe, the tower of the checkpoint against the water, a saddled horse with hobbled legs among the brambles, and the mountains. For an instant the red sun came out from behind a cloud, its last rays glittering playfully over the river, the reeds, the watchtower, and the Cossacks who had gathered in a crowd. Lukashka's fine figure caught Olenin's eye.

Once again Olenin felt completely happy for no apparent reason. He had come out of the forest next to the Nizhnye Prototsky check-point on the Terek, across from the peaceful Chechen village. He greeted the Cossacks and, not finding any ready opportunity to do good, entered their hut. There too, he found no opportunity to do good. The Cossacks received him coldly. He lit a cigarette. The Cossacks ignored him, first because he was smoking and also because they were preoccupied: The brother of the slain Chechen warrior had come down from the mountains with a scout to buy back his body. The Cossacks were waiting for a lieutenant from the Cossack Regiment to arrive.

The dead man's brother was tall and well-built, with a cropped beard dyed red. He was calm and majestic as a Czar, despite his tattered coat and sheepskin hat, and bore a remarkable resemblance to his dead brother. He did not deign to look at anyone and did not even glance at the corpse but squatted in the shadows smoking a pipe and spitting, uttering from time to time forceful, guttural sounds, to which his companion responded respectfully. It was clear that he was a warrior who must have encountered Russians under very different circumstances, and that Olenin did not interest him in the least. Olenin walked over to the dead man and stood gazing at him, but the dead man's brother, looking past him, uttered curt, angry words, and the scout quickly covered the dead man's face. Olenin was impressed by the majesty and sternness of the brother's expression. He tried to start a conversation, asking him what village he was from, but the Chechen barely glanced at him, spat, and turned away. Olenin was so taken aback that this Chechen showed no interest in him that he imagined the man either must be a fool or simply did not understand Russian. Olenin turned to the Chechen's companion, the scout who was acting as interpreter. He was a restless man, wearing clothes that were also tattered, but his hair was black instead of red, and he had gleaming white teeth and sparkling black eyes. The scout seemed eager to talk and asked for a cigarette.

"They were five brothers," the scout told Olenin in broken Russian. "This is the third brother the Russians killed, only two left. This one's a warrior, big warrior," he said, pointing at the Chechen. "When they killed his brother—his name was Ahmed-Khan—this warrior was sitting in the reeds across the river. He saw it all: how they put him in the boat, how they took him to the riverbank. He sat there till nightfall. He wanted to shoot an old man he saw there, but the others said no."

Lukashka joined Olenin and the scout, and sat down.

"What village are they from?" Lukashka asked.

"There, from those mountains," the scout replied, pointing beyond the Terek toward a bluish, misty gorge. "You know Syuk-su? It's some ten versts beyond."

"You know Girei Khan from Syuk-su?" Lukashka asked, evidently proud that he knew him. "He's a blood brother of mine."

"He's my neighbor," the scout said.

"A good man!" Lukashka said and with keen interest began talking to the scout in Tatar.

The Cossack lieutenant and the village elder arrived on horseback, accompanied by two Cossacks. The lieutenant, a recently commissioned Cossack officer, greeted the men, but they did not return the greeting with a "Good health, Your Honor!" the way soldiers of the Russian army would greet a lieutenant, and only a few of the Cossacks even bothered to acknowledge him with a nod. Some of the men, including Lukashka, got up and stood at attention. The sergeant reported that at the checkpoint all was well. Olenin thought this was very funny— it was as if the Cossacks were playing at being soldiers. But the formalities were quickly dropped, and the lieutenant, who was as much a dashing Cossack as the others, was soon in lively conversation in Tatar with the scout. The Cossacks wrote up some kind of document, handed it to the scout, took the money he held out to them, and then gathered around the dead man.

"Which one of you is Luka Gavrilov?" the lieutenant asked.

Lukashka took off his hat and stepped forward.

"I sent a report about your feat to the colonel. I don't know what will come of it, but I've put you up for a medal. You're too young to be made sergeant. Can you read and write?"

"No, I can't."

"But you're a fine fellow!" the lieutenant said, continuing to play the commanding officer. "You can put your hat back on. Which of the Gavrilovs is he from? Broad-back Gavrilov?"

"He's his nephew," the sergeant replied.

"Ah, I see. Well, men, lend the Chechens a hand," he said, turning to the Cossacks.

Lukashka's face shone with joy, and he looked even handsomer than usual. He put his hat on and sat down again next to Olenin.

The Chechen's body was placed in a boat, and his brother walked down to the riverbank, the Cossacks stepping aside to let him pass. He pushed the boat away from the bank with his powerful leg and jumped on. For the first time, Olenin noticed, the Chechen quickly ran his eye over the Cossacks and gruffly asked his companion a question. The scout, still on the bank, said something and pointed at Lukashka. The Chechen looked at him and, turning away, gazed at the opposite bank. There was no hatred in his eyes, only cold contempt. He again said something.

"What did he say?" Olenin asked the restless scout.

"Your men slaughter ours, ours butcher yours," the scout said, clearly making it up. He laughed, baring his white teeth, and jumped into the boat.

The dead man's brother sat motionless, his eyes fixed on the opposite bank. He was filled with such contempt that there was nothing on the Cossacks' side of the river that could arouse his curiosity. The scout stood at the back of the boat, talking continuously as he steered, dipping the paddle skillfully now on one side, now on the other. The boat grew smaller and smaller as it cut across the current, the Chechens' voices barely audible, until the Cossacks saw it reach the opposite bank, where horses were waiting. The Chechens lifted the body out of the boat and carried it to one of the horses, laying it, though the horse shied, over its saddle. They mounted their horses and slowly made their way along the road that led past the Chechen village, from which a crowd of people had come to look.

Back on their side of the river, the Cossacks were very pleased. The men joked and laughed, and the lieutenant and the village elder went inside the hut to drink some vodka. Lukashka sat down cheerfully next to Olenin, his elbows resting on his knees as he chipped away at a stick. He tried to give his expression a serious look.

"Why are you smoking?" Lukashka asked, feigning interest. "Is it really good?" He was saying this only because he had noticed that Olenin was uncomfortable among the Cossacks, who were ignoring him.

"It's just a habit," Olenin said. "Why?"

"Well, if one of us smoked, there'd be trouble!" Lukashka said. "Look how close the mountains seem," he added, pointing toward the gorge. "But you'll have a hard time reaching them. How are you going to get back to the village alone in the dark? I can take you there, if you want—but you have to ask the sergeant."

"What a fine fellow!" Olenin thought, looking at Lukashka's cheerful face. He thought of Maryanka and of the kiss he had heard by the gate, and felt sorry for Lukashka and his rough ways. "What nonsense this is!" he thought. "A man kills another and is happy, pleased, as if he had done the most wonderful thing. Can Lukashka not be aware there is nothing to be cheerful about? That happiness lies not in killing but in sacrificing oneself?"

"You'd better not run into that Chechen again," one of the Cossacks, who had seen the boat off, said to Lukashka. "Did you hear him asking about you?"

Lukashka raised his head. "My godchild?" he replied, meaning the Chechen he had killed.

"Your godchild won't be asking any more questions—I mean that redheaded brother of his."

"Let him thank God my bullet wasn't aimed at him," Lukashka said, laughing.

"Why are you so happy?" Olenin asked. "If it had been your brother who was killed, would you be happy?"

Lukashka looked at him with a twinkle in his eye. It was as if he understood Olenin but was above such considerations. "Well, isn't that how things are? Aren't they killing our brothers too?"

22

The lieutenant and the village elder left. Olenin, as a favor to Lukashka, and so that he would not have to go through the dark forest alone, asked the sergeant to give Lukashka leave to accompany him back to the village, and the sergeant complied. Olenin thought that Lukashka wanted to see Maryanka and was quite pleased at having the companionship of such a handsome and gregarious Cossack. Involuntarily he united Lukashka and Maryanka in his imagination and found pleasure in thinking of them together. "He loves Maryanka," he thought, "and I could love her too." A new and powerful feeling of tenderness took hold of him as they walked through the dark forest. Lukashka also felt lighthearted. Something resembling love touched these two young men, who were so different from one another. Whenever their eyes met, they wanted to laugh.

"Through which gate are you going into the village?" Olenin asked.

"The middle one. But I'll take you as far as the marsh; after that you won't have anything to fear."

"Why? Do you think I'm afraid? You can head back to the checkpoint," Olenin said, laughing. "I'll manage well enough on my own."

"It's not as if I have anything else to do. But how come you're not afraid—I am!" Lukashka said, also laughing.

"In that case, come over to my place. We'll talk, we'll drink, and you can go back tomorrow morning."

"You think I can't find myself a place to spend the night?" Lukashka said with a grin. "But the sergeant told me I had to be back tonight."

"I heard you sing a song last night, and then I saw you . . ."

"You did, did you?" Lukashka replied with a nod.

"Is it true you're getting married?" Olenin asked.

"My mother wants me to. But I don't even have a horse."

"Aren't you a regular soldier?"

"No, no! I've only just enlisted. I don't have a horse yet, and there's no way I can get one. That's why I can't get married."

"How much does a horse cost?"

"The other day some men were trying to buy a horse across the river, and they wouldn't give it to them for sixty rubles—but it was a Nogai horse."

"Would you like to come along on the campaign as my orderly?" Olenin asked suddenly. "I can see to everything, and give you a horse too. Really, as it is I have two."

"What do you mean?" Lukashka said, laughing. "Why should you give me such a present? I'll make do, with God's help."

"I mean it! Or don't you want to be an orderly?" Olenin said, happy that he had thought of making Lukashka a present of his horse. Yet for some reason he suddenly felt ill at ease and ashamed, and did not know what to say.

Lukashka was the first to break the silence. "So, you have your own house back in Russia?" he asked.

Olenin could not refrain from telling Lukashka that he had not one house but several.

"Good houses? Bigger than ours?" Lukashka asked good-naturedly.

"Much bigger, ten times bigger, and three stories high."

"And you have horses as good as ours?"

"I have a hundred horses, even better than yours, each worth three or four hundred rubles, and I mean silver rubles. Racing horses, you know. But I like the ones here better."

"Did you come here of your own free will, or were you drafted?" Lukashka asked banteringly. "See this? This is where you got lost," he added, pointing at a path beside them. "You should have headed to your right."

"I came here of my own free will," Olenin said. "I wanted to see your land and go on campaigns."

"I'd love to go on a campaign!" Lukashka said. "Do you hear those jackals howling?" he added, stopping to listen.

"Aren't you frightened because you killed a man?" Olenin asked.

"Why should I be frightened? I'd love to go on a campaign!" Lukashka repeated. "I really would!"

"Maybe we can go together. My company is going to march before the holiday, and the Cossack Regiment too."

"You came to the Caucasus of your own free will? You have houses, you have horses and serfs? I would do nothing but carouse! So, what's your rank?"

"I'm a cadet, but I've been put up for a commission."

"If your house is as big as you say it is, and you're not bragging, I would have stayed there. I'd never go anywhere! Do you like living among us?"

"Yes, very much," Olenin replied.

It was completely dark by the time the two men arrived at the village. They were still immersed in the black gloom of the forest. The wind moaned in the treetops. The jackals seemed to be howling, cackling, and crying right next to them, but from the village ahead came the sound of women talking and dogs barking, and the two men could clearly see the outline of the houses. Fires flickered, and the aroma of burning dung hung in the air. That evening Olenin felt, more than ever before, that his home, his family, all his happiness were here in the village, and that he would never live anywhere as happily as he did here. That evening he was filled with love for everyone, particularly Lukashka. When they came to his lodgings, Olenin led the horse he had bought in Grozny out of the barn. It was not the one he always rode but the other one—not a bad horse, though no longer young. To Lukashka's great surprise, Olenin gave it to him.

"Why would you give me your horse?" Lukashka asked. "I haven't done anything for you yet."

"Don't worry, it's nothing to me," Olenin replied. "Take it. Perhaps you will give me a present someday. We might ride out on a campaign together."

Lukashka was embarrassed. "But why are you giving it to me? An animal like that costs a lot of money," he said, without looking at the horse.

"Go on, take it! If you don't, I'll be offended. Vanyusha, take the horse over to his house."

Lukashka took hold of the reins. "Well, thank you very much. I never expected this, never!"

Olenin was as happy as a twelve-year-old boy.

"You can tether her here. She's a good horse, I bought her in Grozny. You should see her gallop. Vanyusha, bring us some Chikhir. Let's go inside."

The wine was brought, and Lukashka sat down and picked up a mug. "God grant that I may be of service to you," he said, emptying it. "What's your name?"

"Dmitri Andreyevich."

"Well, Dmitri Andreyevich, God save you! We'll be blood brothers. You must come and visit us—we're not rich people, but we know how to treat a blood brother. I'll tell my mother to give you clotted cream, grapes, anything you need. And if you come out to the checkpoint, you can count on me for hunting, crossing the river, anything you want. You should have seen the wild boar I killed a few days ago! I shared the meat with the other Cossacks, but if I'd known, I'd have given it to you."

"That's all right, thank you anyway. By the way, don't harness the horse, she's never pulled a cart."

"I'd never harness her! Ah, and you know," Lukashka said, lowering his head, "I have a blood brother, Girei Khan. He wants me to lie in ambush with him by the road that leads down from the mountains. If you want, you can come along. I won't tell anyone. I'll be your *murid*."*

"Ah yes, I will come along one of these days."

Lukashka seemed to have calmed down. His composure surprised Olenin, and even put him off a little. They talked for a long time, and it was late at night when Lukashka, who had drunk a lot but was not intoxicated (for he was never intoxicated), shook hands with Olenin and left. Olenin looked out the window to see what he would do. He was walking quietly, his head lowered. He led the horse out the gate, suddenly shook his head briskly, sprang into the saddle like a cat, grabbed the reins, and with a whoop galloped down the street. Olenin had thought Lukashka would cross the courtyard to celebrate his good fortune with Maryanka, but even though Lukashka did not do that, Olenin was in high spirits as never before. He could not refrain from telling Vanyusha not only that he had made Lukashka a present of the horse but also his whole theory of happiness. Vanyusha objected to this theory and declared that since *l'argent il n'y a pas,* the whole thing was foolish.

Lukashka rode home, jumped off the horse, and told his mother to send it out to graze with the Cossack herd, as he had to return to the checkpoint. His deaf-mute sister offered to take care of the horse and

* *Murid* in Tatar, lit. "discipline," here "scout."

mimicked with signs that if she saw the man who had given it to him, she would bow down to the ground before him. The old woman only shook her head, certain that Lukashka had stolen the horse, and so told her daughter to take it out to the herd well before dawn.

Lukashka returned to the checkpoint alone, puzzling over why Olenin had given him the horse. He knew it was not a particularly good one, but it was worth at least forty rubles, and he was very pleased with the gift. But he could not understand why the gift had been made and so was not in the least thankful. Quite the opposite: Vague suspicions that Olenin might be harboring wicked intentions filled his head, but he could not figure out what these might be, nor could he accept the idea that a stranger would make him a present of a forty-ruble horse out of the goodness of his heart. If Olenin had been drunk and swaggering about, it would have made some sense. But he had been sober, and might well have intended the horse as a bribe to get him to do something bad. "We'll find out soon enough," Lukashka thought. "I got the horse, and we'll see what's next! I'm nobody's fool! We'll see who'll get the better of whom! We'll see!" he thought, convinced that he would have to be on his guard. Feelings of hostility toward Olenin stirred in him.

Lukashka did not tell anybody how he got the horse. When asked, he answered evasively or simply said that he had bought it. Back in the village, however, everyone soon knew the truth. When Maryanka, Cornet Ilya Vasilyevich, Lukashka's mother, and the other Cossacks found out about the puzzling gift Olenin had made, their suspicions grew, and they began to fear him. And yet, notwithstanding their fear, his action also awakened in them great respect for his "simplicity" and wealth.

"You heard?" one of the Cossacks said. "The cadet billeted on Ilya Vasilyevich has thrown away a good fifty-ruble horse on Lukashka! He must be rich!"

"Yes, I heard!" another Cossack replied. "Lukashka must have done him some great service. Let's wait and see what will become of the boy. What luck Lukashka the Snatcher has!"

"But these cadets are a devilish bunch!" a third said. "Just watch him set fire to the house or something."

2 3

Olenin's life went on placidly. He had few dealings with his commanding officers or fellow soldiers, and was not sent out for work or training. In this way, being a wealthy cadet in the Caucasus Regiment was particularly advantageous. As a result of the campaign, he had been put up for a commission and so was left in peace, and as the officers considered him an aristocrat, they behaved in a dignified way before him. Their card games and evenings of drinking and song, which he had experienced while on the campaign, did not attract him, and so he avoided their company while they were quartered in the village. The life of an officer in a Cossack village has always had its own special character. While every soldier stationed at a fort will drink stout, play cards, and discuss the honors to be won on a campaign, in a Cossack village he will drink Chikhir with his hosts, treat girls to tasty morsels of food and honey, and tag along after a Cossack woman, with whom he will fall in love and sometimes even marry.

Olenin had an instinctive aversion to following the crowd and had always lived in his own way. Here in the village too he did not follow the well-trodden path of the Caucasus officer. He woke up at dawn of his own accord, drank tea, and sat on his porch admiring the mountains, the morning, and Maryanka. Then he put on his tattered ox-skin coat and his rawhide shoes, slipped a dagger into his belt, took his rifle and a bag with some lunch and tobacco, called his dog, and by six in the morning was already on his way into the forest surrounding the village. He returned in the evening around seven, tired, hungry, and with five or six pheasants hanging from his belt. Sometimes he also brought back an animal he had shot. His lunch and the cigarettes in his bag lay untouched. Had the thoughts in his head lain like the cigarettes in his bag, it would have been clear that throughout the day not a single thought had moved. He returned home refreshed, strong, and utterly happy. He would not have been able to say what he had been thinking about all that time, for what flitted through his head were not thoughts, or memories, or dreams, but fragments of all three. If he suddenly stopped and asked himself what he was thinking about, he might find himself imagining that he was a Cossack working in an orchard with his Cossack wife, or a Chechen warrior in the mountains, or a boar trying to escape from Olenin the hunter. And all the while he would be watching and listening for a pheasant, a boar, or a deer.

Uncle Eroshka now came over every evening. Vanyusha brought them a jug of Chikhir, and the two men would quietly chat, drink, and then contentedly go to sleep. The next day there was more hunting, more healthy tiredness, and more conversation, drink, and contentment. Sometimes, on a feast day or a Sunday, Olenin would spend the whole day at home. Then his main occupation was Maryanka. He eagerly watched her every move from his window or porch, though he was unaware he was doing this. He looked at her and was in love with her (or thought he was), the way he was in love with the beauty of the mountains and the sky, and had no thought of trying to enter into any sort of rapport with her. He felt that he could not have the relationship that Lukashka had with her, and even less the kind that was possible between a rich Russian officer and a Cossack girl. He was sure that were he to take the approach some of his comrades had, he would trade his delightful contemplation for an abyss of suffering, disappointment, and remorse. He had already managed a feat of selflessness in not approaching Maryanka, and this gave him much pleasure. But the main reason he did not approach her was that he was frightened of her, and under no circumstances would he have ventured to address a playful word of love to her.

One day during the summer—Olenin was at home, not having gone out hunting—a Moscow acquaintance, a very young man he had met in society, knocked quite unexpectedly at his door.

"I say, *mon cher,* my dear fellow! How pleased I was when I heard you were here!" the young man said in Moscow French, peppering his speech with more French words as he continued. "They told me Olenin is here! Which Olenin, say I. As you can imagine, I was overjoyed! Well, so Fate has thrown us together again! Tell me how you are—all the tos and fros." But then Prince Beletsky went on to tell Olenin his own story: how he thought it might be fun to join the regiment for a while, how the commander in chief had asked him to be his aide-de-camp, and how he might well take him up on the offer after the campaign, though he had to confess he was not in the least interested. "Serving here in this godforsaken place one at least has to make a career for oneself, get a medal, rank, a transfer to the Guards," Prince Beletsky said. "All that is quite obligatory, *mon cher,* if not for oneself then for one's family and one's friends. I must say, the commander received me very well; a decent fellow indeed!" he continued, without pausing for breath. "He's put me up for a St. Anna Medal for the expedition. So I think I'll stay here till we set out on the campaign. This is a marvelous place, though. What women! So, how is life treating you here? I was told by our captain—you know, that poor old fool Startsev, nice fellow, though—he told me that you are living the life of the savage, and that the fellows here have seen neither hide nor hair of you. Not that I blame you, *mon cher,* for not wanting to have too much to do with the officers here. Though I am happy that we will see one another! I'm staying at the local sergeant's house. There's a girl there—a Ustenka—marvelous, I tell you!" And more and more French and Russian words poured forth from the world that Olenin thought he had abandoned forever.

Beletsky was considered by all a pleasant and good-natured fellow. And perhaps that is precisely what he was. But notwithstanding his handsome, agreeable face, to Olenin he seemed extremely unpleasant. Beletsky exuded all the vileness that Olenin had renounced. What vexed him most was that he could not, that he simply did not have the strength to, push away this man who had come from that other world. It was as if that former world had an irrefutable hold on him. He was angry with Beletsky and with himself, and involuntarily peppering his conversation with French words and phrases, he found himself interested in the affairs of the commander in chief and their Moscow acquaintances. Because he and Beletsky were the only two men in this village who spoke that special Moscow brand of French, Olenin looked down on the other officers and the Cossacks and was cordial to Beletsky, promising to drop by at his place and inviting him to come over again. But Olenin did not go to visit him. Vanyusha approved of Beletsky, saying that he was a true gentleman.

Beletsky immediately settled into the life of the rich officer stationed in a Cossack village. Within a month he had become like a local resident: he plied the old Cossacks with wine, had parties and went to parties that the village girls arranged, bragged of feats, so much so that the womenfolk for some reason called him Grandpa. The Cossacks could relate to a man like him who loved women and wine. They got used to him, and even liked him better than Olenin, who remained a mystery to them.

24

It was five in the morning. Vanyusha was out on the porch, fanning the flames beneath a samovar with a boot. Olenin had already ridden off to the river to bathe. (He had recently come up with a new diversion, riding with his horse into the river.) His landlady was already lighting the stove in the milk shed, and thick black smoke was rising from its chimney. Maryanka was in the shack milking one of the cows. "She won't stand still, damn her!" came her impatient voice, followed by the rhythmic sound of milking. The lively clatter of hooves sounded in the street outside, and Olenin rode up to the gate, bareback on his handsome gray horse that was still glistening and wet. Maryanka's pretty head, covered in a red kerchief, poked out of the shack and disappeared again. Olenin was wearing a red silk shirt, a tall sheepskin hat, and a white Circassian coat belted with a strap from which his dagger hung. He sat with self-conscious elegance on his well-fed horse and, with his rifle slung behind him, leaned forward to open the gate. His hair was still wet, and his face shone with youth and vigor. He thought himself handsome and stylish, and felt that he resembled a Chechen warrior. But he was wrong. Anyone from these regions could see in an instant that he was just a Russian soldier. When he noticed Maryanka's head poking out of the shack, he leaned forward with added bravura, swung the gate open, and holding the reins tightly, rode into the courtyard flourishing his whip.

"Is the tea ready, Vanyusha?" he called out cheerfully, without looking toward the shack. With pleasure he felt his handsome steed tensing its rear, pulling at its bridle, every muscle quivering, ready to leap. Its hooves clattered on the hardened clay of the yard.

"*C'est prêt!*" Vanyusha called back. Olenin thought Maryanka's pretty head might still be peering out of the shack, but he did not turn to look. As he jumped from his horse, his rifle banged against the

porch, and he slipped but caught himself. He quickly threw a frightened glance toward the shack but saw nothing. All he could hear was
the rhythmic sound of milking.

He went into the house and after a while came out again with a
book and a pipe of tobacco and sat down to drink tea in a corner of the
porch that was still shaded from the slanting rays of the morning sun.
That day he had decided to stay home until lunch in order to write
some long-postponed letters. And yet for some reason he could not
bring himself to leave his comfortable little corner on the porch. He
resisted going back inside, as if the house were a prison. His landlady,
Old Ulitka, had lit the stove, and Maryanka had let the cattle out and
was now gathering up the cow dung and piling it along the fence.
Olenin was reading, but without taking in a single word. He kept looking up from his book to gaze at the strong young woman moving about
before him. He was afraid that he might miss a single movement as she
entered the damp morning shadows cast by the house, or walked into
the middle of the yard, lit by the sun's cheerful, young rays, her shapely
figure in its bright smock shining as it cast a black shadow. He watched
with delight how freely and gracefully she leaned forward, her pink
smock clinging to her breasts and shapely legs, and how she straightened up, her rising breasts outlined clearly beneath the tight cloth. He
watched her slender feet lightly touching the ground in their worn red
slippers, and her strong arms with rolled-up sleeves thrusting the
spade into the dung as if in anger, her deep, black eyes glancing at him.
Though her delicate eyebrows frowned at times, her eyes expressed
pleasure and awareness of their beauty.

"I say, Olenin! You look like you've been up for a while!" Beletsky
called out, entering the yard in an officer's coat.

"Ah, Beletsky!" Olenin replied, holding out his hand. "You're up
early."

"I had no choice, *mon cher,* I was driven out," he said. "There's to be
un petit bal at my place tonight. Maryanka, you're coming over to
Ustenka's this evening, aren't you?" he called out to her.

Olenin was taken aback at the ease with which Beletsky addressed
her. But Maryanka looked down as if she had not heard and marched
off to the milk shed, her spade on her shoulder.

"Look how shy she is, the sweet thing," Beletsky said as she disappeared into the shed. "Shy in front of you, *mon cher*," he added and smiling cheerfully ran up the steps of the porch.

"There's going to be a ball at your place?" Olenin asked. "And what do you mean, you were driven out?"

"My landlady's daughter, Ustenka, is throwing *un petit bal,* and you are invited. When I say *un petit bal,* I mean pies will be served and girls will gather."

"But why should we go?"

Beletsky grinned and with a wink nodded toward the milk shed.

Olenin shrugged his shoulders and blushed. "I say, Beletsky, what a strange fellow you are!"

"Come on, I want to hear all about it!"

Olenin frowned. Beletsky saw his frown and smiled with a sudden air of interest. "Come, come," he said, "you're practically living in the same house with her, and I must say she's a splendid girl, a wonderful girl, a perfect beauty . . ."

"She is amazingly beautiful!" Olenin quickly said. "I have never seen such a beautiful woman."

"Well then, what's the problem?" Beletsky asked, completely confused.

"This may strike you as peculiar," Olenin replied, "but there is no point in hiding the truth: From the day I arrived here, it is as if women no longer exist for me. And I like it that way, I really do! After all, what can men like you and me possibly have in common with these women? If you ask what I have in common with Uncle Eroshka, for instance, that's entirely different. He and I share a passion for hunting."

"What do we have in common with these women? Well, if you put it that way, what did I have in common with Amalia Ivanovna back in Moscow? Why should this be any different? If you tell me that the women here aren't all that clean, well that's another matter. *A la guerre comme à la guerre!*"

"I never knew any Amalia Ivanovnas, nor did I have anything to do with them," Olenin replied. "One cannot respect such women, but these women I do respect."

"Well, go ahead and respect them, *mon cher,* who's stopping you?"

Olenin remained silent. It was clear that he wanted to finish what he was saying, as the matter lay close to his heart. "I know that I'm an exception," he said with obvious embarrassment. "But the way I am living now, I see no reason to change my rules. I could not live here, let alone live as happily as I do, if I lived like you. So I am seeking something very different in these women."

Beletsky raised his eyebrows in disbelief. "Be that as it may, I still hope you will come over this evening. Maryanka will be there, and I will introduce you. You must come. If you are bored, you can always leave. Will you come?"

"I would, but to tell you the truth I'm worried that I might be swayed in my resolve."

"Ho ho ho!" Beletsky shouted. "If you come, I will see to it that you won't be swayed. You will come, won't you? You'll give me your word?"

"I would come, but to be honest—I'm not at all sure what we're supposed to do there, or what role we are to play."

"Please! You must come!"

"Well, perhaps I will," Olenin said.

"Why do you want to live the life of a monk when there are such splendid women here, women the likes of which you won't find anywhere else in the world? It's simply unbelievable! Why waste your life and not put to good use what's at hand? By the way, have you heard that our company is to head out to Vozdvizhesnkaya?"

"Not from what I hear. I was told that the Eighth Company was going to go," Olenin replied.

"No, I received a letter from the adjutant. He writes that the commander himself is intending to march in the campaign. I'm looking forward to seeing him again. I admit, this place is beginning to bore me a little."

"I heard that we'll be launching an attack soon," Olenin said.

"I haven't heard anything. What I heard was that Krinovitsin got a St. Anna Medal for a sortie. He was expecting to be made lieutenant," Beletsky said, laughing. "What a disappointment, no? He marched straight over to headquarters to complain."

Twilight was approaching, and Olenin began thinking about the party. The invitation was tormenting him. He wanted to go, but he found it strange and a little frightening to imagine what it would be like. He knew that none of the Cossack men or any of the old women would be there—only the girls. How would it be? How was he to comport himself? What was he to say to them, and what would they say to him? What rapport could there be between him and those wild Cossack girls? Beletsky had told him of the strange relationship, cynical and yet strict, that he had with them. Olenin felt uncomfortable about being in the same room with Maryanka, and perhaps even having to talk with her. But the idea seemed impossible when he remembered her regal bearing. And yet Beletsky kept emphasizing how simple it would be. "Is it possible that Beletsky treats Maryanka with the same familiarity as he does the other girls?" Olenin wondered. "Very interesting. No, it's better if I don't go. Oh, this is all so horrible and vulgar, so pointless!" The question of what would happen at the party kept tormenting him, though he felt he had to go since he had already given his word. He left the house without having decided what he was going to do, but then headed over to Beletsky's.

The house in which Beletsky lived was very much like Olenin's. It stood on posts about three feet off the ground and had two rooms. In the front room, into which Olenin climbed up a steep ladder, lay featherbeds, carpets, blankets, and pillows attractively arranged in the Cossack manner along the wall facing the door. On the side walls brass pans and weapons hung. Watermelons and pumpkins lay under the bench. In the second room there was a large stove, a table, benches, and Old Believer icons. This was where Beletsky was quartered, with his camp bed, his bags, and his weapons that were hanging on a wall carpet. His toiletries and miniature portraits were arranged on a table, and his silk dressing gown lay discarded on the bench. Beletsky, fresh and handsome, was lying on the bed in his undergarments reading *Les Trois Mousquetaires.*

"What do you think? Haven't I settled in nicely here?" he said, jumping up. "Marvelous, no? I'm glad you came! The girls are working up a storm. Do you know how they make their pies? Dough with a filling of pork and grapes! But that's not all—look at the commotion out there!" Through the window they saw bustling in the landlady's house, the girls running in and out carrying all kinds of things.

"Are you ready yet?" Beletsky called out to them.

"Almost! Are you hungry, Grandpa?" And peals of laughter came from inside the house.

Pretty Ustenka, plump and flushed, came hurrying with rolled-up sleeves into Beletsky's room to collect the plates. "Get away from me, you'll make me drop everything!" she squealed at Beletsky, and then, turning to Olenin, she laughed and called out, "Don't just stand there, come and pitch in! Go get some nice sweets for us girls!"

"Is Maryanka here yet?" Beletsky asked.

"Of course! She's the one who brought the dough," Ustenka said, hurrying out the door.

"You know, if one were to dress Ustenka, clean her up and prune her a little, she'd be better than all our beauties back home," Beletsky said to Olenin. "Have you seen the Cossack woman Borshcheva, who married the colonel? Amazing, the *dignité* that woman has! One wonders where they get it!"

"I haven't met the colonel's wife, but if you ask me, I prefer the way the Cossack women dress."

"Well, I am the sort of man who takes to any way of life!" Beletsky said with a cheerful sigh. "I'm off to see what the girls are up to." He threw on his dressing gown and hurried out. "Don't forget to see to the sweets!" he shouted.

Olenin called in Beletsky's orderly and told him to go get some spice cakes and honey. Olenin handed him the money but suddenly felt the action was vile, as if he were somehow trying to bribe him, and he didn't know what to say when the orderly asked him how many spice cakes and how much honey he was to get.

"Um . . . yes . . . as much as you like," Olenin quickly said.

"Shall I spend all the money?" the old soldier asked, eager to serve. "There are mint spice cakes and honey spice cakes, but the mint ones are more expensive. They sell them for sixteen!"

"Yes, yes, spend it all," Olenin said and sat down by the window, surprised that his heart was pounding as if he were bracing himself for something dire. He saw Beletsky enter Ustenka's house, heard squeals and shouts from the girls inside, and a few moments later saw Beletsky come jumping down the ladder, followed by more squeals, shouts, and laughter.

"They chased me out!" he told Olenin.

A few minutes later Ustenka came over and solemnly invited the two men to the party, announcing that everything was ready. As they entered her house they saw that everything was indeed ready. She had arranged all the pillows neatly along the wall, and a disproportionately small piece of cloth lay on the table, on which stood a carafe of Chikhir and a plate of dried fish. The whole house smelled of dough and grapes. Six or seven girls in their best quilted coats, their heads uncovered, stood huddled in the corner behind the stove, whispering and tittering.

"I beg you to do homage to my patron saint, St. Ustinya," Ustenka said, motioning her guests to the table.

Olenin saw Maryanka among the girls, all of whom were beautiful without exception, and he felt sad and vexed that he was meeting her under such awkward and tasteless circumstances. He felt foolish and ill at ease, and decided to follow Beletsky's example and do as he did. Beletsky walked over to the table with an air of easy solemnity and elegantly drank a glass of wine to Ustenka's health, bidding the others do the same. Ustenka declared that the girls did not drink.

"But we might drink if you mix some honey into the wine," one of the girls said.

The orderly, who had just returned from the store with honey and cakes, was called in. He glared at the two carousing gentlemen with a mix of envy and contempt, and carefully handed them the spice cakes and a chunk of honey wrapped in paper. He began to explain the price of everything and to count out the change, but Beletsky waved him away.

Beletsky filled the glasses with Chikhir, mixed in some honey, and arranged the spice cakes on the table. He then dragged the girls one by one from their corner, sat them at the table, and began dividing the cakes among them. Olenin noticed Maryanka's small, suntanned hand take two round mint cakes and one brownish one, uncertain what to do with them. The conversation was awkward and unpleasant, in spite of Ustenka's and Beletsky's ease and their attempts at livening up the company. Olenin kept falling silent and tried hard to think of something to say. He felt that he was drawing attention to himself, perhaps even provoking ridicule and infecting the others with his unease. He blushed. He sensed that he made Maryanka feel particularly uneasy. "I'm sure they must be expecting us to give them money!" he thought. "But what would the best way to do that be, and what is the quickest and easiest way out of here?"

25

"How is it possible that all this time you haven't met your own lodger?" Beletsky asked Maryanka.

"How can I meet him if he never comes over to see us?" Maryanka replied, glancing at Olenin.

Olenin was suddenly gripped by fear. His face flushed and, not knowing what he was saying, he spluttered, "I'm frightened of your mother . . . she gave me such a scolding the first time I came to your house."

"And so that frightened you off?" Maryanka asked, looking at him and then turning away.

It was the first time Olenin actually saw her face, for it had always been covered by a kerchief. It was not surprising that Maryanka was considered the most beautiful girl in the village. Ustenka was pretty enough: small and plump, with rosy cheeks, cheerful brown eyes, and a perpetual smile on red lips that were always laughing and chattering. Maryanka was not pretty—she was beautiful. And yet her features might almost have been considered a little too masculine, even coarse, were it not for her fine figure, her shapely breasts and shoulders, her severe yet tender black eyes with their dark eyebrows, and the gentle expression of her mouth as she smiled. She rarely smiled, but when she did, it was striking. She exuded strength and health. All the girls were pretty, but everyone in the room—the other girls, Beletsky, even the orderly who brought the cakes and honey—only had eyes for

Maryanka. It was as if every word spoken was spoken to her. She stood among them like a czarina.

Beletsky tried to keep the spirit of the party going, fussing and chatting away, having the girls pass the Chikhir around, and repeatedly making improper remarks in French to Olenin about Maryanka's beauty. He called her "la vôtre," and urged Olenin to follow his example with the girls. Olenin felt increasingly morose. He was trying to think up an excuse to escape when Beletsky proclaimed that, as it was Ustenka's name day, she had to offer them a glass of Chikhir followed by a kiss. She agreed, but on condition that a gift of money would be placed on her plate, the way it was done at weddings.

"The Devil brought me to this disgusting revelry!" Olenin muttered to himself and got up to leave.

"Where are you off to?"

"I want to get some tobacco," he replied, intending to escape, but Beletsky seized him by the arm.

"I have money," Beletsky said in French.

Olenin was very angry at his own awkwardness. "I see you can't leave this place without paying," he thought bitterly. "Why can't I simply do as Beletsky is doing? I should never have come here, but now that I'm here I shouldn't ruin their fun. I must drink as a Cossack would!" He picked up a wooden bowl that held a good eight glasses of wine, filled it with Chikhir, and drank it down. The girls watched this unseemly action in horror and disbelief. Ustenka brought him and Beletsky another glass of Chikhir and gave each a kiss.

"So, girls, we're going to have some fun," she called out, jingling the four coins the men had put on her plate.

Olenin no longer felt awkward and became quite talkative.

"It's your turn, Maryanka!" Beletsky said, taking hold of her arm. "We want a glass of wine and a kiss!"

"This is the kind of kiss you'll get from me!" she said brightly, raising her hand as if to strike him.

"You can kiss Grandpa without him having to give you a coin!" another girl bantered.

"What a good idea!" Beletsky said and gave Maryanka a kiss as she struggled to get away. "No, you must offer your lodger a glass!" He seized her by the arm, led her to the bench where Olenin sat, and made her sit down next to him.

"What a beautiful girl!" Beletsky said, touching her cheek and turning her head into profile. Maryanka did not resist and gazed at Olenin with a proud smile.

"What a beauty!" Beletsky repeated.

"Yes, I am a beauty!" her eyes seemed to say. Olenin, forgetting himself, threw his arms around her and leaned forward to kiss her. But she tore herself away, pushing Beletsky over and capsizing the table as she rushed toward the stove. There were shouts and laughter. Beletsky whispered something to the girls, and he and they quickly ran out of the room, locking the door behind them.

"Why will you kiss Beletsky but not me?" Olenin asked Maryanka. "Don't you like me?"

"I just don't want to kiss you, that's all," she replied, biting her lip with a frown. "Beletsky's our grandpa," she added with a smile. She went to the door and began banging on it. "Why did you lock the door, you devils?"

"Let them stay outside!" Olenin said, approaching her.

She scowled and roughly pushed him away. Again he was struck by her beauty and her regal bearing. Suddenly he came to his senses and was ashamed at his behavior. He went to the door and began to tug at it. "Beletsky! Unlock the door! This foolishness really won't do!"

Maryanka broke into bright, happy laughter. "So you *are* frightened of me!" she said.

"Of course I am! You're just like your mother when you get angry!"

"You should spend more time with Eroshka—then all the girls will fall in love with you." She smiled and looked him straight in the eyes, her face close to his.

He did not know what to say. "And if I came to visit you?" he asked her abruptly.

"Well, that would be different," she said with a nod.

Beletsky suddenly pushed the door open, and Maryanka fell back against Olenin, her thigh knocking his leg.

"My thoughts about love, selflessness, and Lukashka's right to Maryanka were all such nonsense!" flashed through Olenin's mind.

"Happiness is all that matters: He who is happy is right!" And with a force that took even him by surprise, he seized Maryanka and kissed her forehead and cheeks. She laughed out loud and ran to join the other girls.

That was the end of the party. Ustenka's mother returned from the fields and, scolding the girls, chased them all out.

26

"If I don't rein myself in a little, I'll fall wildly in love with that Cossack girl!" Olenin said to himself as he walked home. He lay down to sleep with this thought but felt that it would all pass and that he would be fine in a day or two.

But it did not pass. His relationship with Maryanka began to change. The wall that had separated them crumbled. Olenin now greeted her every time they met. The cornet, having collected the rent money from Olenin and realizing how wealthy and generous he was, invited him over to his house. Old Ulitka now received him warmly, and since the day of the party Olenin often went over to visit them in the evenings and stayed until late at night. To all outward appearances, his life in the village was unchanged, but in his soul everything had changed. He spent his days in the forest but with the approach of dusk went to visit the cornet and Old Ulitka either alone or with Uncle Eroshka. They had become so accustomed to his visits that they would have been surprised if he failed to come one evening. He paid well for the wine and was a quiet man. Vanyusha always brought him his tea. Olenin always sat in the corner by the stove while the old woman continued unperturbed with her chores and he and the cornet, sipping tea or Chikhir, chatted about Cossack affairs, neighbors, and Russia. Olenin was asked many questions about Russia, which he answered at great length. Sometimes he brought a book with him, which he would read quietly. Maryanka crouched like a gazelle by the stove or in a dark corner. She never took part in the conversation, but Olenin saw her eyes and face, heard her movements and heard her cracking sunflower seeds, and felt that she was listening to him with all her being. He felt her presence as he silently read. At times he imagined that her eyes were fixed on him as he talked, and encountering their radiance, he would fall silent and gaze at her. She immediately covered her face, and he, pretending to be immersed in conversation with the old woman, listened to Maryanka's breath and movements and waited for her to look at him again. When others were present she was cheerful and kind toward him, but when they were alone, her tone became abrupt and rough. Sometimes he came to visit before Maryanka had returned from herding the cattle back into the yard and suddenly would hear her strong tread and see her blue cotton smock flashing by the open door. She would walk into the room, see him, and her eyes would smile at him with a tenderness that was barely discernible, and he would feel both joy and fear. He neither expected nor wanted anything from her, but her presence became increasingly vital to him.

Olenin had immersed himself so entirely in the life of the village that his past seemed completely foreign to him, and his future, particularly a future outside the world in which he now lived, did not interest him at all. Receiving letters from friends and relatives, he was offended that they evidently grieved over him as over someone lost. Here in his village he considered those lost who did not live a life like his. He was convinced that he would never regret having torn himself away from his previous life to settle down in the Caucasus in such a solitary and idiosyncratic way. On campaigns and in the forts he had felt fine. But it was only here, under Uncle Eroshka's wing, in the forest and in his house at the edge of the village, and when he thought of Maryanka and Lukashka, that he saw clearly what a lie he had lived in the past. This lie had distressed him even back then, but now it seemed to him inexpressibly laughable and vile. With every passing day he felt freer and more like a human being. He saw the Caucasus now very differently from what he had once imagined it to be: he did not find anything that remotely resembled what he had dreamed of, or read, or heard. "All that nonsense about cloaks, rapids, Ammalat-beks, heroes and villains," he thought. "The people here exist as nature does. They die, they are born, they copulate, again they are born, they fight, eat, drink, rejoice, and again die, without any terms except for the unchanging terms that nature imposes on sun, grass, beast, and tree. They have no other laws."

When he compared these people to himself, they seemed so strong, wonderful, and free that he felt ashamed and unhappy. He often considered throwing everything to the wind and registering as a Cossack, buying livestock and a house in the village, and marrying a Cossack woman. But not Maryanka! He would graciously concede Maryanka to Lukashka. He would live with Uncle Eroshka, go hunting and fishing with him, and march with the Cossacks on their campaigns. "Why don't I do this? What am I waiting for?" he asked himself. "Am I afraid of doing what I find reasonable and right?" he wondered, both inciting and chastising himself. "Is the dream of being a simple Cossack, of living close to nature without harming my fellow human beings, of doing good, a more foolish dream than what I dreamt before?" he thought. "Dreams of being an imperial minister or a regimental commander?"

But an inner voice told him to wait. He was held back by the vague awareness that he was not quite capable of living life the way Eroshka or Lukashka did. His idea of happiness was so different from theirs. He was held back by the thought that happiness lay in selflessness. The horse he had given to Lukashka continued to fill him with joy. He was always on the lookout for occasions to sacrifice himself for others, but these occasions did not arise. At times he forgot this newfound recipe for happiness and felt he might well be able to immerse himself in the kind of life Eroshka led. But then he would suddenly catch himself and quickly grasp at the idea of selflessness, and once again calmly and proudly gaze at others and their happiness.

27

At the start of the grape harvest Lukashka rode into the village to see Olenin. He appeared even more dashing than usual.

"So, you are getting married?" Olenin asked cheerfully as he came out to meet him.

"I exchanged the horse you gave me, across the river," Lukashka said, avoiding the question. "This one's a real beauty. A Kabardinian horse from the great Lov stud. I know my horses."

They examined the new horse, and Lukashka did wild stunts riding through the yard. It was an exceptionally fine bay with a long, broad body, a glossy coat, a thick tail, and the soft, delicate mane and withers of the thoroughbred. The horse was so well fed that one could stretch out and sleep on its back, Lukashka said. Its hooves, eyes, and teeth were fine and sharply outlined, as one sees only in the purest breed lines. Olenin could not help admiring the horse—it was the first time he had come across such a beauty in the Caucasus.

"And what a step he has!" Lukashka said, patting the horse's neck. "He's really clever, too. He follows me everywhere!"

"When you exchanged the horse, did you have to pay a lot in addition?" Olenin asked.

"No, I just threw in whatever I had," Lukashka answered with a grin. "I got him from a blood brother."

"He's a wonderful horse! How much would you sell him for?" Olenin asked.

"I've been offered a hundred and fifty rubles, but I'd give him to you for nothing," Lukashka said cheerfully. "Say the word, and he's yours. I'll unsaddle him and you can take him away. Just give me any old horse so I can ride out on sorties."

"No, no, you must keep him!"

"Well, I've brought you a present anyway," Lukashka said, loosening his belt and pulling out one of his two daggers. "I got it across the river."

"Thank you!"

"And my mother says she'll bring you some grapes."

"She needn't do that. I'm sure you and I will have a chance to settle things someday. Look, I'm not even offering you any money for this dagger you're giving me."

"Money? But you and I are blood brothers, just like I am with Girei Khan across the river! He took me to his house and told me to choose something I like for myself. So I took this sword. That's how we do things here."

Olenin and Lukashka went inside the house and drank a glass of Chikhir.

"Are you going to stay in the village for a while?" Olenin asked.

"No, I just came to say good-bye. I'm being sent from the checkpoint to one of our squadrons across the Terek. I'm leaving right now with my friend Nazarka."

"So when's the marriage going to be?"

"Well, next time I get a day's leave I'll get betrothed," Lukashka said reluctantly.

"You won't be staying a little longer to see your future bride?"

"No. What do I need to see her for? By the way, when you'll be out marching on a campaign, don't forget to ask for Lukashka the Snatcher. You should see all the wild boars out there! I've already killed two. I'll take you out hunting."

"Good-bye! May God protect you!"

Lukashka mounted his horse without first crossing the yard to Maryanka's house and, doing stunts on the saddle, rode down the street to where Nazarka was waiting.

"Are we going to Yamka's?" Nazarka asked, winking in the direction of the house where she lived.

"I'll join you there in a while," Lukashka said. "Here, take along my horse, and feed him if I'm late. By morning I'm sure to be at the squadron."

"Did the cadet give you anything else?"

"No, he didn't," Lukashka said, dismounting and handing the reins to Nazarka. "As it is, I'm glad I gave him my dagger as a present, otherwise he might well have wanted my horse."

Lukashka slipped past Olenin's window into the yard and crossed over to the main house. It was quite dark already. Maryanka, wearing only her smock, was combing her hair and getting ready for bed.

"It's me," the Cossack whispered.

Her stern expression suddenly brightened. She opened the window and leaned out with a mix of fear and joy.

"What do you want?" she asked.

"Open up," Lukashka said. "Let me in for a minute. I'm tired of waiting." He touched her cheek through the open window and kissed her. "Come on, let me in."

"I've already told you I wouldn't do that!" she replied. "Are you here for long?"

He did not answer but continued kissing her, and she did not ask further.

"I can't even hug you properly through the window," Lukashka said.

"Maryanka!" came her mother's voice. "Who are you talking to?"

Lukashka took off his white sheepskin hat so it would not give him away and crouched down by the window.

"Go, quickly!" Maryanka whispered and then called out to her mother: "It's Lukashka, he's looking for Father."

"Tell him to come over here."

"He's gone already! He said he was in a hurry!"

Lukashka ran through the yard, ducking beneath the windows, and headed over to Yamka's. Olenin was the only one to see him. Lukashka and Nazarka drank two mugs of Chikhir and then left the village.

The night was warm, dark, and quiet. They rode in silence, the horses' hooves the only sound. Lukashka began singing a song about the Cossack Mingal, but before he finished the first verse he turned to Nazarka. "Can you believe she wouldn't let me in?"

"So she didn't?" Nazarka replied. "Well, I knew she wouldn't. Yamka told me that the cadet has started going over to her house. Uncle Eroshka's been bragging that the cadet gave him a rifle for getting him Maryanka."

"He's lying!" Lukashka said angrily. "She's not that kind of girl. If that old devil doesn't shut his mouth I'm going to shut it for him!" And he began singing his favorite song.

> From the gardens of a warrior lord
> In the distant town of Ishmael
> A bright and shining falcon soared,
> Leaving the cage it knew so well.
>
> The warrior rode on his handsome horse
> From his gardens in distant Ishmael,
> And held out his hand in deep remorse
> To the shining falcon he loved so well.
>
> "Beckon me not with bejeweled hand,
> I was, my lord, your prisoner too long.
> I shall fly to the lakes of a distant land,
> And feast on the meat of the whitest swans."

28

The betrothal was held at the cornet's house. Lukashka had returned to the village for the day but did not come to see Olenin, and Olenin did not go to the betrothal, although the cornet had invited him. He felt more dejected than at any time since he had settled in the village. He had seen Lukashka, dressed in his best clothes, walk with his mother to the cornet's house and was tortured by the thought that Lukashka was acting so coldly toward him. Olenin shut himself in his room and started to write in his diary.

"Lately much has changed, and I have reflected on many things," he began, "and the way things have turned out, I seem to be back where I started. To be happy, one needs only one thing: to love. To love self-lessly, to love everyone and everything, to spread a web of love in all directions and catch whoever falls into it. I have caught Vanyusha, Uncle Eroshka, Lukashka, and Maryanka this way."

Just as Olenin was writing these words, Uncle Eroshka came into the room. He was in the best of spirits. A few days earlier Olenin had dropped by to see him, and had found him sitting proudly in his yard adroitly skinning a boar with a tiny knife. His dogs, among them Lyam, his favorite, gently wagged their tails as they watched him work. Urchins were staring respectfully at Eroshka through the fence, not taunting him the way they usually did, and the women of the neighborhood, not usually kind to him, called out greetings and brought him flour, clotted cream, and jugs of Chikhir. The following morning Eroshka was sitting in his storeroom, covered in blood, handing out pounds of boar meat in exchange for money or wine. His face seemed to say: "God sent me good fortune and I killed a boar! You see? Uncle has become useful again!"

As was to be expected, he began drinking, and four days later was still drinking without having left the village. And he drank quite a bit at the betrothal too. He had come stumbling to Olenin's place from the cornet's house with a red face and a matted beard, but he was wearing a new quilted coat, red and trimmed with gold lace, and was clutching a balalaika made from a large gourd. He had often promised Olenin that he would play and sing for him, and as he was now very much in the mood to do so, was disappointed to find him writing.

"Ah, keep writing, keep writing, my friend," Eroshka said in a whisper, as if some sort of spirit might be lurking between Olenin and the paper, and the old man sat down quietly on the floor, as if worried he might frighten the spirit away. When Uncle Eroshka was drunk, his favorite place was on the floor. Olenin turned and looked at him, called for some wine, and continued writing. Eroshka was bored with drinking alone. He wanted to talk. "I was at the cornet's house, you know, at the betrothal. . . . What pigs they are! I can't stand them, so I've come over to you."

"Where did you get that balalaika?" Olenin asked, continuing to write.

"I went across the river, that's where I got it," Eroshka whispered. "I'm a balalaika master, I can play anything: Tatar, Cossack, rich men's songs, poor men's songs, whatever you want."

Olenin looked at him again, smiled, and continued writing. His smile encouraged the old man. "Forget them, my friend, just forget them!" Eroshka suddenly said. "They've hurt you, so forget them! Spit on them! What's the point of writing and writing? What's the point?" And he mimicked Olenin, tapping his fat fingers on the floor as if he were scribbling something, his rough face drawn into a haughty grimace. "What's the point of writing all those nasty documents, show some spirit!" Eroshka could not imagine there was any form of writing other than pernicious legal briefs.

Olenin laughed, and so did Eroshka, who jumped up off the floor, eager to show Olenin his talent in playing the balalaika and singing Tatar songs.

"What's the point of writing? You'd do better to listen! I'll sing you something! Once you're dead, there'll be no more listening to songs! We need fun! Fun!"

First he sang one of his own songs, to which he also danced.

—Ay, diddle-diddle-dee
When you saw him where was he?
—I did not have to look too far,
He's selling pins at the bazaar.

Then Eroshka sang a song he had learnt from his old friend the sergeant major.

> It was Monday when I fell in love
> All Tuesday did I weep and cry,
> Wednesday I asked: "Will you be my dove?"
> Thursday I waited for her reply.
> Friday she said: "I cannot love."
> Saturday I knew I had to die.
> But Sunday I took a little stroll
> And thought: "No, I think I'll save my soul!"

And then again:

> —Ay, diddle-diddle-dee
> When you saw him where was he?

Then he winked and began to dance and shake his shoulders, as he sang:

> I will kiss you, I will hug you
> Give you ribbons white and blue,
> Nadyezhda, Nadyezhda,
> I hope you love me too!

He became so excited that he began to play faster and faster, jumping and turning skillfully as he danced around the room.

Songs like "Ay, diddle-diddle-dee" and the sergeant major's song he sang only for Olenin. But then, having drunk another three or four glasses of Chikhir, he remembered the old days and began singing real Cossack and Tatar songs. In the middle of one of his favorite songs, his voice suddenly began to tremble, and he fell silent as he continued to strum the strings of his balalaika.

"Ah, my friend, my dear friend!" he said.

Hearing the strange tone in Eroshka's voice, Olenin turned to look at him. The old man's eyes were filled with tears, and one rolled down his cheek. He was crying.

"My days have gone forever, they won't be coming back," he sobbed. "Drink! Why aren't you drinking?" he suddenly shouted in his booming voice, not wiping away his tears.

A song from Tavlinskaya was particularly moving for the old man. It had only a few words, but all its magnificence lay in the sad refrain "Ay! Dai, dalalai!"

Eroshka translated the Tatar words for Olenin. A dashing young man had driven his sheep from the village into the mountains to graze. The Russians came, set fire to the village, killed all the men, and took all the women prisoner. When the young man came back from the mountains, there was nothing where the village had once stood. His mother was gone, his brothers were gone, the house was gone. Only a single tree remained. The young man sat beneath the tree and wept. "I am alone now, alone like you," he said to the tree. "Ay! Dai, dalalai!"

Eroshka sang the heartrending refrain over and over and, suddenly seizing one of the rifles off the wall, ran out into the yard and fired off both barrels into the air. Then he sang even more somberly, "Ay! Dai, dalalai!"

Olenin followed him out onto the porch and gazed into the starry sky where the shots had flashed. There were lights and voices in the cornet's house across the yard, and a crowd of girls had gathered on the porch and by the windows, some of them hurrying between the shed and the front room. At Uncle Eroshka's refrain and rifle shots, a group of whooping Cossacks came bursting out of the house and joined in the song.

"Why aren't you at the betrothal?" Olenin asked Eroshka.

"Forget them, forget them," the old man said. Obviously, they had offended him somehow. "I don't like them, I don't like them at all. Terrible people! Let's go back inside. They can carouse at their place and we'll carouse at ours!"

Olenin followed him into the house. "What about Lukashka, is he happy? Won't he come over to see me?" he asked.

"Lukashka? They told him I was going to get you his girl," the old man said in a whisper. "Ha! His girl! If we want her we can have her. Give them enough money, and she's ours. I can fix it up for you!"

"No, Uncle, money is of no use if she doesn't love me. Please don't speak of this again."

"No one loves us, you and me—we're outcasts!" Uncle Eroshka said suddenly, and began to cry again.

Olenin drank more than usual while listening to the old man's stories.

"Now my friend Lukashka is happy," Olenin thought, but he himself felt sad.

That evening the old man drank so much that he could no longer get up off the floor, and Vanyusha had to call some soldiers to help him drag him out. Vanyusha spat. He was so furious at Eroshka's behavior that he did not even say anything in French.

29

It was August. For days there had not been a cloud in the sky. The sun was scorching, and a burning wind had been blowing since morning, raising clouds of hot sand above the dunes, carrying the sand over reeds, trees, and villages. Grass and leaves were covered with dust. The paths and salt marshes lay bare and crackled underfoot. The waters of the Terek had long receded, and its runlets were drying up. The slimy banks of the pond near the village had been trodden flat by cattle, and the splashing and shouting of boys and girls rang out all day long. The reeds and dunes were drying out in the steppe, and the lowing cattle headed for the fields. Wild animals moved to distant marshes and mountains beyond the Terek. Clouds of gnats and mosquitoes hovered over the lowlands and the villages. The snow-covered peaks were hidden in gray mist. The air was dry, reeking. Every evening, the sun set in a glowing red blaze. It was rumored that Chechen marauders had crossed the shallow river and were on the prowl.

This was the busiest season. The villagers were swarming over the melon fields and over the vineyards that lay in the stifling shade, clusters of ripe black grapes shimmering among broad, translucent leaves. Creaking carts heaped high with grapes made their way along the road leading from the vineyards, and grapes crushed by the wheels lay everywhere in the dust. Little boys and girls, their arms and mouths filled with grapes and their shirts stained with grape juice, ran after their mothers. Tattered laborers carried filled baskets on powerful shoulders. Village girls, kerchiefs wound tightly across their faces, drove bullocks harnessed to loaded carts. Soldiers by the roadside asked for grapes, and the women climbed onto the rolling carts and threw bunches down, the men holding out their shirt flaps to catch them. In some courtyards the grapes were already being pressed, and the aroma of grape-skin leavings filled the air. Bloodred troughs stood beneath awnings, and Nogai laborers with rolled-up trousers and stained calves were working in the yards, while grunting pigs devoured the leavings and wallowed around in them. The flat roofs of the sheds were covered in dark, amber-colored clusters drying in the sun, and flocks of ravens and magpies fluttered over them, picking at seeds.

The fruits of the year's labor were being cheerfully gathered, and this year the harvest was exceptionally good. Laughter, song, and the happy voices of women came from within a sea of shadowy green vines, through which their smocks and kerchiefs peeked.

At noon Maryanka was sitting in the vineyard, in the shadow of a peach tree, pulling the family lunch from the shade beneath an unharnessed cart. Her father the cornet, who had returned from the school for the grape harvest, sat nearby on a horse blanket, washing his hands with a jug of water. Her little brother, who had just come running from the pond, stood there panting and wiping the sweat off his forehead with his sleeve, and looked at his mother and his sister, hungry for food. Old Ulitka, her sleeves rolled up over her powerful, sunburnt arms, was busy laying out grapes, dried fish, clotted cream, and bread on a low, round Tatar table. The cornet dried his hands, took off his hat, crossed himself, and went over to the table. The boy took the jug and drank greedily. Mother and daughter sat down and made themselves comfortable at the table. It was unbearably hot even in the shade, and a stench hung in the air. The strong, hot wind blowing between the branches did not bring coolness but only swayed the tops of the pear, peach, and mulberry trees that dotted the vineyards. The cornet crossed himself again, picked up a jug of Chikhir covered with a vine leaf, drank from the jug, and handed it to his wife. He had taken off his jacket and was sitting in his unbuttoned shirt, revealing his hairy, muscular chest. His thin, cunning face was cheerful, and neither his pose nor his speech gave any sign of his usual attempt at decorum. He looked contented and relaxed.

"Do you think we'll finish picking as far as beyond the shed by this evening?" he asked, wiping his wet beard.

"I think so," the old woman replied, "as long as the weather doesn't hold us back. The Demkins haven't brought in even half their harvest yet," she added. "Ustenka's working there all alone, she's killing herself."

"What do you expect from them?" he said archly.

"Here, drink, Maryanushka!" Old Ulitka said, handing her daughter the jug. "Lord willing, there'll be enough now for your wedding!"

"That'll be a while yet," the cornet said with a frown.

Maryanka hung her head.

"Why can't I talk about it?" the old woman said. "It's already settled, and it won't be long now."

"Don't plan so far ahead," the cornet said. "Let's keep to our grape picking now."

"Have you seen Lukashka's new horse?" the old woman asked. "He doesn't have the one Dmitri Andreyevich gave him anymore—he traded it."

"No, I haven't seen it yet," the cornet said. "I just spoke to that servant fellow of his, and he says they just sent Dmitri Andreyevich another thousand rubles from Moscow!"

"A rich man," the old woman said.

The whole family was cheerful. Work was moving ahead well, and there were more grapes than they had expected.

After lunch, Maryanka gave the oxen some hay, rolled her quilted coat into a pillow, and lay down under the cart on the flattened, lush grass. She was wearing only her faded blue calico smock and a red silk kerchief, but the heat was almost unbearable. Her face was burning, and she did not know where to put her feet. Her eyes were moist with exhaustion and sleep. Her lips parted, and her chest rose and fell heavily.

The work season had begun two weeks earlier, and the unremitting labor had taken over her life. She rose at dawn, quickly washed her face with cold water, wrapped herself in her shawl, and ran barefoot to tend the cattle. Then she put on her slippers and quilted coat, wrapped some bread into her bundle, and harnessed the oxen to ride out to the vineyards, where she worked for the whole day picking grapes and carrying baskets, resting only for an hour. In the evening she returned to the village, cheerful and full of life, leading the oxen by a rope and goading them with a long switch. She tended the cattle at dusk, tucked some pumpkin seeds into the wide sleeve of her smock, and went to the corner to chat with the other girls. But as darkness fell she returned home to eat with her family, then sat dozing on the bench above the stove, listening to her parents talking with Olenin. She lay down to sleep the moment he left, and slept soundly till morning. The following day was the same. She had not seen Lukashka since their betrothal but was calmly waiting for the wedding. She had grown used to Olenin, and felt his gaze upon her with pleasure.

30

There was no escaping the heat in the vineyard. Mosquitoes were swarming all around, and Maryanka's little brother kept nudging her as he turned in his sleep. She was just dozing off when Ustenka came over from the neighboring vineyard and crawled under the cart to lie down next to her. "Time for a nap, time for a nap!" she sang. "No, wait a moment," she said, crawling out again. She broke off two green branches, slid them into one of the wheels, and hung her jacket over them to ward off the sun.

"Shoo!" she called to Maryanka's little brother as she crawled back under the cart. "A big Cossack like you napping with the girls? Shoo!"

Alone with Maryanka, she seized both her hands, hugged her, and began kissing her cheeks and neck. "My sweet boy, my handsome darling," she crooned, breaking into a shrill titter.

"Stop it! I see 'Grandpa' has taught you some nice things," Maryanka said of young Beletsky, pushing her away. The two girls began to laugh uncontrollably, and Maryanka's mother called to them to keep quiet.

"Why, are you jealous of me and my handsome 'grandpa'?" Ustenka asked Maryanka in a whisper.

"No, I'm not! Let me sleep. What did you come over here for, anyway?"

"Don't worry, I'll tell you why."

Maryanka raised herself on her elbow and rearranged her kerchief. "Well?"

"I know a thing or two about your lodger," Ustenka whispered.

"What's there to know?"

"Aha, I see your lips are sealed!" Ustenka said, nudging Maryanka's elbow and laughing. "Doesn't he come over to see you?"

"Yes. So what?" Maryanka said, suddenly blushing.

"Well, unlike you I'm a straightforward girl," Ustenka said. "I don't hide anything from my friends—why should I?" And her cheerful, rosy face became pensive. "After all, I'm not doing anybody any harm. I love him, and that's that."

"You're in love with Grandpa?"

"Yes, I am."

"But that's a sin!" Maryanka protested.

"Ah, Maryanka! When's a girl to have fun, if not while she's still young and free? One day I'll marry a Cossack, bear children, and have my share of worry. Wait till you marry Lukashka—there'll be no more time for fun. All you can look forward to is children and work."

"Some girls marry and live happily, though!" Maryanka replied calmly.

"But tell me just this once if anything has happened yet between you and Lukashka."

"What should have happened? We got betrothed. My father wanted me to marry in a year, but now it's been decided for autumn."

"What did Lukashka say to you?"

Maryanka smiled. "You know exactly what he said. He said he loves me, and kept asking me to go into the vineyards with him."

"The devil! You didn't, did you?" Ustenka whispered. "Though he *is* dashing, the best fighter in the village! I hear he carouses out there in the squadron too. The other day our Kirka came back and said that Lukashka had exchanged his horse for a *really* good one. But I suppose he still misses you. What else did he say?"

"You always want to know everything," Maryanka whispered back, tittering. "He rode up to my window one night when he was drunk—he wanted to come in."

"And you didn't let him?"

"Didn't let him? I said I wouldn't and I won't!" Maryanka replied sharply. "Once I've made up my mind, that's that!"

"But he's so handsome! No girl would refuse him!"

"So let him go to a girl that won't refuse him," Maryanka said proudly.

"Don't you feel sorry for him?"

"Yes, but I'm not about to do anything foolish. It's a sin."

Ustenka suddenly hugged Maryanka and nestled her head on her chest, trying to smother her laughter. "You're such a silly girl," she said, gasping for breath. "I see you don't want to be happy!" And she began tickling her.

"Stop it!" Maryanka squealed, laughing.

"Just look at those two devils!" The old woman's sleepy voice came from beyond the cart. "Never a peaceful moment!"

"You don't want to be happy," Ustenka repeated in a whisper, propping herself up a little. "You're so lucky—how they all love you! You're rough with them, but they still love you. If I were in your shoes, you'd see how fast I'd wind that lodger of yours around my little finger. I was watching him at my party: he was ready to gobble you up with his eyes. You should see the things Grandpa has given me, and your lodger is even richer. His servant says he has his own serfs."

Maryanka also propped herself up a little and smiled, lost in thought. "You know what he told me once—our lodger, I mean," she said, chewing on a blade of grass. "He told me: 'I want to be a Cossack, like Lukashka, or your little brother, Lazutka.' I wonder why he said that."

"Lies! He's just saying whatever comes into his head," Ustenka replied. "You should hear some of the things my 'grandpa' says—you'd think his mind's unhinged!"

Maryanka lay her head on her rolled-up jacket, rested her arm on Ustenka's shoulder, and closed her eyes. "He wanted to come and work in the vineyards with us. My father told him he could," Maryanka said, and after a few moments of silence fell asleep.

31

The sun came out from behind the pear tree shading the cart, and its hot, slanting rays cut through the branches Ustenka had arranged and touched the faces of the sleeping girls. Maryanka woke up and retied her kerchief. She looked around and saw Olenin talking to her father beyond the pear tree. She nudged Ustenka and pointed at him with a smile.

"I did go yesterday, but I didn't find a thing," Olenin was saying, looking around uneasily but unable to see Maryanka through the branches on the cart.

"You should ambulate in an arc into those regions over there," the cornet said, reverting to his attempt at elegant speech. "You will come upon an abandoned vineyard—I should in actual fact denominate it as a vacant plot—but one can always encounter hares there!"

"A fine thing to be walking about looking for hares during the busiest time of the year," Old Ulitka said cheerfully. "You'd do better to come over here and pitch in. You'd get to work a bit with the girls." She turned and called to them. "Come on, girls, time to get up!"

Maryanka and Ustenka, whispering back and forth, could barely restrain their laughter.

From the moment the cornet and Old Ulitka had heard that Olenin had given Lukashka a fifty-ruble horse, they had become more friendly toward him. The cornet in particular seemed pleased to see Olenin's growing interest in his daughter.

"But I don't know how to do that sort of work," Olenin said, trying not to look through the green branches, where he had noticed Maryanka's blue smock and red kerchief.

"Come, I'll give you some dried apricots," the old woman said.

"An ancient Cossack custom of hospitality, just a bit of old woman's foolishness," the cornet proclaimed, as if attempting to correct his wife's words. "I imagine that in Russia you partook not merely of dried apricots but even of pineapple marmalade and preserves to your heart's content!"

"So you say there are some hares in the abandoned vineyard," Olenin said. "I'll go over there right away." And throwing a quick glance at the cart, he raised his sheepskin hat and hurried through the straight, green rows of vines.

By the time Olenin returned to his landlord's vineyard, the sun had already dipped beneath the fence and its broken rays were shining through the translucent leaves. The wind had settled, and a cool freshness began spreading through the vines. As if instinctively, his eyes were drawn to Maryanka's blue smock glimmering among the leaves in the distance. He began picking grapes as he made his way toward her, his panting dog snapping at low-hanging clusters with its drooling mouth. Maryanka was nimbly cutting large bunches of grapes and dropping them into a basket, her face flushed, her sleeves rolled up, her kerchief tied beneath her chin. Without letting go of the vine, she stopped, smiled at Olenin, and then continued working. He came nearer and hung his rifle over his shoulder to free his hands. He wanted to say, "Good heavens, are you working all alone? Where is everyone else?" But he only raised his hat without a word. He felt awkward being alone with Maryanka, yet came nearer, as if to torture himself on purpose.

"You'll be shooting women, with your rifle dangling like that," she said.

"No, I won't."

Both were silent.

"How about helping me?"

He took out his knife and began cutting grapes. He found a thick cluster weighing a good three pounds, the grapes so tightly bunched together that they flattened each other, and held it up for her to see.

"Should I cut all of these? Aren't they too green?"

"Wait, I'll do it."

Their fingers touched. Olenin took her hand, and she looked at him and smiled.

"So you'll be getting married soon?" he said.

She turned away without replying, then looked at him with stern eyes.

"So you love Lukashka?"

"What's that to you?"

"I envy him."

"I don't believe you."

"I do. You're so beautiful."

He suddenly felt ashamed of what he had just said. His words had sounded so vulgar. He flushed and seized her hands.

"Whatever I am, I'm not for you!" Maryanka said. "Why are you making fun of me?" But her eyes revealed she knew he was serious.

"I'm not making fun of you! If you only knew how I . . ."

His words sounded even more vulgar, even less expressive of what he felt. But he went on. "There's nothing I wouldn't do for you!"

"Stop!"

But her face, her sparkling eyes, her taut breasts and shapely legs were saying something very different. He felt she was aware of the vulgarity of his words but was too pure to take offense. He felt she knew what he was struggling to tell her but wanted to hear how he would say it. How could she not know, he thought, when everything he wanted to tell her was what she herself was? But she did not want to understand, she did not want to answer him!

"Hello there!" Ustenka's crooning voice called from beyond the nearby vines, followed by her chirping laughter. Her naïve little face poked out from behind the leaves. "Come here and help me, Dmitri Andreyevich! I'm working all by myself!"

Olenin did not move. Maryanka continued picking grapes but constantly looked over to Olenin. He was about to say something but stopped, shrugged, and marched quickly out of the vineyard, his rifle over his shoulder.

32

Olenin stopped two or three times, listening to Maryanka's and Ustenka's echoing laughter. They were calling something after him. He spent the whole afternoon hunting in the forest and was back in the village by dusk without having killed anything. As he walked through the courtyard, he noticed that the door to the milk shed stood open and caught a glimpse of a blue smock. Eyeing the shed, he called to Vanyusha more loudly than usual to announce his presence and sat down on the porch. The cornet and Old Ulitka had already returned from the vineyard. He saw them come out of the shed and go into their house without calling him over. Maryanka went out to the gate twice. In the twilight, it seemed to him that she might have turned to look at him. He greedily watched her every move but could not bring himself to go over to her. She disappeared into the house, and he came down from the porch and began pacing back and forth in the yard, but she did not come out. Olenin spent the whole night in the yard, listening to every sound in his landlord's house. He heard them talking throughout the evening, heard them eating their supper, preparing their featherbeds, and lying down to sleep. He heard Maryanka laugh at something, and then everything fell silent. There was a whispered conversation between the cornet and his wife, and there was a sigh. Olenin went into his house. Vanyusha lay asleep in his clothes. Olenin felt a pang of envy and went out into the yard again and paced up and down, waiting for something to happen. But nobody appeared, nobody moved. All he could hear was the regular breathing of three people. He knew Maryanka's breathing, and kept listening to it and to the beating of his heart.

The village now lay in silence. The waning moon appeared, and Olenin could see the cattle huffing in the yards, laboriously lying down and getting up again. He angrily asked himself what it was he wanted, but he could not tear himself away. Suddenly he heard footsteps in the landlord's house and a creaking of floorboards. He rushed toward the front door. But again there was silence, except for even breathing. A cow lying in the yard sighed heavily, moved, and slowly heaved herself onto her knees and got up, swishing her tail. He heard something plopping evenly onto the dry clay, and with a sigh the cow lay down again in the hazy moonlight. Olenin wondered what he should do and decided to go to bed. But again he heard sounds, and in his mind the image sprang up of Maryanka coming out into the misty, moonlit night. He rushed toward her window and again heard footsteps. Just before dawn he finally knocked on her shutters, ran over to the door, and then really did hear a sigh and footsteps. He grabbed hold of the latch and began rapping. He heard bare feet treading carefully toward the door, the floorboards scarcely creaking. The latch moved, the door rasped lightly, there was an aroma of herbs and pumpkins, and the figure of Maryanka appeared. He saw her only for an instant in the moonlight. She slammed the door shut and, whispering something, ran back with light steps. Olenin began knocking softly, but no one answered. Suddenly he was startled by a man's shrill voice.

"Aha!" a short Cossack in a white sheepskin hat called out, marching through the yard toward Olenin. "Aha! I saw it all!"

Olenin recognized Nazarka and was at a loss for what to do or say.

"Aha! I'm going over to the village elder right this minute!" Nazarka shouted. "I'm going to tell him everything, and her father too! Ha! A cornet's daughter indeed! I see one man isn't enough for her!"

"What do you want from me?" Olenin spluttered.

"Nothing! I'm going to tell the village elder, that's all!" Nazarka called out, obviously for all to hear. "How sly you cadets are!"

Olenin stood pale and shivering. "Come with me! Come!" he hissed, grabbing Nazarka by the arm and tugging him roughly toward his house. "Nothing happened! She wouldn't let me in, and I didn't do ... She's an honest girl!"

"The village elder will decide how honest she is," Nazarka replied.

"All the same, I'll give you ... Here, wait a moment."

Nazarka fell silent. Olenin hurried into the house and came back with ten rubles.

"Nothing happened, I tell you! But it's all my fault, so here you go. But for God's sake, nobody must find out! You see, nothing happened ..."

"A good day to you," Nazarka said and left.

Nazarka had come that night to the village at Lukashka's bidding to find a place to hide a stolen horse, and while he was heading down the street to his own house he had heard Olenin pacing the yard. Later that morning, when he returned to the squadron, he bragged to Lukashka how cleverly he had earned himself ten rubles.

When Olenin ran into the cornet and Old Ulitka that morning, he was relieved to see that they knew nothing of the incident. He did not speak to Maryanka, but she giggled whenever she looked at him. He also spent the following night pacing the courtyard in vain and then went hunting all day and in the evening, to escape himself, dropped by to see Beletsky. His feelings frightened him, and he promised himself he would no longer visit his landlord.

The following night his sergeant major woke him up, for the company had been ordered to set out immediately on a sortie. Olenin was relieved, and considered not coming back to the village anymore. The sortie lasted four days. Afterward, the commander asked to see Olenin, who was a relation, and suggested that he remain at headquarters. But Olenin declined. He could not live without his village, and asked for permission to return. He was awarded a military cross, which in the past he had longed for but which now left him indifferent. He was even more indifferent about his promotion to officer, the order for which had not yet come. He rode back with Vanyusha a few hours before his company and arrived in the village without incident.

All evening he sat on his porch gazing at Maryanka. All night he paced the yard vacantly and without aim.

33

The following morning Olenin woke up late. The cornet and his family had already gone to the vineyard. Olenin did not go out hunting but read a little, sat on the porch for a while, and then went back inside to lie down again. Vanyusha wondered if he was ill. In the evening Olenin got up again and began writing late into the night. He wrote a letter that he would not send; as it was, nobody else would understand what he wanted to say, nor was there any point in anyone understanding. This is what he wrote:

> I receive letters of condolence from Russia—my friends are afraid I will perish, buried in this wasteland. They say: He will run wild, lose touch with the times, will begin drinking, and God forbid, might even marry a Cossack woman. Didn't General Yermolov* say that any man who serves for ten years in the Caucasus either drinks himself to death or marries a dissolute woman? How dreadful! And yet I would be ruining myself were I to have the great honor of becoming the husband of Countess B., or a chamberlain, or a marshal of the nobility. How pitiful and vile you all are! You know nothing about life, nothing about happiness! Life must be

---

* General Alexei Yermolov was the commander in chief of the Russian troops in the Caucasus from 1816 to 1827.

experienced in all its artless beauty! You would have to see and understand what I see before me every day: the eternal snow of the mountains and a noble woman of the pristine beauty with which the first woman must have sprung from our Creator's hands! If you could see what I see, you would understand who is on the path to destruction, you or I; whether I am living a true life, or you. If only you realized how loathsome and pitiful you are in your delusions! I am more disgusted than I can say when, instead of my hut, my forest, and the beautiful woman I love, I imagine those Moscow women with their pomaded hair and false curls, their pouting lips, their corseted, deformed bodies, and the drawing-room prattle that calls itself conversation but is not worthy of the name. I picture those dull faces and those wealthy girls whose eyes tell you: "Feel free to make up to me, even though I'm a rich bride." The interminable arranging and rearranging of seats, the barefaced pandering, and the eternal gossip and pretense! The never-ending rules—who to shake hands with, who to nod to, who to exchange a few words with! And at the end of it all, that eternal boredom that flows in our blood from generation to generation, with everyone convinced how inevitable it all is. I want you to understand this, I want you to believe it! Once you understand what truth and beauty are, everything you think and say, your wishes for your happiness and mine, will crumble to dust. Happiness is living in nature, speaking with nature, seeing nature. I can hear you saying with heartfelt compassion: "He might even, God forbid, marry a simple Cossack woman and be forever lost to society!" But that is precisely what I want. I want to be lost, utterly lost, in your eyes. I want to marry a simple Cossack woman. And if I don't have the courage, it is only because it would represent the height of happiness of which I am not worthy.

Three months have passed from the first time I saw a young Cossack woman by the name of Maryanka. The ideas and prejudices of the world I had left behind were still fresh within me. In those days I did not believe that I could love this woman. I admired her as I admired the beauty of the mountains and the sky, and I could not help admiring her because, like the mountains and the sky, she is beautiful. The sight of her beauty became a necessity in my life, and I began to wonder whether I was not in love with her. But nothing I felt resembled what I had always imagined love to be. What I felt was not like the melancholy of loneliness or the desire for marriage, nor did it resemble platonic love—carnal love even less. I needed to see her, hear her, know that she was close. And if I was not happy, at least I was at peace. After a party at which I spoke to her for the first time, at which I touched her, I felt that between this woman and myself an indissoluble bond existed, even if unacknowledged, against which I must not struggle. But I did struggle. I asked myself if one can love a woman who will never understand one's most profound interests. Can one love a woman merely for her beauty, as if she were a statue? I asked myself this though I was already in love with her, even if I did not yet believe in what I was feeling.

After that party our relations changed. Until then I had seen her as a foreign though noble object of nature. After the party, I saw her as a person. I began meeting her, speaking to her, and going to her father's vineyard. I spent whole evenings visiting at their house. Even in this close proximity she remained in my eyes as pure, unapproachable, and noble as before. She always replied to everything I said with the same calmness and pride, the same lighthearted indifference. There were times when she was friendly, but for the most part every glance, every word, every movement expressed this indifference, which was not contemptuous but overwhelmingly bewitching. Every day, with a forced smile on my lips, I tried to play a role, addressing her playfully while torments of passion and desire raged in my heart. She saw that it was all a sham but looked at me directly and cheerfully. This situation became unbearable. I did not want to lie to her. I wanted to tell her everything I thought, everything I felt. I was so agitated! We were in the vineyard. I began to tell her of my love in words that I am ashamed to remember—ashamed because I should not have dared speak to her like that, for she stands on a far loftier plane than those words or the feelings they express. I said no more, and from that day on my situation has been unbearable. I did not want to debase myself by continuing my previous lightheartedness, and yet I felt that I was not up to a straightforward relationship with her. In desperation I wondered what I should do. In absurd dreams I imagined her as either my mistress or my wife, but I rejected both ideas in disgust. Turning her into a harlot would be terrible. It would be murder. But turning her into a lady, the wife of Dmitri Andreyevich Olenin, like one of the local Cossack women whom our officer married—that would be even worse! If I could become a Cossack like Lukashka, steal herds of horses, drink my comrades under the table, sing wild songs, kill men, and climb drunk through her window to spend the night without a thought about who I am or what I am doing—if I could do that, then it would be another matter. Then she and I would understand one another, and I would be happy. I tried to give myself up to that kind of life, but became even more aware of how weak and ungainly I am. I could not forget myself and the difficult, discordant past that is so repulsive to me. And I see my future as even more hopeless. Every day I see before me the distant, snow-covered mountains and that happy, noble woman. But there is no possibility in this world for me to be happy. This woman is not for me! What is sweetest and most terrible is that I feel I understand her, but she will never understand me. Not because she is lower than me. Quite the opposite. She simply *must* not understand me. She is happy. She is unruffled, calm, and self-sufficient, like nature. And I, a weak and corrupted being, should want her to understand my repulsiveness and torment? I could not sleep at night but wandered aimlessly beneath her windows, refusing to admit to myself what was happening to me. On the eighteenth, our company rode out on a sortie. I was away from the village for three days. I felt dejected and didn't care about anything. I found the singing, the cards, the drinking, and the talk of honors in the detachment more revolting than usual. I have just now gotten back, seen her, my house, Uncle Eroshka, seen the snowy mountains from my porch, and was seized by such a powerful new feeling of joy that I understood everything. I love this woman with what for the first and only time in my life is true love. I know what has happened to me. I am not afraid of debasing myself, I am not ashamed of my love but proud of it. I am not to blame for falling in love. It happened against my will. I tried to escape it by self-lessness, and tried to find happiness in the love between Maryanka and the Cossack Lukashka, but I only stirred up my own love and jealousy. This is not the kind of ideal, so-called exalted love I felt earlier. It is not the kind of attraction in which you admire your feelings of love and sense that you yourself are generating these feelings, that you are doing everything yourself. I have experienced that too. It is even less the desire for pleasure. It is something entirely different. Perhaps what I love in her is nature, the personification of everything wonderful in nature. Yet I am not acting of my own free will: an elemental force loves her through me, the whole of God's world, the whole of nature forces this love into my soul and tells me: "Love!" I love her not with my mind, not with my imagination, but with all my being. Loving her, I feel that I am an inseparable part of God's blissful creation. I wrote earlier of the new conviction that I came to in my solitary life. But nobody will ever know how difficult it was to achieve this conviction, or with what joy I became aware of it and saw a new road opening before me. Nothing was more important to me than this conviction. But then I fell in love, and now this conviction is gone, as are any regrets over it. It is difficult for me even to conceive that I could have prized such a cold, one-sided way of thinking, Beauty came and scattered to the winds all that laborious, seething inner toil—and I have no regrets! The idea of selflessness is nonsense, rubbish! Selflessness is nothing but pride, an escape from self-imposed misery, a salvation from envying others' happiness. Live for others, and do good? Why should I, when in my soul there is nothing but love for myself, when all I wish for is to love her and live the life of a Cossack with her? Now I no longer desire happiness for Lukashka or for others. I do not love these others now. Not long ago I would have told myself that this was bad. I would have tortured myself with questions, such as what will become of her, of me, of Lukashka. Now I do not care. Now I do not live of my own accord: something stronger than me is leading me. I am tortured. But in the past I was dead, and it is only now that I am alive. I shall go to her house right away and tell her everything.

34

After finishing the letter late in the evening, Olenin went to the cornet's house. Old Ulitka was sitting on the bench behind the stove unwinding silk cocoons, and Maryanka, her head uncovered, was sewing by the light of a candle. Seeing Olenin come in, she jumped up and hurried to the stove, snatching up her kerchief.

"Come here, Maryanka," her mother said. "You can sit with us."

"No, my head is bare," she replied and quickly climbed onto the bench above the stove. Olenin could see only one of her knees and a shapely, dangling calf. He gave the old woman a packet of tea, and she offered him some clotted cream, which she sent Maryanka to get. Maryanka put the bowl of cream on the table and climbed back onto the bench. Olenin felt her eyes peering at him. He and Ulitka spoke about household matters, and Ulitka, carried away by the rough, proud village hospitality of people who come by their bread through hard work, began piling plates of grape preserves and raisin cake onto the table and brought out the best wine. Though her rudeness had shocked Olenin when they first met, he was now increasingly touched by her simple tenderness, especially toward her daughter.

"Why anger God by complaining?" Old Ulitka said. "God praised, we have everything we need. We've pressed our grapes, we've made our preserves, we'll be selling at least three or four barrels of it, and there'll still be enough grapes for all our wine. You know, you shouldn't be thinking of leaving us too soon—we'll have such fun at the wedding!"

"When's the wedding going to be?" Olenin asked, feeling the blood suddenly rush to his cheeks, his heart beating irregularly and in agony. He heard the creaking of the bench above the stove and the cracking of pumpkin seeds.

"Next week, if it were up to me. As it is, we're ready," the old woman replied simply, as if Olenin were not present, as if he did not exist. "I've prepared everything for my Maryanushka. We'll be handing her over very nicely. But there's just one thing that isn't right: Our Lukashka's been carousing too much lately. Much too much! He's been up to no good, you know. The other day one of the Cossacks from his squadron said that Lukashka went riding out into Nogai land."

"He should be careful they don't catch him," Olenin said.

"And I told him: 'Lukashka, you must stop this. We all know what young men are like, but there's a right time for everything. You've done your raiding, you've rustled horses, you've killed a Chechen fighter—you've proven yourself! Now you must settle down, Lukashka,' I told him, 'or there'll be trouble.' "

"Yes," Olenin said. "I saw him two or three times at our detachment. He's always carousing, and he's sold another horse." He glanced over to the stove, where a pair of dark eyes flashed at him angrily. He felt ashamed for what he had just said.

"So what, he's not doing anyone any harm," Maryanka suddenly exclaimed, "and if he's carousing, it's his own money." She lowered her legs from the bench, jumped down, and left the room, slamming the door behind her. He waited, staring at the door, oblivious to what Old Ulitka was saying. A few minutes later an old man, who turned out to be Ulitka's brother, came in, accompanied by Uncle Eroshka, followed by Ustenka and Maryanka.

"Good evening all," Ustenka squeaked and then turned to Olenin. "Still enjoying the festival?"

"Yes, I am," he replied and for some reason suddenly felt ashamed and awkward. He wanted to leave but could not. He also felt that sitting there silently would be impossible. But Ulitka's brother came to his rescue, calling for some wine, and he and Olenin drank a glass. Then Olenin drank another glass with Eroshka, and another with an old Cossack from the neighborhood who dropped in. The more Olenin drank, the heavier his heart was. But the old men were intent on having fun. The two girls climbed up onto the bench above the stove and sat whispering, watching them drink one glass after another. Olenin sat silently, drinking more than the others. The old Cossacks began shouting and singing. Ulitka tried to make them leave, refusing to give them any more Chikhir. The girls laughed at Uncle Eroshka's antics, and it was already ten o'clock when they all went out on the porch. The old men invited themselves over to Olenin's house to drink through the night, and Eroshka led the way. Ustenka hurried home, and Old Ulitka went to the milk shed to close it up for the night. Maryanka stayed alone in the house. Olenin suddenly felt fresh and cheerful, as if he had just woken up. He seized the opportunity and, letting the old men go on ahead, hurried back to the cornet's house, where Maryanka was getting ready to go to bed. He went up to her and wanted to say something, but his voice broke. She sat down on her bed, pulled up her legs, and moved back to the furthest corner. She looked at him with wild, startled eyes. She was clearly frightened. Olenin felt this. He was sad and ashamed but at the same time proud and pleased that he could awaken any kind of feeling in her.

"Maryanka!" he said. "Will you never take pity on me? I love you more than I can say!"

She shrank back even further. "It's the wine that's speaking. You'll get nothing from me."

"No, it's not the wine. Don't marry Lukashka. I'll marry you!" he said, and then thought: "What am I saying? Will I be able to say it tomorrow?" But an inner voice answered: "I will, of course I will!"

"Marry me?" she asked, looking at him gravely, her fear apparently gone.

"Maryanka! I will go out of my mind, I'm not myself! I will do whatever you command!" And a stream of crazed, tender words poured from him.

"Stop babbling," she interrupted, suddenly seizing the hand he held stretched out to her, gripping it tightly with her strong, hard fingers. "Since when do gentlemen marry simple Cossack girls? Go away!"

"But will you? Everything I . . ."

"And what about Lukashka? What would we do with him?" she asked, laughing.

He tore his hand out of her grip and threw his arms around her, but she sprang up like a wild deer and ran barefoot out onto the porch. He came to his senses and was horrified at himself. He again felt vile in comparison to her but did not for an instant repent what he had said. He went home. Ignoring the old men drinking there, he went to bed and slept more soundly than he had for a long time.

35

The following day was the day of the festival. In the evening all the villagers came out into the streets, their finery sparkling in the setting sun. More wine than usual had been pressed, and the villagers were finally free from their labor. The Cossacks were going to embark on a campaign within a month, and many families were quickly preparing weddings.

Most of the people had gathered on the square in front of the village council and near two stores, one of which sold sweets and sunflower seeds, the other kerchiefs and calico. Outside the council, old men in somber gray and black coats without gold trim or other decoration were sitting and standing. In placid voices they talked among themselves about the wine harvest, village matters, and the old days, while they gazed on the younger generation with regal indifference. Women and girls stopped to bow to them, and young men respectfully slowed their gait, raised their hats, and held them for a while above their heads. The old men looked at the passersby, some sternly, some kindly, and slowly raised their hats in response.

The girls had not yet gathered into a circle for the round dance. They sat chatting and laughing in little groups on the ground and on the mounds that surrounded the houses, wearing bright jackets and white kerchiefs tied over their heads and faces. Children were running about the square, shouting and squealing, throwing a ball high into the clear sky. At the other end of the square some of the older girls had already begun their round dance, singing in weak, timid voices. Young Cossacks who were not on active duty, or who had just returned from their squadrons for the feast, cheerfully walked arm in arm in twos and threes, wearing dapper white or red Circassian coats with gold trim. They walked among the groups of girls, stopping to banter and flirt. The Armenian storekeeper, in a gold-trimmed jacket of delicate blue cloth, stood smugly in front of his open door, through which could be seen piles of folded colored kerchiefs. He waited for customers with the pride of the Oriental tradesman. Two red-bearded Chechens who had come from across the Terek to see the feast were squatting barefoot outside the house of a Cossack they knew. They nonchalantly smoked their small pipes and spat, throwing quick, guttural words at each other as they eyed the crowd. From time to time a drab Russian soldier in an old coat hurried across the square through the brightly colored crowd. Some of the carousing Cossacks were already beginning to sing drunken songs. All the houses were locked up, and the porches had been washed clean the night before. Even the old women were out in the streets, which by now were littered with the husks of melon and pumpkin seeds. The air was warm and still, and the clear sky crystalline and blue. The dull, white mountains beyond the roofs seemed close and glowed pink in the rays of the setting sun. Now and then the distant boom of a cannon came from across the river, and a blend of cheerful, festive sounds echoed over the village.

Olenin had paced up and down the yard all morning, waiting to catch a glimpse of Maryanka. But she had put on her finery and gone to mass at the chapel, after which she and the other girls sat outside the house, cracking seeds and hurrying in and out, Maryanka throwing cheerful glances at Olenin. He was afraid of addressing her in a familiar tone in front of others. He wanted to continue the conversation of the night before and make her give him a definite answer. He was waiting for another opportunity to be alone with her, but it did not arise, and he felt he no longer had the strength. She came out into the street again, and a few minutes later he followed her. He passed the corner where she was sitting, radiant in her blue satin jacket, and with a heavy heart heard the girls' laughter behind him.

Beletsky's house was on the square. As Olenin walked past, he heard Beletsky calling him and went inside. They chatted for a while, then sat by the window. A little later Uncle Eroshka joined them in his new jacket and sat next to them on the floor.

"What an aristocratic gathering," Beletsky said with a smile, pointing his cigarette at the brightly colored crowd on the square. "Look, mine's there too—the one in red. A new dress!" And leaning out the window he shouted, "Hey, when will the dances start?" He turned to Olenin and continued, "Let's wait till the sun sets, then we'll go too. And after that we'll invite them all over to Ustenka's. We'll arrange *un petit bal* for them."

"I'll come to Ustenka's too," Olenin said abruptly. "Will Maryanka be there?"

"Yes, she will! You must come!" Beletsky said, without a hint of surprise. "But I must say, all this is very attractive," he added, again pointing at the colorful crowd.

"Yes, very," Olenin agreed, trying to appear nonchalant. "I'm always surprised that people at these festivals are suddenly so cheerful and pleased simply because today, for instance, might be the fifteenth. You can see the festival in everything—everything is festive: people's eyes, faces, voices, movements, clothes, the air, the sun. Yet back in Russia we don't have festivals anymore."

"Indeed we don't," Beletsky replied, irritated at such musings, and turning to Eroshka said, "But you're not drinking anything!"

Eroshka winked at Olenin and nodded toward Beletsky. "He's a good host, your blood brother here!"

Beletsky raised his glass. *"Allah birdi!"** he said, and emptied it.

"Saul bul!"† Eroshka replied with a smile, emptying his glass. "You think this is a festival?" he said to Olenin, standing up and looking out the window. "This isn't what *I'd* call a festival, my friend! You should have seen what they were like in the old days! The women all came out in real finery, with gold trimmings and coin necklaces, and golden

---

* *Allah birdi* means "God gave." This is a common toast Cossacks use when drinking with one another. [Tolstoy's note]

† *Saul bul* means "Health to you!" [Tolstoy's note]

headdresses, and you should have heard the clink-clink-clink of the gold when they walked! Every woman looked like a princess, and they came out in flocks, singing songs. There was carousing all night long. The men would roll barrels into the yards and sit drinking till dawn, and then they would all walk through the village arm in arm. They went from house to house, and took along anyone they met. They drank and danced for three whole days. I remember my father would come home without his hat, all bloated and red, his clothes ripped to shreds, and lie down to sleep. Mother knew exactly what to do: She brought him fresh caviar and some Chikhir for his hangover, and then she'd go through the village looking for his hat. And Father would sleep for two whole days! That's how people were back then, and look at them now!"

"And the girls back then in their finery, what were they doing? They weren't carousing too, were they?" Beletsky asked.

"Yes, some of them were. The men would call out to each other, 'Let's break up the girls' dances!' Then they would ride over to where the girls were, and the girls would grab cudgels and go at them. On Shrovetide young men would ride up to a line of girls and get a real beating—the girls would beat them and their horses too—but if one of the men managed to break through the line of girls, he could grab hold of whichever one he liked and ride off with her. Believe me, he could love her as much as he liked. Ah, those girls! They were like czarinas!"

36

Just then two Cossacks rode into the square from a side street. One was Nazarka, the other Lukashka, sitting jauntily on his well-fed Kabardinian bay, which stepped lightly on the hard mud of the street, tossing its handsome head and fine, glossy mane. Lukashka was riding in from a distant, dangerous place, his rifle hanging in its sling, his pistol jutting from his belt, and his cloak rolled into a bundle behind the saddle. His rakish bearing, the casual flick of his hand as he tapped the horse's flank with his whip, and the way his flashing black eyes narrowed as he looked about expressed the strength and conceit of youth.

Have you ever seen a more dashing Cossack? his eyes seemed to say. The stately horse with its ornamented silver bridle, the fine rifle, and Lukashka's handsome looks drew the attention of the whole square, while Nazarka, scrawny and short, cut a sorry figure.

Lukashka rode past the old men and stopped to raise his sheepskin hat from his closely cropped head.

"I hear you've rustled quite a few Nogai horses," a thin old man said, glaring at him with a dark frown.

"You've counted them, have you, Grandpa?" Lukashka replied, turning away.

"At least don't take Nazarka with you," the old man said, his frown growing darker.

"The old devil knows everything," Lukashka muttered to himself, a worried expression flitting over his face. But he saw a large group of girls gathered at the corner of the square and rode over to them.

"Good evening, girls," he called out in his powerful, sonorous voice, reining in his horse. "How you've all grown while I was away, you witches you!" he added with a grin.

"Greetings, Lukashka, greetings!" the girls cheerfully called back.

"Brought back a lot of money?"

"Treat us to some tasty sweets!"

"Are you back for long?"

"It's been such a while since you were here in the village!"

Lukashka tapped his horse with his whip and rode closer to the girls. "Me and Nazarka have ridden in for a night of fun."

"You've been away so long that Maryanka's forgotten all about you," Ustenka squeaked and, giggling, nudged Maryanka with her elbow.

Maryanka moved away from the horse, threw back her head, and gazed calmly at Lukashka with large, glittering eyes.

"Yes, it has been a while, hasn't it! Are you trying to trample us with that horse of yours?" she said sharply and turned away. Maryanka's cold words took him aback, and his face, which had been sparkling with joy and bravado, suddenly darkened. "Jump up onto my horse and I'll gallop to the mountains with you!" he called out to her, as if trying to chase away his dark thoughts, and went riding through the crowd of girls doing stunts on the saddle in a wild display of horsemanship. Riding past Maryanka, he shouted: "Wait and see how I'll kiss you! Wait and see!"

Their eyes met. She blushed and stepped back. "Really! Your horse is going to trample me!" she said. She lowered her eyes and glanced at her pretty feet in their tight blue stockings and red slippers trimmed with silver lace. Lukashka rode up to Ustenka, and Maryanka sat down next to a Cossack woman who was holding a baby. The baby reached out to her, its fat little hands grabbing for the coin necklace hanging across her blue jacket. Maryanka leaned toward the baby, watching Lukashka out of the corner of her eye. Lukashka reached into his jacket pocket, took out a packet of sweets and seeds, and handed it to Ustenka. "These are for you girls," he told Ustenka, glancing at Maryanka with a smile.

Embarrassment flitted over Maryanka's face, and her beautiful eyes misted over. She pulled the kerchief from across her face and, quickly leaning toward the baby that was holding on to her necklace, began covering its little white face with kisses. The baby opened its toothless mouth and screamed, pushing against Maryanka's breasts.

"You'll smother him!" the baby's mother said, pulling it away from Maryanka and opening her smock to feed it. "You'd do better to be talking to your young man over there."

"I'll just see to my horse, and then me and Nazarka will come back! We're going to drink and dance all night," Lukashka said, flicking his horse with the whip and riding off with Nazarka. The two men rode into a side street and headed for their houses, which stood side by side.

"Here we are at last! Come back as fast as you can!" Lukashka called out to his friend, dismounting at his own gate. He carefully led his horse into the yard.

"Hello, Stepka!" he called to his deaf sister. She was out on the street, dressed up for the festival like the other girls, but hurried back into the yard to take his horse. With signs he asked her to take the horse into the stable but not unsaddle it. She hummed and smacked her lips, pointing at the horse and kissing it on its muzzle, indicating that she thought it a fine animal.

"Hello, Mother!" he called, steadying his rifle as he jumped onto the porch. "How come you're not outside with the others?"

The old woman opened the door for him. "Well, look who's here!" she said. "Kirka told us you wouldn't be coming back tonight."

"Can I have some Chikhir? Nazarka will be coming over to celebrate the holiday."

"I'll get you some right away," the old woman replied. "All the girls are out having fun, your sister too." She took the keys and hurried to the shed.

Nazarka, after putting away his rifle and seeing to his horse, went over to Lukashka's house.

37

"To your health!" Lukashka said, taking a full cup of Chikhir from his mother and carefully raising it to his lips.

"The thing is," Nazarka said, "Uncle Burlak was asking how many horses you've already rustled. It looks like he knows something."

"The old devil!" Lukashka replied, tossing his head. "I don't care! The horses are all across the river already—I'd like to see him go out looking for them."

"It's not good though, is it?"

"What's not good? Take him some Chikhir tomorrow and everything will be fine. Let's have some fun now! Drink!" Lukashka shouted the way old Eroshka always did. "We'll go out into the streets and join the girls for some fun! Go buy sweets and honey, or I'll find my sister and send her. We'll have fun all night!"

Nazarka grinned. "Are we staying in the village for long?"

"Let's have fun! Go get some vodka, here's the money!"

Nazarka obediently headed over to Yamka's. Uncle Eroshka and Ergushov, swooping down like birds of prey where fun and liquor were to be had, came staggering into Lukashka's house.

"Bring out another jug of Chikhir!" Lukashka called to his mother.

"Will you tell us where you rustled those horses, you young devil?" Eroshka shouted. "Good boy! I love you!"

"Ha! You love me?" Lukashka replied laughing. "If you love me, then why do you bring my girl sweets from that Russian cadet, you old devil!"

"That's a lie! That's a lie!" the old man shouted with a guffaw. "But you should have seen that rogue begging me! Go over to her, he begged, fix things up for me! He even gave me a rifle. But I didn't do it, by God! It would have been easy enough, but I felt sorry for you. So, tell me where you've been!" Eroshka added, slipping into Tatar.

Lukashka began talking vigorously in Tatar, and Ergushov, who did not speak it too well, interjected something in Russian here and there. "One thing I know," Ergushov said, "is he's rustled those horses. I'm certain of it!"

"We set off with Gireika," Lukashka said. That he called Girei Khan by a nickname like Gireika was a sign to the other Cossacks of Lukashka's boldness. "Across the river Gireika kept bragging that he knows the steppe like the back of his hand and would show us the way. But when darkness came we were still riding and riding—old Gireika had gotten lost, and we didn't know which way we were heading anymore. He couldn't find the village. I think we had veered off too far to the right. It was midnight and we were still looking. But then finally we heard the dogs barking."

"What fools!" Eroshka said. "We too used to lose our way on the steppe at night—it's a devil of a place—but what I used to do was ride up onto a hillock and start howling like a wolf. Like this!" He put his hands to his mouth and began to howl. "Then the dogs in the village howled right back. So, go on. Did you find the horses?"

"We rounded them up, but then Nazarka was almost caught by some Nogai women."

"Yes, they almost caught me," Nazarka said in an offended tone as he came back in with the vodka.

"We rode off, and Gireika got lost again! We ended up in the dunes. We thought we were riding toward the Terek, but it turned out we were going in the opposite direction."

"You should have looked at the stars," Uncle Eroshka said.

"Yes, you should have," Ergushov chimed in.

"That's easy enough to say, but you should have seen how dark it was. We rode this way, we rode that way. Finally I got off my horse and put the saddle on one of the mares we had stolen. I thought maybe my horse would take us back. So what do you think? Well, the horse snorts, then snorts again, puts his nose down to the ground, and off he gallops, straight back to our village. And not a minute too soon, because it was getting light already. We barely managed to hide the horses in the forest. Nagim came from across the river and led them away."

Ergushov shook his head. "Very smooth! Did you make a lot?"

"It's all here," Lukashka said, slapping his pocket. But his mother came back into the room, and he did not continue.

"Drink, everybody!" he shouted.

"Many years ago, Girchik and I rode out late one night," Eroshka began.

"We'll never hear the end of this," Lukashka interrupted. "I'm off!" He emptied his cup of wine, tightened his belt, and went out into the street.

38

It was already dark outside. The autumn night was fresh and still. A golden full moon floated above the black poplars standing on one side of the square. Smoke was rising from the milk sheds and mixing with the light fog spreading over the village. Lights shone in some of the windows. The smell of dung, pressed grapes, and mist hung in the air. The buzzing sound of talking, laughing, singing, and the cracking of pumpkin seeds was more distinct than during the day. White kerchiefs and sheepskin hats gleamed in the dark near fences and houses.

On the square, outside the open door of the brightly lit store, the crowd shimmered black and white. There was laughter and talking, and voices singing loud songs. The girls danced in a large circle, holding hands, stepping smoothly over the dusty square. A thin, ugly girl was leading the song:

> Near the trees of a dark and distant wood
> Two handsome Cossack warriors stood,
> Ai-da-lyuli! Ai-da-lyuli!
> They walked all day, all day they walked,
> They walked all day through the vineyards green,

Where the emerald vines, the emerald vines,
Hid the prettiest maid they had ever seen.
Ai-da-lyuli! Ai-da-lyuli!
The warriors then spoke angry words
The warriors drew their flashing swords,
Each claiming the maiden as his own,
Ai-da-lyuli! Ai-da-lyuli!
"Spill not your blood," the maiden said.
"Pierce not each other's brotherly heart!
I shall choose which of you to love instead,
To cherish and love till death do us part."
Ai-da-lyuli! Ai-da-lyuli!

The old women were standing nearby listening to the song, and little boys and girls chased each other through the darkness. The men stood in groups, from time to time pulling girls out of the circle as they danced past and entering the ring themselves. Beletsky and Olenin were standing in a dark doorway wearing Circassian coats and tall sheepskin hats. They spoke quietly to one another in their Moscow speech, aware that they were drawing attention to themselves. Dancing near them in the circle were plump little Ustenka, in a red jacket, and Maryanka, majestic in her new dress.

Olenin and Beletsky were chatting about how they might pull Maryanka and Ustenka out of the circle. Beletsky thought Olenin just wanted to have some fun, but Olenin was waiting for his fate to be decided. He desperately wanted to see Maryanka alone, to tell her everything, to ask her to be his wife. Even though he felt this question had long been answered in the negative, he hoped he would have the strength to tell her everything he felt, so that she would understand him.

"Why didn't you say before that you wanted to see her?" Beletsky whispered. "I would have gotten Ustenka to arrange things. You're such a strange fellow!"

"What can I do? Someday, someday very soon, I will tell you everything. But for God's sake, I beg you to arrange for her to come to Ustenka's!"

"That's easy enough," Beletsky said. For propriety's sake he walked up to Maryanka first and asked her: "Who will *you* choose to love instead: surely the handsome warrior of the song, and not Lukashka." Not waiting for a reply, he turned to Ustenka and whispered that he wanted her to bring Maryanka along. But a new song began, and the girls started dancing the round again.

In the vineyards,
In the vineyards,
In the vineyards dark and green,
Walked a handsome man,
A handsome man,
The handsomest ever seen.
Past my window,
Past my window,
Past my window sunny and bright,
He kept walking,
He kept walking,
He kept walking day and night.
"Come down to the vineyards,
To the vineyards dark and green,
Don't turn away,
Don't turn away,
Come be my glorious queen."
I went down to the vineyards,
To the vineyards dark and green,
And I dropped my silken kerchief
At the foot of the ravine.
"I bring you back your kerchief,
Your kerchief gold and green,
Five kisses,
Five kisses,
Come be my glorious queen.
Be happy now and cheerful,
And dance with ribbons red,
For when you marry me,
When you marry me,
A thousand tears you'll shed."

Lukashka and Nazarka broke into the dancing ring and walked around the line of girls. Lukashka beckoned to them and began singing along in a sonorous voice. "Well," he called out, "won't one of you girls join me?" The girls began pushing Maryanka, but she did not want to leave the circle. The sound of tittering whispers and little slaps and kisses mingled with the song. Lukashka nodded pleasantly to Olenin.

"Ah, Dmitri Andreyevich, so you've come to watch?"

"Yes, I have," Olenin replied coldly.

Beletsky leaned toward Ustenka and whispered something in her ear. She wanted to reply, but the line of girls moved on. When she passed Beletsky again, she said quickly, "Fine, we'll come."

"Maryanka will come too?" Beletsky asked.

Olenin leaned forward to Maryanka. "Will you? Please come, even if only for a little while. I need to speak to you."

"The other girls are coming, so I'll be coming too."

"Will you give me an answer to what I asked you?" he asked, leaning toward her again. "You seem so happy."

The row of girls moved on, and Olenin followed Maryanka.

"Will you answer me?"

"Answer you what?"

"What I asked you three days ago," Olenin whispered. "Will you marry me?"

Maryanka thought for a few moments.

"I'll answer you," she said. "I'll answer you soon enough."

Her eyes twinkled merrily at Olenin through the darkness. He kept following her. He was happy at the opportunity to be so close to her. But Lukashka, continuing to sing, pulled her out of the ring of dancers into the middle.

"You must come to Ustenka's," Olenin barely managed to say and then went back to join Beletsky. The song ended. Lukashka's lips parted, as did Maryanka's, and they kissed.

"No, five kisses, five kisses," Lukashka said.

Talk, laughter, and boisterousness replaced the smooth dance and soft sounds. Lukashka, who seemed already quite tipsy, was handing out sweets to the girls. "These are for you!" he said with a proud satisfaction both comical and touching. "But any girl who goes off to celebrate the feast with Russian soldiers has to leave the dancing ring now!" he added suddenly, glaring in Olenin's direction.

The girls clamored to take the sweets, laughing and jostling one another. Beletsky and Olenin moved to the side. Lukashka, as if ashamed of his generosity to the girls, took off his hat, wiped his forehead with his sleeve, and went over to Maryanka and Ustenka. "Don't turn away, don't turn away," he said, echoing the words of the song that had just ended. "Don't turn away," he repeated angrily. "For when you marry me, when you marry me, a thousand tears you'll shed!" And he embraced Maryanka and Ustenka. Ustenka struggled free and slapped him so hard on the back that she hurt her hand.

"Are you dancing another round?" he asked.

"The other girls might," Ustenka snapped, "but I'm going home, and Maryanka's coming with me."

"Don't go, Maryanushka," he said. "This is the last chance we'll have for some fun. Go to your house and I will come to see you."

"What should I do at my house? This is a festival, I want to have some fun—I'm going to Ustenka's."

"But I'll be marrying you."

"Good," Maryanka replied, "and when we're married, then we'll see."

"So you're going?" Lukashka said sternly. He pressed her to him and kissed her on the cheek.

"Stop it!" she said, tearing herself away.

Lukashka shook his head reproachfully. "Maryanka, Maryanka, things will turn out badly. A thousand tears you'll shed." And turning away, he called to the girls, "A song, another song!"

Maryanka seemed frightened and angered by what he had said. She followed Ustenka but then stopped. "What will turn out badly?" she asked him.

"That will."

"What?"

"That you're having fun with that Russian soldier, that lodger of yours, and won't love me anymore," he said.

"Don't tell me who to love and who not to love! You're not my father or my mother. I'll love whoever I want to!"

"Well, good!" Lukashka said. "But just remember what I said!" And he went to the store. "Girls!" he shouted. "Why have you stopped? Another dance! Nazarka, here, get more Chikhir!"

"Will she come too?" Olenin asked Beletsky.

"Yes, she will," Beletsky replied. "Let's go, we have to prepare *un petit bal* for the girls."

39

It was late at night when Olenin came out of Beletsky's house with Maryanka and Ustenka. Maryanka's white kerchief shimmered in the dark street. The golden moon was sinking into the steppe, and a silvery fog hung over the dark houses. The village lay in silence, only the girls' retreating footsteps were to be heard. Olenin's heart was pounding. His burning cheeks cooled in the damp air. He looked up at the sky and then at the house from which he had just come—the candles inside had gone out—and then looked again at the girls' retreating shadows. Maryanka's white kerchief disappeared in the fog. He felt a horror at being left alone. He was so happy. He jumped off the porch and ran after the girls.

"What are you doing? Someone will see you!" Ustenka hissed.

"I don't mind."

Olenin threw his arms around Maryanka. She did not resist.

"How much more are you going to kiss?" Ustenka said. "There'll be time enough for that once you're married, but enough now."

"Good night, Maryanka, tomorrow I shall speak to your father. Don't tell him anything yourself."

"What is there for me to tell him?" Maryanka replied.

The girls hurried away. Olenin walked on alone, reliving the last few hours. He had spent the whole evening with her in the corner by the stove. Ustenka had not left the room for a moment but had been having fun with Beletsky and the other girls. Olenin had spoken to Maryanka in whispers.

"Will you marry me?" he had asked her.

"You're making fun of me. I know you'll never marry me," she had answered gaily.

"But do you love me? Tell me, for God's sake!"

"Why should I not love you, it's not as if you were one-eyed or a hunchback," she had said, laughing, her rough hands squeezing his. "What sweet little white hands you have, they're soft as cream."

"I'm serious. Tell me, will you have me?"

"Why not? If my papa gives me to you."

"You know that I'll be driven out of my mind if you're making fun of me. Tomorrow I shall go to your mother and father and ask to be betrothed to you."

Maryanka had burst out laughing.

"What is it?" he had asked.

"It's so funny."

"I'm not joking. I'll buy an orchard, a house, I'll register as a Cossack, and . . ."

"And you'd better mind you don't go after other women! That would make me very cross."

Olenin blissfully repeated these words in his mind. Remembering them filled him with pain and made him breathless with happiness. He felt pain because she had seemed so unperturbed, speaking to him as she always did. This new situation had not seemed to trouble her in the least. It was as if she did not believe him and did not give their future any thought. It seemed as if she loved him only at that moment and did not imagine a future with him. But he felt happy because everything she had said seemed true, and she had agreed to belong to him. "Only when she is mine will she and I understand one another. Such a love cannot be defined in words—one needs a lifetime, a whole lifetime. Tomorrow everything will be made clear. I can no longer live this way, tomorrow I will tell her father, Beletsky, the whole village!"

Lukashka had drunk so much at the feast after two days of endless carousing that for the first time in his life he could not stand up, and he ended up sleeping at Yamka's.

40

The following morning Olenin woke up earlier than usual and in his first waking moments joyfully remembered what was awaiting him that day, and thought of her kiss, of her rough hands squeezing his, and of her words, "What sweet little white hands you have." He jumped out of bed, ready to go straight to the cornet's house to ask for Maryanka in marriage. The sun had not yet risen. There seemed to be an unusual commotion in the street. He heard voices and horses' hooves. He threw on his jacket and hurried out onto the porch. Across the yard at the cornet's house, everyone was still asleep. He saw five mounted Cossacks talking loudly among themselves, Lukashka riding in front on his sturdy Kabardinian steed. Olenin could not make out what they were saying, as they were all shouting at the same time.

"We're riding out to the upper checkpoint!" one of the men yelled.

"Come on, saddle up and catch up with us!" another called to some Cossacks who had come out of their houses.

"It's closer if we go out the other gate!"

"Nonsense!" Lukashka declared. "We must go out the middle gate!"

"Yes, it's closer that way," another Cossack riding a mud-spattered, sweating horse called out.

Lukashka's face was flushed and puffy after his night of drinking, and his sheepskin hat sat crookedly on his head. He called out orders as if he were the officer in charge.

"What's going on?" Olenin shouted, struggling to catch the Cossacks' attention. "Where are you all off to?"

"We're going to get some Chechens who've holed up in the dunes! But we don't have enough men yet!"

The Cossacks rode down the street, calling others to join them. Olenin suddenly felt that it would look bad if he did not ride out with them. But if he did, he wanted to come back early. He dressed, loaded his rifle, jumped onto his horse, which Vanyusha had quickly saddled, and caught up with the Cossacks at the village gate. They had dismounted and were standing in a circle, passing around a wooden cup of Chikhir and drinking to the success of the sortie. Among them was a young fop of a cornet who happened to be in the village at the time and who now tried to assume command. But even though he outranked the others, they were prepared to take orders only from Lukashka.

Nobody paid any attention to Olenin. The Cossacks remounted and set out again. Olenin rode up to the cornet and asked what was going on, but the cornet, though usually a friendly fellow, treated him with contempt. Olenin nevertheless managed to get out of him that Cossack scouts had spotted a group of Chechen marauders in the dunes some eight versts from the village. The scouts had surrounded the Chechens, who were trying to shoot their way out, refusing to give themselves up alive. The sergeant who had headed the party of scouts had sent one of them back to the village to get help.

The sun was beginning to rise. About three versts from the village, the steppe opened out on all sides, a monotonous, sad, dry expanse speckled with cattle tracks, tufts of grass, and in the hollows low-growing reeds. There were a few overgrown paths, and far away on the horizon some Nogai tents. The absence of shade and the austerity of the steppe were striking. There the sun always rises and sets red. When the wind blows, it brings with it mountains of sand. When the air is calm, as it was that morning, the silence is particularly striking. Even though the sun had already risen, a heavy gloom hung over the steppe. It was somehow particularly deserted and blurred. There was not a breath of wind. The only sounds were of hooves and snorting horses, and even these echoed weakly and died.

The Cossacks rode for the most part in silence. A Cossack always carries his weapons so that they do not jingle or rattle. Jingling weapons are a great shame for a Cossack. Two other men from the village caught up with the party and called out greetings. Lukashka's horse suddenly became restless, having stumbled or caught its hoof in the grass—a bad omen in Cossack lore. The others looked at Lukashka and then quickly looked away, as if they had not noticed. Lukashka pulled the reins and frowned. He gnashed his teeth and flourished the whip above his head, his horse suddenly tensing its legs, as if uncertain which one to step on before it soared into the air. But Lukashka struck its sturdy flanks with his whip, struck again, and then a third time. The horse, baring its teeth, its tail fanning out, rose snorting on its hind legs, staying back a few paces from the rest.

"A good steed!" the young cornet said. That he said *steed* instead of *horse* showed his appreciation of the animal.

"A lion of a horse," said one of the older Cossacks.

They rode at a slow gait, at times breaking into a trot, the only interruption of the solemnity of the ride.

As they headed for the dunes, they encountered only a Nogai cart with a tent pitched on it, slowly rolling along a trail some distance away. A Nogai family was crossing the steppe to another camp. The Cossacks also came across two broad-faced Nogai women with baskets on their backs, which they were filling with dung patties left behind by cattle. The young cornet, who spoke only a little Kumik, asked the women something, but they could not understand him and looked at each other in fear. Lukashka rode up to them and energetically uttered the usual Kumik greeting. The Nogai women, visibly relieved, greeted him back as freely as if he were their brother.

"Ai, ai, kop abrek!" they said plaintively, pointing in the direction the Cossacks had been riding in.

Olenin understood that they were saying "Many Chechen fighters." He had never experienced anything like this, having only heard about such sorties from Uncle Eroshka, and he wanted to ride with the Cossacks and see everything. He admired them, watching and listening closely, trying to remember everything. He had taken his sword and his loaded rifle with him, but seeing how the Cossacks avoided him, he decided not to take part in the fray. As it was, he felt he had already proven his courage sufficiently back in his detachment, but more important, he was too happy thinking about Maryanka.

Suddenly a shot was heard in the distance.

The young cornet became agitated and began yelling orders at the Cossacks, how to split up and from which side they should attack. But the men did not pay the slightest attention, following only Lukashka's orders. Lukashka's face and bearing were calm and solemn. He spurred his horse into a gallop that the other horses struggled to keep up with, and he kept his narrowed eyes fixed ahead.

"I see a horseman out there," he called, reining in his horse so the others could catch up.

Olenin peered into the distance but could see nothing. Yet soon they were able to make out two horsemen trotting calmly toward them.

"Are those Chechen marauders?" Olenin asked.

The Cossacks did not reply to this nonsensical question, for no Chechen would ever be foolish enough to cross the river into Cossack territory with a horse.

"Isn't that old Rodka waving to us?" Lukashka shouted, pointing at the horsemen, who were now quite visible. "He's coming toward us."

Within a few minutes it was clear that the horsemen were a scout and the sergeant.

41

"Are they far?" Lukashka called out immediately. At that moment a shot was fired not more than thirty paces away. The sergeant smiled. "That's our Gurka. He's firing at them," he said, nodding in the direction of the shot.

They rode on and found Gurka behind a sand dune, reloading his rifle. He was bored and to pass the time was shooting at the Chechens who were hiding behind the next dune. A Chechen bullet came whistling overhead.

The young cornet had turned ashen and confused. Lukashka jumped off his horse, threw the reins to one of the Cossacks, and went over to Gurka. Olenin also dismounted and followed him, crouching low. No sooner had they reached Gurka than two bullets came whistling past. Lukashka ducked and turned to Olenin, laughing. "They'll shoot you down, Dmitri Andreyevich. You'd better go back. This has nothing to do with you."

But Olenin wanted to see the Chechens at all costs. He could make out their hats and rifles jutting from behind the dune not more than two hundred paces away. He saw a sudden puff of smoke, and another bullet came whistling over. The Chechens were hiding in a marsh behind the dune. Olenin was impressed with the terrain: it looked just like the rest of the steppe, but the fact that the Chechens were holed up where they were somehow gave it a special character. He felt it was the perfect place for Chechens to be hiding. Lukashka went back to his horse, and Olenin followed him.

"What we need is a hay cart," Lukashka said. "Otherwise they'll kill us all. I saw one over there behind that mound."

The cornet and the sergeant agreed with Lukashka, and the hay cart was brought over. The Cossacks hid in it, covering themselves with hay, and Olenin rode to a nearby hillock from which he could watch. The cart began to roll. The Chechens—there were nine of them—were sitting in a row, knee to knee, and did not fire.

There was silence. Suddenly strange sounds came from the Chechen side: it was a song reminiscent of Uncle Eroshka's "Ay! Dai, dalalai!" The Chechens knew that they could not escape and had strapped their knees together to avoid the temptation to flee. They were loading their rifles and singing a dirge.

The Cossacks drew closer with their hay cart, and Olenin waited from one second to the next for the first shots, but the silence was broken only by the Chechens' dirge. Suddenly the song stopped, a sharp shot rang out, the bullet hitting the front of the cart, followed by the Chechens' yells and curses. One shot followed another, the bullets hitting the cart. The Cossacks did not shoot back, though they were now not more than five paces away. A few more seconds passed, and the Cossacks, led by Lukashka, came out whooping from behind both sides of the cart. Olenin heard only a few shots, shouts, and moans. He saw smoke and thought he also saw blood. Abandoning his horse, not knowing what he was doing, he ran to join the Cossacks. He was blinded by horror. He couldn't make out anything and only understood that it was all over. Lukashka, white as a shroud, was holding a wounded Chechen and shouting, "Don't shoot this one! I want him alive!" The Chechen was the same red-haired man who had come to buy back the body of his brother, the one Lukashka had killed. Lukashka forced the Chechen's arms behind his back, but the man suddenly broke free, drew a pistol, and shot at him. Lukashka fell. There was blood on his stomach. He jumped up but fell again, swearing in Russian and Tatar. There was more and more blood on him and under him. The other Cossacks, among them Nazarka, came running and loosened his belt. Nazarka tried to sheathe his sword but had trouble doing so because the blade was thick with blood.

The Chechens, red-haired and with cropped beards, lay dead, hacked to pieces. Only the man who had fired at Lukashka was still alive, though badly wounded. Like a hawk shot down by a hunter, he crouched on his haunches, pale and gloomy, his teeth clenched, his eyes darting around, ready to defend himself with his drawn dagger. He was covered with blood that was flowing from beneath his right eye. The young cornet approached him and then, edging away as if to avoid him, quickly shot him in the ear. The Chechen flung himself at the cornet but fell dead.

The Cossacks, puffing and panting, dragged the dead bodies together and gathered the weapons. Each red-haired Chechen was a human being, each face had its own expression. Lukashka was carried to the cart, still writhing and cursing in Russian and Tatar, "You bastard, I'll strangle you with my own hands! You won't get away! *Ana seni!*"* Soon he fell silent with weakness.

Olenin returned to the village. That evening he heard that Lukashka was dying, and that a Tatar from across the river was trying to heal him with herbs.

The bodies had been brought to the village council, and women and children had hurried over to look at them.

Olenin had returned around dusk and for a long time could not recover from what he had seen. But with nightfall, the memories of the previous evening with Maryanka came rushing back. He looked out the window. Maryanka was doing chores, going from the house to the storeroom and back. Her mother had gone to the vineyard, and her father was at the village council. Olenin, unable to wait until she finished her chores, went over to speak to her. As he entered the room, she turned away, which he took to be out of shyness.

"Maryanka," he said. "You don't mind if I come in, do you?"

She turned around abruptly. There was a trace of tears in her eyes. Her face was touched by a beautiful sadness. She looked at him silently and imperiously.

* *Ana seni:* Tatar, "Your mother," a curse.

"Maryanka, I've come . . . ," he began.

"Leave me alone," she said, her expression not changing, tears pouring down her cheeks.

"Why are you crying? What happened?"

"What happened?" she asked in a rough, harsh voice. "Cossacks have been killed, that's what's happened!"

"You're worried about Lukashka?"

"Go away!"

"Maryanka!" Olenin said, approaching her.

"You'll never get anything from me!"

"Don't say such things," Olenin begged.

"Go away, I hate you!" she shouted, stamping her foot and coming toward him threateningly. Her face expressed such contempt, hatred, and disgust that Olenin suddenly knew he had nothing to hope for, and that his original impression that she was inaccessible to him had been right. He ran out of the house.

42

Back in his room he lay motionless on his bed for two hours, then he went to his company commander to ask for a transfer to headquarters. Without bidding anyone farewell, and settling his accounts with the cornet through Vanyusha, he prepared to set out to the fort where the regiment was stationed. Only Uncle Eroshka came to see him off. They drank a glass, then another, and then another. Just as when he left Moscow, a troika stood waiting outside the door. But Olenin did not deliberate with himself, as he had back then, nor did he tell himself that everything here he had thought and done was "not quite right." He no longer promised himself that he was embarking on a new life. He loved Maryanka more than ever but knew that she would never love him.

"Farewell, my dear friend," Uncle Eroshka said. "When you're on your expedition, be more clever than I was! Listen to the words of an old man! When you are out on a sortie—I am an old wolf and have seen it all—and they start shooting, don't go running to huddle with the other soldiers in a group. When you Russian soldiers get frightened, you all crowd together, thinking you're hog-free when there's a lot of you. But it's the worst thing you can do! The first thing the enemy always does is shoot at a crowd. In my day, I always saw to it that I got as far away from the others as I could, and I wasn't hit even once! Ah, the things I've seen in my time!"

"But you've got a bullet in your back," Vanyusha said, packing up Olenin's last things.

"Ah well, that was just us Cossacks messing around," Eroshka replied.

"Cossacks? What do you mean?" Olenin asked.

"Simple enough. We were all drinking, and Vanka Sitkin, one of our Cossacks, was roaring drunk, and suddenly, bang, right here in the back."

"Did it hurt?" Olenin asked and turning to Vanyusha added, "Is everything ready yet?"

"What's the rush? I'll tell you all about it. When he shot me, the bullet didn't cut through the bone but stayed right there. And I said to Vanka, 'You've killed me, my friend! Is that what you're trying to do? But don't think I'm going to let you off so easily: You have to stand me a bucket of Chikhir.' "

"But did it hurt?" Olenin asked again, not really listening to Eroshka's tale.

"Let me finish. So he stood me a bucket. We drank it. And all the time, the blood was oozing out. The whole room was full of blood. So Uncle Burlak says to Vanka, 'As the boy's going to croak, you'd better stand us a jug of vodka too, or we'll drag you to court.' So vodka was brought out, and we drank and drank ..."

"Yes, but did it hurt?" Olenin asked again.

"What do you mean did it hurt? Don't interrupt me! I don't like being interrupted. Let me finish. So, we drank and drank till morning, until I fell asleep on the bench above the stove, completely drunk. When I woke up I couldn't straighten up."

"Did it hurt a lot?" Olenin repeated, imagining that this time he would finally get an answer.

"Did I say that it hurt? It didn't hurt, but I couldn't straighten up, I couldn't walk."

"So did it heal?" Olenin asked, so miserable that he didn't even laugh.

"It did, but the bullet's still there. Go on, feel it," Eroshka said, rolling up his shirt to reveal his robust back, where the bullet was lodged near his spine. "See how it rolls?" he added, playfully rolling the bullet like a toy. "Look how far it can roll."

"Do you think Lukashka will live?" Olenin asked.

"Only God knows. There's no doctors here. They went to get one."

"Where from, Grozny?"

"No, my friend," Eroshka said. "If I was the Czar I would have hung all your Russian doctors long ago. All they know how to do is cut a man to pieces. You should see what they did to poor old Baklashev: they cut off his leg and left him half a man. That's the kind of fools they are. Baklashev is worth nothing now. No, my friend, in the mountains there's some real doctors. Like with my blood brother Girchik: on one of the campaigns he was injured right here, in the chest. Your doctors said they could do nothing for him, and so Saib came down from the mountains and cured him. Those doctors know their herbs, my friend!"

"That's all nonsense!" Olenin said. "I'll send a doctor from headquarters."

"That's all nonsense, I'll send a doctor from headquarters," Eroshka mimicked. "What a fool! What a fool! If your doctors could heal anyone, wouldn't all the Cossacks and Chechens go running to them for cures? But as you yourself can see, even your own officers and colonels keep calling in mountain healers. All your doctors are frauds, all of them!"

Olenin said nothing. He agreed only too well that everything in the past world to which he was now returning was a fraud. "What about Lukashka, did you go see him?" he asked.

"He's just lying there like a dead man," Eroshka replied. "He won't eat, won't drink, only vodka. But as long as he's drinking vodka, there's hope. It would be a pity to lose him. He was a good boy, a real fighter, just like me. I was dying like him once—the old women were already wailing over my body. My head was in a fever. They laid me out under the holy icons. So I am lying there, and above me on the stove I see rows of little drummers, tiny ones, all of them drumming the tattoo. I shout at them, but the more I shout, the harder they drum." Eroshka laughed. "The women brought in the priest, they were getting ready to bury me. They said, 'You were a worldly sinner, had fun with women, killed men, ate meat on fasting days, played the balalaika. Confess your sins!' So I began to confess. 'I have sinned,' I said. Whatever the priest asked, I always answered, 'Yes, I have sinned.' He asked me about the balalaika. 'Yes, I have sinned,' I replied. 'Where is the accursed instrument?' the priest shouted. 'Where is it? Give it to me and I will hack it to pieces!' And I said to him, 'I don't have it anymore.' But it was right outside in the shed, hidden under some nets. I knew they wouldn't be able to find it. So they left, and I got well again. But when I went to find the balalaika, I... But what was I talking about before? Ah yes, you must stay away from the crowd during skirmishes, or they'll shoot you like a fool! I'd hate to see that happen to you. You hold your liquor well and I love you. But you Russians always like riding up onto hillocks. There was a fellow here, he'd also come down from Russia, like you, and he kept riding up onto whatever hillock he could find. He always called them 'knolls,' or something strange. No sooner did he clap eyes on a hillock than up he rode! So one day he went galloping up a hillock, very pleased with himself. But a Chechen picked him off and killed him. Ah, how those Chechens can shoot from their rifle rests! They're better than I am. But I don't like it when a fellow gets killed for nothing. I used to watch your soldiers in amazement. What fools! There they'd be, marching away all huddled together with their red collars! How could they not be shot down? One soldier would get killed, fall, get dragged off, and another one would take his place right away. What fools!" the old man repeated, shaking his head. "Why not spread out, and go one by one? That way you can march in an attack, and no one will hit you. That's what you must do!"

"Thank you, Uncle Eroshka. Farewell. God grant that we meet again!" Olenin said, getting up and heading to the door.

The old man remained seated on the floor.

"Is that how friends say good-bye? You fool!" Eroshka shouted. "What is the world coming to! A whole year we drank together, and now it's just good-bye and off you go? And here I am, who love you and feel for you! You who are so sad and alone, always alone. Unloved by anyone! So many nights I couldn't sleep feeling sorry for you! As the song goes: 'It is hard, my brother, to live alone, in distant lands so far from home.' That's just how it's been with you."

"Well, farewell," Olenin repeated.

The old man stood up and gave him his hand. Olenin shook it and turned to go.

"Give me your cheek! Your cheek!" the old man said. He grabbed Olenin's head with his large hands, kissed him three times with his wet mustache and lips, and began to cry. "I love you! Good-bye!"

Olenin climbed onto the cart.

"What? You're leaving just like that? You must give me something to remember you by! Give me your rifle! What do you need two for?" the old man said, sobbing with genuine tears.

Olenin took his rifle and handed it to him.

"The things you've given that old man!" Vanyusha growled. "And he still wants more, the old beggar! These people here are all so grasping," he added, wrapping himself in his coat and sitting down on the box.

"Quiet, you swine!" the old man shouted with a guffaw. "What a miser!"

Maryanka came out of the shed, glanced indifferently at the troika, bowed, and went into the house.

"La fille!" Vanyusha said with a wink and laughed foolishly.

"Let's go!" Olenin shouted angrily.

"Good-bye, my friend! Good-bye! I won't forget you!" Eroshka called out.

Olenin looked back. Uncle Eroshka was chatting with Maryanka, and neither he nor she turned to look at him.

Acknowledgments

I am grateful to my Russian editor, Katya Ilina, for her scholarly input and for checking my translations. At Random House, I would like to thank my editor, Judy Sternlight; production editor Vincent La Scala; and copy editor Susan M. S. Brown for their invaluable help. My warmest thanks to my agent, Jessica Wainwright, for her unflagging encouragement and interest in Russian literature, and Burton Pike, whose advice and translation expertise were a great help throughout the project.

READING GROUP GUIDE

1. "The great Russians have the secret of simplicity," wrote the American novelist and literary critic William Dean Howells. "Tolstoy is, of course, the first of them in this supreme grace ... [his novels] are alike in their single endeavor to get the persons living before you, both in their action and in the peculiarly dramatic interpretation of their emotion and cogitation." Do you agree? If you have read other novels by Tolstoy, such as *Anna Karenina* and *War and Peace*, do you think this opinion of Howells holds up?

2. According to the scholar of Russian literature Ernest J. Simmons, "The natural beauty of Cossack existence transforms Olenin into a philosophical reasoner searching for personal happiness, a kind of Rousseauistic 'natural man.' ... Olenin's conception of the romantic existence of the Cossacks is shattered by the reality of it." Discuss.

3. "Three months have passed from the first time I saw a young Cossack woman by the name of Maryanka," writes Olenin in a letter he will never send. "The ideas and prejudices of the world I had left behind were still fresh within me. In those days I did not believe that I could love this woman" (p. 130). How do Olenin's feelings for Maryanka change over the course of the novel? Can you imagine them ending up together? Would it be a happy marriage?

4. "You and I are blood brothers, just like I am with Girei Khan across the river," Lukashka tells Olenin (p. 111). How would you describe the evolving relationship between these two young men? What draws

them together, and how do they feel about each other, beneath the surface?

5. Describe the traditional roles of men and women in the Cossack community that Tolstoy portrays in such detail. How might this compare to the typical behaviors and responsibilities of men and women in Moscow society in the second half of the nineteenth century? Would you expect the rules of courtship to differ?

6. "A Cossack bears less hatred for a Chechen warrior who has killed his brother than for a Russian soldier billeted with him to defend his village, and who has blackened the walls of his hut with tobacco smoke," writes Tolstoy (p. 17). Which scenes in *The Cossacks* best exemplify these cultural tensions? What are the root causes of the hostility and discomfort that these groups feel when they interact with each other?

7. Why is Uncle Eroshka so successful at getting along with his fellow Cossacks, the Russian soldiers, and (according to his own stories) the Chechens?

8. Tolstoy was a young man when he began writing *The Cossacks* in 1852, and he finished the short novel a decade later. Does it feel like the work of a young man? How would you compare his later works with this early, semiautobiographical novel?

9. After Lukashka has been wounded in the confrontation with the Chechens, Olenin approaches his beloved Maryanka and she shouts, "Go away, I hate you!" Why does Maryanka react this way?

10. In Chapter 20, Olenin sets out on a solo hunting expedition in the forest. There, he finds himself "gripped by such a strange feeling of groundless joy and love for everything that, in a habit he had had from childhood, be began crossing himself and expressing his thankfulness" (p. 82). What sparks this extraordinary feeling in Olenin, and what conclusion does he draw from it? Does he undergo a permanent change in the course of his year in the Caucasus, or is it just temporary? How would you describe this transformation?

11. In her Introduction, Cynthia Ozick invites readers to "set aside the somber claims of history, at least for the duration of this airy novel. *A Midsummer Night's Dream* pays no heed to the Spanish Armada; *Pride and Prejudice* happily ignores the Napoleonic Wars; *The Cossacks* is unstained by old terrors." Is it the responsibility of fiction writers to incorporate a moral consciousness and sense of history into their narratives? What are some major literary classics or popular contemporary works that accomplish this feat?

ABOUT THE TRANSLATOR

PETER CONSTANTINE was awarded the 1998 PEN/Book-of-the-Month Club Translation Prize for *Six Early Stories*, by Thomas Mann, and the 1999 National Translation Award for *The Undiscovered Chekhov*. He is one of the editors of *A Century of Greek Poetry: 1900–2000*. Widely acclaimed for his recent translation of the complete works of Isaac Babel, he also translated Gogol's *Taras Bulba* and Voltaire's *Candide* for the Modern Library. His translations of fiction and poetry have appeared in many publications, including *The New Yorker, Harper's,* and *The Paris Review.* He lives in New York City.